RIVER OF STONE

RIVER OF STONE

Fictions and Memories

RUDY WIEBE

VINTAGE BOOKS

A Division of Random House of Canada

VINTAGE BOOKS CANADA EDITION, 1995

Canadian Cataloguing in Publication Data

Wiebe, Rudy, 1934
River of stone: fictions and memories

ISBN 0-394-28078-4

I. Title.

PS8545.I38R58 1995   C813'.54   C95-P30492-4
PR9199.3.W54R58   1995

First Edition

Printed and bound in Canada

*The people travelled all over the land, so
every place was home.... The elders always
said the Creator walks the land and takes
care of us, and it gave the people confidence.*

— GEORGE BLONDIN,
When the World Was New

TABLE OF CONTENTS

LOVE LETTERS FROM
LAND AND SEA

NORTH AND WILDERNESS. When I consider my country as a place distinct and particular from all the other places I have seen and lived in, that's it: north and wilderness.

Never mind that I live in a modern city: my travels and any map tell me wilderness and north are no more than a few minutes away from anywhere in Canada by air. And air travel is the Canadian way: this century's plane or helicopter is our continuation of the canoe, carried on endless streams of air with endless stories of long flights and crashes in our turbulent air's weather rapids. Canada reaches so far north that air will carry you in that direction until suddenly you will be going south.

And somewhere there is tiny Hedwen Island; at the outermost tip of the giant Dehcho (Mackenzie River)

Delta, anchored between Richards and Summer Islands in Kugmallit Bay. One hundred and twenty kilometres northwest of Tuktoyaktuk as the helicopter flies its island-sea route, where the July-green land undulates gently above the grey ice-ridden water of the Beaufort Sea.

I slide one hundred and twenty metres down sand cliffs to the rippled beach, and walk west singing. Centuries of Dehcho driftwood caught in the hollows of bays; a loon's pre-emptory nest of waterplants smeared on a spit between sweet water and salt, its long, deep-brown egg dappled black; three pieces of hollow petrified bone sticking out of a headland eroding steadily into the sea: what animal were they? Dinosaur seventy million years ago when the globe tilted differently and tropical trees flourished here two metres thick? The loon, most ancient of birds, calls where it rides between ice-pans; perhaps longing for its solitary dappled egg.

A flash of red beyond the nest in the hard sand: a detergent container, crushed, but containing a bleached mass of aluminum foil. I complete the break, shake out the black sand; and disclose a message from the sea.

"BEAUFORT SEA'S ARCTIC / 1986," I read on paper mottled by seepage. "August 1986 / Arnak Drilling Rig / Kenting 32 / Esso Resources Canada Ltd." Twenty-two signatures under "Names" and as many dates and places under "Date of Departure" — everything from August 1 for Aklavik to August 18 for Australia. And under that, curled tight, a second sheet with twenty-one more names and departures. Only three names have comments: "Flo

Keir (No. 1 Cook YAH)" and "Les R . . . " bracketing to his indecipherable signature "(Homo)", and the last name: "Thora Reid — Fifteen years of missed boats."

Somewhere in the Beaufort Sea on a manufactured steel and gravel island, forty-three people, five years ago.

I walk on, trying to imagine at least one of those lives, the sea nudging an occasional beluga whale rib near my boots. And discover beside me the ice that undergirds the world here: a crumbling cliff and beneath a few centi-metres of moss the massive black ice wedge that holds the land up and reaches down, hundreds of metres down, down to the limits of the permafrost. Geologists tell me later this may be the black ooze of prehistoric glaciers which here still give shape to the land. Or, some theorize, much of northernmost Canada may be supported on ice wedged somewhere kilometres down into the yet un-discovered texture of the earthen earth: they cannot tell for sure.

What is obvious: without the ice, the island would not exist.

I climb and slither and sink up the oozing cliff, between floating tussocks of moss brilliant with tundra flowers, bot-tomless sand, vanishing water. I touch, fondle, lick this black ice, this primordial cold which solidified here before the existence of humanity.

"Forget me not," the last words on the last sheet from the sea, serrated by sand and water, ask of me. If I am ignorant, forgetting is impossible. Only this bit of knowl-edge allows me to promise: "I will remember."

PASSAGE BY LAND

I NEVER SAW A MOUNTAIN or a plain until I was twelve, almost thirteen. The world was poplar and birch-covered; muskeg hollows and stony hills; great hay sloughs with the spruce on their far shores shimmering in summer heat, and swamps with wild patterns burned three and four, sometimes five feet into their moss by some fire decades before, filled with water in spring but dry in summer and sometimes smoking faintly still in the morning light where, if you slid from your horse and pushed your hand into the moss, you could feel the strange heat of it lurking.

In such a world, a city of houses with brick chimneys, telephones, was less real than Grimms' folktales, or Greek myths. I was born in what would become, when my father and older brothers chopped down enough trees for the house, our chicken barn; and did not speak English until I went to school, though I can't remember learning it. Perhaps I never have (as one former professor insists when he reads my novels); certainly it wasn't until years later I discovered that the three miles my sister and I had meandered to school, sniffing and poking at pussy-willows and ant hills, lay somewhere in the territory Big Bear and Wandering Spirit had roamed with their warriors always just ahead of General Strange in May and June, 1885. As a child, however, I was for two years the official flag raiser (Union Jack) in our one-room school, and during the war I remember wondering what it would be like if one day, just as I turned the corner of the pasture with the cows, a huge car would wheel into our yard, Joseph Stalin emerge and from under his moustache tell my father he could have his farm back in Russia, if he wanted it. Then I would stand still on the cow path trodden into the thin bush soil and listen, listen for our cowbells; hear a dog bark some miles away, and a boy call; and wonder what an immense world of people — I could not quite imagine how many — was now doing chores and if it wasn't for the trees and the curvature of the earth (as the teacher said) I could easily see Mount Everest somewhere a little south of east. Or west?

My first sight of the prairie itself I do not remember. We were moving south, leaving the rocks and bush of northern Saskatchewan forever, my parents said, and I was hanging my head out of the rear window of the hired car, vomiting. I had a weak stomach from having been stepped on by a horse, which sounds funny though I cannot remember it ever being so. Consequently, our first day in south Alberta the driver had me wash his car and so

I cannot remember my first glimpse of the Rocky Mountains either. It was long after that that anyone explained to me the only mountain we could see plainly from there was in the United States.

But sometimes a fall morning mirage will lift the line of Rockies over the level plain and there they will be, streaked black in crevices under their new snow with wheat stubble for base and the sky over you; you can bend back forever and not see its edge. Both on foot and from the air I have since seen some plains, some mountains on several continents; jungles; the Danube, the Mississippi, even the Amazon. But it was north of Oldman River one summer Sunday when I was driving my father (he had stopped trying to farm and he never learned to drive a car) to his week's work, pouring concrete in a new irrigation town, that we got lost in broad daylight on the prairie. Somewhere we had missed something and the tracks we were following at last faded and were gone like grass. My father said in Low German, "Boy, now you turn around."

I got out. The grass crunched dry as crumbs and in every direction the earth so flat another two steps would place me at the horizon, looking into the abyss of the universe. There is too much here, the line of sky and grass rolls in upon you and silences you thin, too impossibly thin to remain in any part recognizably yourself. The space must be broken somehow or it uses you up, and my father muttered in the car, "If you go so far and get lost, at least there's room to go back. Now turn around." A few moments thereafter we came upon a rail line stretched in a wrinkle of the land — the prairie in Alberta is not at all flat, it only looks like that at any given point — white crosses beside rails that disappeared straight as far in either direction as could be seen. We had not crossed a railroad before but the tracks could no more be avoided here than anything else and some connecting road to the new town must be eventually somewhere beyond.

In that wandering to find it is rooted, I believe, the feeling I articulated much later; the feeling that to touch this land with words requires an architectural structure; to break into the space of the reader's mind with the space of this western landscape and the people in it you must build a structure of fiction like an engineer builds a bridge or a skyscraper over and into space. A poem, a lyric, will not do. You must lay great black steel lines of fiction, break up that space with huge design and, like the fiction of the Russian steppes, build giant artifact. No song can do that; it must be giant fiction.

The way people feel with and live with that living earth with which they are always labouring to live. Farmers or writers.

THE DARKNESS INSIDE THE MOUNTAIN

NUMBER THREE HIGHWAY west of Lethbridge, paved,
leads through Fort Macleod where at seven-thirty
in the morning the black Hutterite men are already
swinging off their staked cattle truck in front of the New
American Café — "To buy ice-cream cones till the back
door of the beer parlour opens," Daddy tells me, laughing
— and then there's the high prairie of the Piegan lands —
"Watch for Horse-drawn Vehicles" — and in the empti-
ness against the foothills a tree has been set up. It couldn't
have grown there so thick and all alone, its huge sawn-off
branches holding up what at that distance looks like a
platform of branches and blankets.

"That's the way Indians bury them," Daddy says.
"Chiefs. High for the crows."

"Crows?" I can see one flapping across the summer
shimmer of heat already buckling the hills.

"It's okay, better to fly off than be dragged deeper by worms."

That was one reason Mama didn't want me to go with him all day on his truck run to the Crowsnest Pass. "A girl of ten, Wendell, doesn't need *soaking* in cynicism." "Don't 'Wendell' me." "I didn't give you your name." "You don't have to use it, 'you' is enough." So I am in the red Coca-Cola truck he has driven since spring, bottles leaping in their crates when he can't miss a pothole, the mountains south of Pincher Creek like broken teeth with very bad fillings. The three Cowley elevators drone past, then Lundbreck with half-boarded-up square storefronts — "There's no mine here now, not even a sawmill" — and the pavement ends with a crash and slither of gravel, the bottles going crazy. The railroad bounces doubly under us and against a hill, curves, and suddenly the road silence of a bridge, and thunder. Spray in clouds between cut rock —

"Daddy! Daddy!"

"Yeah, Lundbreck Falls. We'll have a look coming back."

The falls are gone behind an inevitable shoulder of rock and I'll have to wait with a memory of water hanging like brushed grey corduroy, vivid grey, not like irrigation falls, and the quick flash of rapids between trees and rocks, a shimmer spreading behind my eyelids as I squeeze them shut. When I open them there is the smoking cone of the Burmis sawmill but a tiny church also, you'd have to bend to go in, and over a hump the peaked and mortared stone walls of a — no, surely a castle! With all the wooden core of it burned out by a year-long siege, don't tell me! — and I look at Daddy and he doesn't, just grins and gestures ahead to the sudden upthrust of Crowsnest Mountain. Straight down the highway, over the narrow railroad track that cuts the gravel at right angles in front of Bellevue slouched on little hills ahead. We have to stop there while a string of mine cars tugs across the road in front of us.

"You must be good luck," Daddy says. "I never seen them going down the mine before."

Past our broad red nose the little cars are now all seated tight with blackish men facing each other knee to knee, hip-roofed lunch buckets in their laps. Each single giant monster eye on the top of each head turns, stares, and one by one they slide into the hole in the hillside, click *click*, click *click*, box after box of them slipping past where the sunlight of the trees and the blue sky stops like a wall. And for one instant that single eye glares from the darkness, and is gone, click *click*, click *click*.

The sun sits on the eastern mountains and I would like to curl up, arrange all this behind my eyelids, there is too much already, how can I possibly remember it all, but Bellevue is there, old stores cut into hillsides and a Chinese café and a Ukrainian café with bottle cases stacked in cellars, behind gaping fences, crashing as my father heaves them about single-handedly and the blackish faces of the off-work miners leaning across the porch rail of the Bellevue Hotel swivel with us as our long red truck flashes past in the window behind them. We bend around a large grey school and the road splits, straight ahead or down into the valley to a scatter of houses across the river and around a green hill. We drive straight on.

"What about those?"

"There's nobody there," Daddy says, "in Hillcrest, there's nothing there now."

Behind my eyelids I imagine I can see into one of those little houses, look inside its one large room, and there is no ear to hear it as slowly, without a sound, the floor crashes soundlessly into the dark hole of the cellar below and the corners of black begin to move — I jerk my eyes open and a girl, tiny like me, tilts against the iron fence of the schoolyard with her hands up as if wired there and I wave, she is the first girl I have seen and I wave with both hands, desperately, but she does not move. Her face is early-summer brown like mine but she does not even blink, only her head turns like a mechanism and then we are plunging into the pale limestone wilderness of the Frank Slide under the ruptured face of Turtle Mountain. The highway and the railroad so smooth over and through it, a monumental cemetery for eighty people buried in two minutes; 1903, Daddy says, and on the edge of it they found a baby still sleeping in its cradle untouched. Through piled fields of boulders and past a store beside Gold Creek and then Turtle Mountain Playgrounds, and we stop in the noon shadow of that threatening overhang to eat sandwiches. Last night my mother packed them, and we wash their dryness down with Coca-Cola ice cold because my father exchanges two of our extras for cold bottles from the cooler he services inside.

"See that man," he says, chewing. "He's starting on his third million. Finished the first two, too."

A slim man — he has arms, legs just like everyone, how could you see he is rich? — opens the door of a silvery green convertible for a thinner woman with hair like a cloud of gold piled upon her head. O, she is. Rich. The convertible murmurs, spins away, their heads leaning back together, they almost touch.

"He was just born," my father says, "that's how he got all that."

Blairmore is one long street facing lower green mountains, the CPR station, and the water tower. And a longer alley black with heat and the fried stink of food, the blackness moving, settling, settling down out of the sky like granular snow in the blistering day, everywhere. I sort bottles, my hands like the miners' faces but sticky with pop too, and my father stacks cases five-high and hauls them in and out, up and down on the two-wheeled dolly until finally we drive the length of the street again, bumping through the sunken sewer ditches that cross in front of every business and past green mine timbers squared up like tunnels on the cinder space beside the railroad — a banner, "Welcome to the 52nd Annual Mine Rescue Games" — and finally, finally, there is air at the open window and only the grainy blue of Crowsnest Mountain. By itself like a blessing, and the road folded left and upward in green arcs towards Coleman. My father is sweating; his thick hands shake as he rides back and forth through his ten gears into the hills.

"I can't work a whole day on that horse-p — " He gestures behind him but looks straight ahead. "Not such a killer day."

I had never thought he could. After three grocery and one drug store, four cafés, the miners' clubs and the Canadian Legion, he pulls up tight against the bright shade of the alley behind the hotel — "Take a rest, I won't be long" — and is gone. I lock the doors, stretch out and fall into sleep that breaks in sweat, I am gasping on the sweat-hot seat. I pull myself loose, clamber out and up, hand and toe up to the top of the cases on the truck. The bottles burn my fingers. And I cannot open them anyway like my father does by levering two caps together because my hands are far too small, and weak.

"I'll open one for you." A whiskered man, grey, his layers of clothing so black with dirt they shine below me in the terrific sun. He reaches up, his horned, gleaming hand takes one bottle from me and his lips draw back on his teeth and he places the top of the bottle there and at one slight grind of his head the hot liquid boils out between his whiskers and over his chin and down his layered front, but he does not notice. Just spits out the cap oks up at me easily, offering me the hissing bottle. make you sick," he says. His voice is as gentle as uching me. "Hot like that."

But I cannot put the bottle to my mouth. Not where his enormous teeth have been. He is something that has risen out of this day, out of the black and overwhelming power of these towns strung between and under mountains and over mines, a heat-blister out of the day, his green eyes glittering through his hair with the snore of the fan blowing beer fumes over me.

"Did you deliver in Hillcrest?" his soft voice asks.

"Hillcr…wha…no, no…no."

"You wouldn't. Not today, that's when it happened, June 19, 1914. Forty years, today."

His hands clutch the top cases and I cannot move. He is so close the dirt stands grained and polished in his skin bit by bit.

"A tiny fire jumped up, poof! In those miles of tunnels crossing each other two thousand feet inside Hillcrest Mountain, and then the fire licked along the methane gas bleeding along the tops of the tunnels and found the coal dust, here, there, the pockets where the miners were working and it exploded…waugggghhh!…and the ventilator shafts blew out and then all the oxygen left in the tunnels burned, bright blue like thunder and lightning breaking, and all the miners…" his face, hands, body are changing like a rubber horror mask, bursting from one contortion into another, his body curling up, jerking open spastically… "they breathe fire…the last oxygen burning, explosion after explosion…in the darkness inside the mountain they begin to come apart."

Gradually his face hardens again, his arms, head, shoulders are all there, together.

"Only their brass identification tags gleam in the stinking smoke when the rescue lamps...Hillcrest Collieries Limited, June 19, 1914. One hundred eighty-nine men. From Peter Ackers to Michael Zaska."

The coated bottle still sticks in my hand. The truck is twenty cases long: each narrow body is a row of cases, to lay them tight side by side will take nine...nine and a half....

"That was my shift," his soft voice goes on. "I was called, yes, I was called but my leg ached. So my friend took my shift. There was never a body found with his brass tag on it. His unchangeable number. We found, we assembled one hundred eighty-eight bodies, and then we had one leg left over."

The sun winks between the four chimneys, the immense crossed tipple of Coleman Collieries. A tiny smoke forms there, disappears grey into the brilliant sky.

"Forty years ago, today," the old man says. "Listen, I have to tell you their names. Listen, there was Ackers, Peter. Adlam, Herbert. Albanese, Dominic. Albanese, Nicholas. Anderson...."

I have to run, run! But he is below me, between me and the hotel bar door I must reach so I scramble, clanking over the empties and scrape my leg along a case wire but I am down, somehow half-falling and look under the truck — will he move, will he? — and I see one leg there, motionless, beside the tire and then his hair, his head lowers, upside down, it looks like nothing human and at the top of it the terrible mouth is opening on another name and it reaches out for me like a long black tunnel, O sweetest, sweetest Jesus....

"I have only one leg," it whispers, "I have only one...."

The truck spins past me, his head coming up — "Androski, Geor" — and the door under the beer-scummed fan, and darkness. Like a moist hand clapping shut over me...but it is open too, and high everywhere, I reach out my arms and there is nothing. Only this moist, slipping, darkness.

"Daddy...."

But there is a light, behind a high narrow table and a shadow moves there, light and glass, misshapen bottles everywhere. And there are other shadows too: quick little double movements of light that come and go, and then I know suddenly that those are the eyes. Turned to me from the vastness of the cavern which I cannot see the end of, that is breathing around me like an animal opening itself endlessly for me into close, moist terror —

"DADDY!"

"Del," a huge voice from the light and as my heart jerks I feel my father's hands on my shoulders, his big hands hold me as only they can. They lift me, completely, and his chest, his neck is there too. His gentle breath.

"...Prosper. Davidson, John. Demchuk, George," murmurs the mound between wall and telephone post. My father places two warm bottles of Coca-Cola beside it. "Demchuk, Nicholas. Dickenson, Matth...."

The Crowsnest River burbles between boulders around a small island and then bends, vanishes over Lundbreck Falls in quick, slipping silence. In the water I can see that the western sky between the Crowsnest mountains is covered with giant flames. They do not vanish but grow motionlessly larger, upward from the limits of the world and if it were not for the deep sound of water below, I know I could hear the sky burning there.

"The mines are finished," my father says. "Everything's oil and gas now, coal is nothing."

We move slowly east towards the flat darkness of the prairie. I curl up on the seat, my head in the bend of his thigh. I can hear his muscles shift against my ear as he controls the pedals, the levers, and when we are level at last and up to speed his right hand comes to rest heavy and cupped on my hip. But behind my eyelids I am not asleep; in fact, I may never be able to sleep again.

TOMBSTONE COMMUNITY

S CATTERED HERE AND THERE across Western Canada
are communities which stand as tombstones to the
"homestead method" of rural settlement. A number of
them were established during the depression years of the
1930s when, desperate for an honest livelihood, thousands of impoverished families felt that if only they had
land to live on, they could avoid both hunger and the
dole. And there lay such an immensity of Canada beyond
the strip of southern settlement and below the rock of the
Canadian Shield; surely it could be settled in the tried
and proven way: 160 acres and five years with minimum
improvements and the land was theirs. Get enough families to settle in one area and presto! — a stable community had begun.

Prairie governments were nothing loath to encourage
such thinking. Settlers, often enough innocents from
Europe, moved in, registered on their land, and began to
pioneer. In the years that followed they proved again

what had already been discovered with great hardship in the Cypress Hills area twenty years before: that homesteading, which succeeded quite well in founding stable communities in the more fertile black-soil parts of the prairies, broke down completely when a quarter section of thin rocky soil in the short growing season of northern latitudes was counted on to support a family.

The Speedwell-Jackpine community of Saskatchewan where I was born stands as one such tombstone to the one-hundred-and-sixty-acre homestead idea. As a place on the map, Speedwell no longer exists. The vital services of a well-populated, working community — school, post office, store, church — now can be found only twenty miles away — in Glaslyn, a small town some forty miles north of North Battleford. Yet during the early 1940s when I was growing up, Speedwell district had a post office, two stores, two schools of thirty to forty children each, and a vigorous church and social life. On virtually every quarter section along a five-mile road, and for several miles in either direction from it, lived a family of five, eight, sometimes ten or twelve persons. Every one of them was completely involved in helping to dig a home and a living from the poplar-spruce-and-rock-covered soil. And it was not long before even my infant comprehension knew that this work was very hard for all, and impossible for many.

The first settlers in the area did take up homesteads more sensibly than the one-family-to-each-quarter-section pattern. These first were Mennonites from North and

South Dakota, Minnesota, and Kansas who came north in 1925 and 1926 looking for inexpensive, sheltered land. Their homesteads were well scattered to allow a good deal of individual expansion. But the main influx of home-steaders, the Russian Mennonites who began to arrive in Speedwell about 1928, disrupted all this. Having always lived in close-knit villages which farmed the surrounding area intensively, these new Canadians felt that one hun-dred and sixty acres per family a half mile from the near-est neighbour was surely enough land, and surely enough isolation.

It was not the inadequacy of the land but rather its loneliness that first made life hard for the European set-tlers. Russia had been vast; but Canada was not merely vast; it was impassively empty and lonely. My mother still recounts how in those early years she would start out early in the afternoon to look for our few cows on the "free range" that stretched endlessly to the west of our home-stead, listening for the clear tone of the lead cow's bell to guide her. Having wandered far in their grazing, the cattle would often stand motionless among the thick willows to escape the flies and mosquitoes, and no sound would stir the air. Walking, listening, looking, mother would lose all sense of where in the endless bush our small home clear-ing was. The search for the cows became somewhat des-perate then, because they had to be found to lead her home. In the meantime we small children would be wait-ing at home, laughing and chasing each other in glee when we heard the bell coming nearer, but frightened when we saw that the cows had come home by themselves without mother driving them. Then father would come from work and, without pausing to eat, go in search of mother. Standing on a hillock, he would send his high, thin "Halloooo — " into the silent evening. And mother would say when they came home together, father waving a poplar branch around her to chase the mosquitoes, that there never was a finer sound in all the world.

So despite a few warnings to give themselves more "living" room, the Mennonites settling in the Speedwell district in the early thirties were happy to take up every quarter of land. The bush was too huge to face except from a central community. Each step of mastery over it was dependent not only on the iron nerve of the settler but also on the steel stake of the surveyor which, with an impassivity quite equal to that of the vast land itself, stated its cold official statistic impartially in a spruce muskeg or on a stony hilltop. When, as a youngster, my elder brother first made me aware that the surveyors had been all over the country long before we arrived, my imagination could not quite grasp the daring of such exploration. Yet there stood the stake. And beneath its statistic was the inevitable warning, cut deep in the iron: "It is unlawful to remove this marker. Maximum sentence: 7 years imprisonment." It was almost as if the imperturbable surveyor, whoever he was, defied the very wilderness itself to swallow the alien organization he had imposed upon it.

The centre of the community was, quite naturally for the Mennonites, the church. It is the church records that give the statistics of Speedwell-Jackpine community growth. The existence of the church was first noted in the 1928 annual Canadian Mennonite Brethren conference minutes. The 1930 minutes indicate thirty members; with the Russian Mennonite influx, this grew to forty-seven in 1933, ninety-five in 1935, and reached a peak of one hundred and fourteen in 1936. These figures represent about twenty-five families in the church. Add to them the twelve to fifteen families living in the district but not directly connected with the church, and there was a total of forty families or, conservatively, two hundred and fifty persons living on twenty square miles of northern Saskatchewan bushland in the process of being cleared for farming.

The church record indicates that even in the distress of the 1936 depression, permanent settlement on this scale proved impossible. In two years membership dropped by one third — to about seventy members. The families that remained of course took over the claims of those who had left and so they had the advantage of what clearing and breaking had been done. For about eight years, until the end of World War II in 1945, the Speedwell-Jackpine community enjoyed its only relatively stable period, supporting about twenty-five families, that is, some one hundred and fifty persons.

My parents with their six children arrived in Speedwell in 1933. They had lived in south Saskatchewan for a year on relief; that was more than enough. I was born the year after they took up their homestead, and the world which year after year began slowly to register on my

comprehension was the world of pioneer work: the production of necessary food and shelter. To live in a compact
log house carefully plastered with mud against the fury of
winter and sun of summer; to trudge three miles of trails
to a single-room school where the first graders clustered
about a long table and doodled with "Valet" razor blades
on their bench while the harassed teacher was "straightening out" the sixth graders on the opposite side of the school;
to carry a snack of thick bread and cold tea to your father
and brothers where they were scrubbing, with axes and a
team of horses, the poplar- and birch-choked land: that
was the world to me. Towns and cities, with their paved
streets, department stores, motor vehicles, electric lights
and spacious bedrooms, when I learned of them, inhabited
the segment of my imagination reserved for Grimm's fairy
tales and the Greek myths. And certainly the myths and
fairy tales were the more easily understood of the three.

Ours was a world of labour. It was done by all, men,
women and children alike, for the family worked and
lived as a unit. With small fields wrested inch by inch from
the clutch of the bush, the easy life of grain growing, and
harvesting and selling was out of the question. Each member of the family had work to do: in the summer the
smaller children fed the chickens, hoed the garden, herded
the cattle if the fences (after they had been put up) were
insufficient; the older girls and mother cooked, washed,
canned, took the children on berry-picking and seneca-
root-digging trips, expeditions which took place every fine
day as long as the season for either lasted; the older boys

and father cleared land, hayed, broke sod, picked stones and built sod-covered barns. What grain we grew was used to feed chickens, hogs, stock, milk cows and horses. The source of cash income, besides occasional "working out," was the cream cheque which came each week with our returning empty cans. These cheques were never large because poor cows fed largely on slough hay rarely produce either quantity or quality. In winter the children went to school (to grade 8 — after that it was correspondence school if one were interested in higher education) and the women took care of the stock while the men, with as many horses as they could employ, cut and hauled timber for any one of several small mills operating in the bush north of us.

Often when the new spring with its demand for seed and absolutely essential, if elementary, equipment strained the slim family resources too far, my two older brothers, then in their late teens, would walk to Fairholme, the nearest railroad stop, and "ride the rods" six hundred miles to southern Alberta. There they would thin and hoe sugar beets for the summer. The money they earned — sometimes as much as two dollars a day — was brought home in fall to help us through the winter. And on Christmas morning when my Santa Claus plate, as was fitting for the youngest and most inevitably spoiled child of the family, would contain a game that shot glass marbles into tiny pockets of varying scores, my brothers' plates would hold such useful gifts as a package of razor blades each and a bottle of after-shave lotion between them.

It did not matter much that in the last days of the thirties we lived from one year to the next without travelling more than ten miles from home, without seeing either a car or a train. It did not much matter that in a rainstorm the only dry spot in the house was under the kitchen table; that is, if the oilcloth was not entirely worn out. We could work and we had something to eat; that was miracle enough to my parents who had almost starved to death in Russia during the early 1920s. What they told us of these experiences made Canada a miracle even to me, who had never known another land.

Though the hard work remained, during the war years it did become more comfortable in certain areas of life. Social activities centred around the two public schools, Speedwell and Jackpine, and the Speedwell Mennonite Brethren Church. Friendly sports competition in summer was replaced in winter by Christmas concerts and school bazaars. The church had a full weekly program, and for several years two qualified teachers taught a winter Bible school which attracted about thirty young people. We younger children snared rabbits and trapped squirrels and weasels in winter; we thought prices were really very good. Financially things improved so much that we even had an extra horse which could be used to haul my sister and myself to school in the cutter during winter. Well, the youngest children of even a pioneer family invariably grow up weaklings!

But the community showed signs of uneasiness. Despite the difficulties of wartime moving, occasional families, beckoned by the greener fields of the South, would leave. Young people were growing up; some of them had spent ten or twelve years working hard to give their families a bare existence; the leavening experience of younger men returning from the war loud with stories of travel and world wonders had profound effects on Speedwell and its people.

Yet these more or less ideological forces cannot explain the abrupt dying out of the entire community. In early 1946 there were still forty-seven members in the Speedwell Mennonite Brethren Church; it had a lay pastor, three young lay ministers and two deacons. By 1948 there were twelve members left, and a year later one family alone remained. By 1950 the church, and with it the community, had ceased to exist. For several years there was literally no one living in the entire Speedwell district.

I remember well those years of leaving. Only my sister and myself remained at home in our family; the older children had grown up, married local young people, and had moved away to make their living. There was "moving" in the air. You drove to church on Sunday and were almost surprised to meet your neighbour there. He had, apparently, not yet moved that week.

The younger people obviously did not want to stay. There was no way of getting educated beyond eighth grade in the district; life was so much easier elsewhere. Even if they wanted to stay and farm, they would have to begin as their parents — pioneering in the bush, away from the land that was now at least partially cleared. By working in Speedwell there was no prospect of ever having enough money to buy a tractor to do such clearing, and they had no ambition to do it by hand. The prosperity of post-war Canada beckoned everywhere. And if the young people went, why should the now aging parents and the last of the children stay, labouring at the old work with little prospect of more than a subsistence living?

The land, of course, was the root cause for moving. There was little room to expand in the community itself, and the very best wheat one could ever expect, in the very best of years, was a bare No. 2 Northern. Though one need never starve on his farm, one would also never have many comforts. For example, after twenty years of laborious work, only two or three farmers could afford to own and operate an ancient lug tractor, and only one drove a recent model car. Our family never did own either a tractor or car in Speedwell. We drove into the district in 1933 with what equipment we had on a rented truck and we left fourteen years later in exactly the same way.

Tax problems intensified the situation. For many years no one had money to pay taxes. The government knew enough not to make itself ridiculous by insisting on taxes on homesteads during the 1930s. But by 1946 tax notices were getting clamorous, and so rather than work out to earn money to pay taxes on land that they were not too convinced of anyway, a good number of farmers simply left. Not that the back taxes even ten years later were very high. Our family quarter was bought from the municipality in 1957 by a farmer who paid exactly the price of the back taxes — $400. In the first winter after he bought that land he cut $500 worth of spruce on it, but he did it with a chain saw and a tractor.

Caught in the moving fever, drawn by the hope for better land and an easier livelihood, the Speedwell farm-owners left their log houses and their laboriously cleared fields to revert to the government (there were few, if any, buyers for them) and moved south — to Manitoba, Alberta, British Columbia. In the easier, car-transported life they have found in these areas, they often visit one or the other of their old neighbours and reminisce about those hard, yet happy, pioneer years. Time easily erases the greatest hardships, and the romance of having taken part in such pioneering colours all their memories, so that many, if they ever return, will find Speedwell unrecognizable.

Only two families remained living on the periphery of the district in the early 1950s. They lived by farming and trapping. During a wet year beaver appeared from nowhere, dammed up several sloughs which had been fine hay meadows in our time, and the country became known as good hunting territory. Then, about 1955, several of the younger men who had left in the forties and made a bit of capital in southern cities were drawn by the need for land and returned to Speedwell. Using modern mass-farming techniques, they are now doing what the first farmers could not do: making a good living under fairly comfortable circumstances. The grubbing pioneer life is gone now; town is only twenty miles away on a good road: the church has been torn down, the two schools have been closed (the children go to elementary or high school by bus to Glaslyn) and the world is no farther away than the TV screen or the telephone in the living room.

We left Speedwell in 1947; I returned for a visit in the summer of 1963. The poplars grow much taller and straighter than I remember them; there are no spruce left now. The house where we lived seems so much smaller than I thought. It stands tilted, its windows gaping. The three miles I trudged to school seem no distance whatever; the school itself and the hill where we used to slide and ski in winter seem shrinking into themselves. The narrow fields still stretch over the hills, but the poplars and the willows are quickly reclaiming the territory they once lost, very briefly, to axe and plough. Already they grow young and thick in the church cemetery, almost hiding the small tombstone of my sister's grave. And on every quarter section we pass in our car — sometimes too we have to walk because all but the main road is overgrown — there sag the shells of houses that once heard the laughter of families. No one sees them now, from one year end to the next. Their rotting floors will soon crash into their shallow cellars, and no one except wild animals will hear.

But for some years yet these decaying little cabins — for that is really all they are — with their collapsed barns will stand as individual letters on the face of this tombstone community of Speedwell and the homestead idea that once lived, and now is buried, there.

WHERE IS THE VOICE COMING FROM?

THE PROBLEM IS to make the story.

One difficulty of this making may have been excellently stated by Teilhard de Chardin: "We are continually inclined to isolate ourselves from the things and events which surround us...as though we were spectators, not elements, in what goes on." Arnold Toynbee does venture, "For all that we know, Reality is the undifferentiated unity of the mystical experience," but that need not here be considered. This story ended long ago; it is one of finite acts, of orders, or elemental feelings and reactions, of obvious legal restrictions and requirements.

Presumably all the parts of the story are themselves available. A difficulty is that they are, as always, available only in bits and pieces. Though the acts themselves seem quite clear, some written reports of the acts contradict each other. As if these acts were, at one time, too well-known; as if the original nodule of each particular fact had from somewhere received non-factual accretions; or even more, as if, since the basic facts were so clear, perhaps there were a larger number of facts than any one reporter, or several, or even any reporter had ever attempted to record. About facts that are simply told by this mouth to that ear, of course, even less can be expected.

An affair seventy-five years old should acquire some of the shiny transparency of an old man's skin. It should.

Sometimes it would seem that it would be enough — perhaps more than enough — to hear the names only. The grandfather One Arrow; the mother Spotted Calf; the father Sounding Sky; the wife (wives rather, but only one of them seems to have a name, though their fathers are Napaise, Kapahoo, Old Dust, The Rump) — the one wife named, of all things, Pale Face; the cousin Going-Up-To-Sky; the brother-in-law (again, of all things) Dublin. The names of the police sound very much alike; they all begin with Constable or Corporal or Sergeant, but here and there an Inspector, then a Superintendent and eventually all the resonance of an Assistant Commissioner echoes down. More. Herself: Victoria, by the Grace of God, etc., etc., QUEEN, defender of the Faith, etc., etc.; and witness "Our Right Trusty and Right Well-beloved Cousin and Councillor the Right Honourable Sir John Campbell Hamilton-Gordon, Earl of Aberdeen; Viscount Formartine, Baron Haddo, Methlic, Tarves and Kellie in the Peerage of Scotland; Viscount Gordon of Aberdeen, County of Aberdeen in the Peerage of the United Kingdom; Baronet of Nova Scotia, Knight Grand Cross of Our Most Distinguished Order of Saint Michael and Saint George, etc., Governor General of Canada." And of course himself: in the award proclamation named "Jean-Baptiste" but otherwise known only as Almighty Voice.

But hearing cannot be enough; not even hearing all the thunder of A Proclamation: "Now Hear Ye that a reward of FIVE HUNDRED DOLLARS will be paid to any person or persons who will give such information as will lead...(etc., etc.) this Twentieth day of April, in the year of Our Lord one thousand eight hundred and ninety-six, and the Fifty-ninth year of Our Reign..." etc. and etc.

Such hearing cannot be enough. The first item to be seen is the piece of white bone. It is almost triangular, slightly convex — concave actually as it is positioned at this moment with its corners slightly raised — graduating from perhaps a strong eighth to a weak quarter of an inch in thickness, its scattered pore structure varying between larger and smaller on its polished, certainly shiny surface. Precision is difficult since the glass showcase is at least thirteen inches deep and therefore an eye cannot be brought as close as the minute inspection of such a small, though certainly quite adequate, sample of skull would normally require. Also, because of the position it cannot be determined whether the several hairs, well over a foot long, are still in some manner attached to it or not.

The seven-pounder cannon can be seen standing almost shyly between the showcase and the interior wall. Officially it is known as a gun, not a cannon, and clearly its bore is not large enough to admit a large man's fist.

Even if it can be believed that this gun was used in the 1885 Rebellion and that on the evening of Saturday, May 29, 1897 (while the nine-pounder, now unidentified, was in the process of arriving with the police on the special train from Regina), seven shells (all that were available in Prince Albert at that time) from it were sent shrieking into the poplar bluffs as night fell, clearly such shelling could not and would not disembowel the whole earth. Its carriage is now nicely lacquered, the perhaps oak spokes of its petite wheels (little higher than a knee) have been recently scraped, puttied and varnished; the brilliant burnish of its brass breeching testifies with what meticulous care charmen and women have used nationally advertised cleaners and restorers.

Though it can also be seen, even a careless glance reveals that the same concern has not been expended on the one (of two) .44 calibre 1866 model Winchesters apparently found at the last in the pit with Almighty Voice. It is also preserved in a glass case; the number 1536735 is still, though barely, distinguishable on the brass cartridge section just below the brass saddle ring. However, perhaps because the case was imperfectly sealed at one time (though sealed enough not to warrant disturbance now), or because of simple neglect, the rifle is obviously spotted here and there with blotches of rust and the brass itself reveals discolorations almost like mildew. The rifle bore, the three long strands of hair themselves, actually bristle with clots of dust. It may be that this museum cannot afford to be as concerned as the other; conversely, the disfiguration may be something inherent in the items themselves.

The small building which was the police guardroom at Duck Lake, Saskatchewan Territory, in 1895 may also be seen. It had subsequently been moved from its original place and used to house small animals, chickens perhaps, or pigs — such as a woman might be expected to have under her responsibility. It is, of course, now perfectly empty, and clean so that the public may enter with no more discomfort than a bend under the doorway and a heavy encounter with disinfectant. The door-jamb has obviously been replaced; the bar network at one window is, however, said to be original; smooth still, very smooth. The logs inside have been smeared again and again with whitewash, perhaps paint, to an insistent point of identity-defying characterlessness. Within the small rectangular box of these logs not a sound can be heard from the streets of the, probably dead, town.

Hey Injun you'll get hung for stealing that steer
Hey Injun for killing that government cow you'll
get three weeks on the woodpile
Hey Injun

The place named Kinistino seems to have disappeared from the map but the Minnechinass Hills have not. Whether they have ever been on a map is doubtful but they will, of course, not disappear from the landscape as long as the grass grows and the rivers run. Contrary to general report and belief, the Canadian prairies are rarely, if ever, flat and the Minnechinass (spelled five different ways and translated sometimes as "The Outside Hill," sometimes as "Beautiful Bare Hills") are dissimilar from any other of the numberless hills that everywhere block out the prairie horizon. They are bare; poplars lie tattered along their tops, almost black against the straw-pale grass and sharp green against the grey soil of the ploughing laid in half-mile rectangular blocks upon their western slopes. Poles holding various wires stick out of the fields, back down the bend of the valley; what was once a farmhouse is weathering into the cultivated earth. The poplar bluff where Almighty Voice made his stand has, of course, disappeared.

The policemen he shot and killed (not the ones he wounded, of course) are easily located. Six miles east, thirty-nine miles north in Prince Albert, the English cemetery. Sergeant Colin Campbell Colebrook, North West Mounted Police Registration Number 605, lies presumably under a gravestone there. His name is seventeenth in a very long "list of non-commissioned officers and men who have died in the service since the inception of the force." The date is October 29, 1895, and the cause of death is anonymous: "Shot by escaping Indian prisoner near Prince Albert." At the foot of this grave are two others: Constable John R. Kerr, No. 3040, and Corporal C. H. S. Hockin, No. 3106. Their cause of death on May 28, 1897, is even more anonymous, but the place is relatively precise: "Shot by Indians at Min-etch-inass Hills, Prince Albert District."

The gravestone, if he has one, of the fourth man Almighty Voice killed is more difficult to locate. Mr. Ernest Grundy, postmaster at Duck Lake in 1897, apparently shut his window the afternoon of Friday, May 28, armed himself, rode east twenty miles, participated in the second charge into the bluff at about 6:30 p.m., and on the third sweep of that charge was shot dead at the edge of the pit. It would seem that he thereby contributed substantially not only to the Indians' bullet supply, but his clothing warmed them as well.

The burial place of Dublin and Going-Up-To-Sky is unknown, as is the grave of Almighty Voice. It is said that a Métis named Henry Smith lifted the latter's body from the pit in the bluff and gave it to Spotted Calf. The place of burial is not, of course, of ultimate significance. A gravestone is always less evidence than a triangular piece of skull, provided it is large enough.

Whatever further evidence there is to be gathered may rest on pictures. There are, presumably, almost numberless pictures of the policemen in the case, but the only one with direct bearing is one of Sergeant Colebrook who apparently insisted on advancing to complete an arrest after being warned three times that if he took another step he would be shot. The picture must have been taken before he joined the force; it reveals him a large-eared young man, hair brush-cut and ascot tie, his eyelids slightly drooping, almost hooded under thick brows. Unfortunately a picture of Constable R. C. Dickson, into whose charge Almighty Voice was apparently committed in that guardroom and who after Colebrook's death was convicted of negligence, sentenced to two months hard labour and discharged, does not seem to be available.

There are no pictures to be found of either Dublin (killed early by rifle fire) or Going-Up-To-Sky (killed in the pit), the two teen-age boys who gave their ultimate fealty to Almighty Voice. There is, however, one said to be of Almighty Voice, Junior. He may have been born to Pale Face during the year, two hundred and twenty-one days that his father was a fugitive. In the picture he is kneeling before what could be a tent, he wears striped denim over-alls and displays twin babies whose sex cannot be deter-mined from the double-laced dark bonnets they wear. In the supposed picture of Spotted Calf and Sounding Sky, Sounding Sky stands slightly before his wife; he wears a white shirt and a striped blanket folded over his left shoulder in such a manner that the arm in which he cradles a long rifle cannot be seen. His head is thrown back; the rim of his hat appears as a black half-moon above eyes that are pressed shut as if in profound concen-tration; above a mouth clenched thin in a downward curve. Spotted Calf wears a long dress, a sweater which could also be a man's dress coat, and a large fringed and embroidered shawl which would appear distinctly Doukhobor in origin if the scroll patterns on it were more irregular. Her head is small and turned slightly towards her husband so as to reveal her right ear. There is what can only be called a quizzical expression on her crumpled face; it may be she does not understand what is happening and that she would have asked a question, perhaps of her husband, perhaps of the photographers, perhaps even of anyone, anywhere in the world if such questioning were possible for a Cree woman.

There is one final picture. That is one of Almighty Voice himself. At least it is purported to be of Almighty Voice himself. In the Royal Canadian Mounted Police Museum on the Barracks Grounds just off Dewdney Avenue in Regina, Saskatchewan, it lies in the same show-case, as a matter of fact immediately beside that triangular piece of skull. Both are unequivocally labelled, and it must be assumed that a police force with a world-wide reputation would not label *such* evidence incorrectly. But here emerges an ultimate problem in making the story.

There are two official descriptions of Almighty Voice. The first reads: "Height about five feet, ten inches, slight build, rather good looking, a sharp hooked nose with a remarkably flat point. Has a bullet scar on the left side of his face about 1 1/2 inches long running from near corner of mouth towards ear. The scar cannot be noticed when his face is painted but otherwise is plain. Skin fair for an Indian." The second description is on the Award Proclamation: "About twenty-two years old, five feet, ten inches in height, weight about eleven stone, slightly erect, neat small feet and hands; complexion inclined to be fair, wavey dark hair to shoulders, large dark eyes, broad forehead, sharp features and parrot nose with flat tip, scar on left cheek running from mouth towards ear, feminine appearance."

So run the descriptions that were, presumably, to identify a well-known fugitive in so precise a manner that an
informant could collect five hundred dollars — a consid-
erable sum when a police constable earned between one
and two dollars a day. The nexus of the problems appears
when these supposed official descriptions are compared to
the supposed official picture. The man in the picture is
standing on a small rug. The fingers of his left hand touch
a curved Victorian settee, behind him a photographer's
backdrop of scrolled patterns merges to vaguely paradisia-
cal trees and perhaps a sky. The moccasins he wears make
it impossible to deduce whether his feet are "neat small."
He may be five feet, ten inches tall, may weigh eleven
stone, he certainly is "rather good looking" and, though it
is a frontal view, it may be that the point of his long and
flaring nose could be "remarkably flat." The photograph
is slightly over-illuminated and so the unpainted complexion could be "inclined to be fair"; however, nothing
can be seen of a scar, the hair is not wavy and shoulder-
length but hangs almost to the waist in two thick straight
braids worked through with beads, fur, ribbons and cords.
The right hand that holds the corner of the blanket-like
coat in position is large and, even in the high illumination,
heavily veined. The neck is concealed under coiled beads
and the forehead seems more low than "broad."

Perhaps, somehow, these picture details could be rec-
onciled with the official description if the face as a whole
were not so devastating.

On a cloth-backed sheet two feet by two and one-half feet in size, under the Great Seal of the Lion and the Unicorn, dignified by the names of the Deputy of the Minister of Justice, the Secretary of State, the Queen herself and all the heaped detail of her "Right Trusty and Right Well-beloved Cousin," this description concludes: "feminine appearance." But the picture: any face of history, any believed face that the world acknowledges as *man* — Socrates, Jesus, Attila, Genghis Khan, Mahatma Gandhi, Joseph Stalin — no believed face is more *man* than this face. The mouth, the nose, the clenched brows, the eyes — the eyes are large, yes, and dark, but even in this watered-down reproduction of unending reproductions of that original, a steady look into those eyes cannot be endured. It is a face like an axe.

It is now evident that the de Chardin statement quoted at the beginning has relevance only as it proves itself inadequate to explain what has happened. At the same time, the inadequacy of Aristotle's much more famous statement becomes evident: "The true difference [between the historian and the poet] is that one relates what *has* happened, the other what *may* happen." These statements cannot explain the storymaker's activity since, despite the most rigid application of impersonal investigation, the elements of the story have now run me aground. If ever I could, I can no longer pretend to objective, omnipotent disinterestedness. I am no longer *spectator* of what *has* happened or what *may* happen: I am become *element* in what is happening at this very moment.

For it is, of course, I myself who cannot endure the shadows on that paper which are those eyes. It is I who stand beside this broken veranda post where two corner shingles have been torn away, where barbed wire tangles the dead weeds on the edge of this field. The bluff that sheltered Almighty Voice and his two friends has not disappeared from the slope of the Minnechinass, no more than the sound of Constable Dickson's voice in that guardhouse is silent. The sound of his speaking is there even if it has never been recorded in an official report:

> *hey injun you'll get*
> *hung*
> *for stealing that steer*
> *hey injun for killing that government*
> *cow you'll get three*
> *weeks on the woodpile hey injun*

The unknown contradictory words about an unprovable act that move a boy to defiance, an implacable Cree warrior long after the three-hundred-and-fifty-year war is ended, a war already lost the day the Cree watch Cartier hoist his guns ashore at Hochelaga and they begin the long retreat west; these words of incomprehension, of threatened incomprehensible law are there to be heard just as the unmoving tableau of the three-day siege is there to be seen on the slopes of the Minnechinass.

Sounding Sky is somewhere not there, under arrest, but Spotted Calf stands on a shoulder of the Hills a little to the left, her arms upraised to the setting sun. Her mouth is open. A horse rears, riderless, above the scrub willow at the edge of the bluff, smoke puffs, screams tangle in rifle barrage, there are wounds, somewhere. The bluff is so green this spring, it will not burn and the ragged line of seven police and two civilians is staggering through, faces twisted in rage, terror, and rifles sputter. Nothing moves. There is no sound of frogs in the night; twenty-seven policemen and five civilians stand in cordon at thirty-yard intervals and a body also lies in the shelter of a gully. Only a voice rises from the bluff:

We have fought well
You have died like braves
I have worked hard and am hungry
Give me food

but nothing moves. The bluff lies, a bright green island on the grassy slope surrounded by men hunched forward rigid over their long rifles, men clumped out of rifle-range, thirty-five men dressed as for fall hunting on a sharp spring day, a small gun positioned on a ridge above. A crow is falling out of the sky into the bluff, its feathers sprayed as by an explosion. The first gun and the second gun are in position, the beginning and end of the bristling surround of thirty-five Prince Albert Volunteers, thirteen civilians and fifty-six policemen in position relative to the bluff and relative to the unnumbered whites astride their horses, standing up in their carts, staring and pointing across the valley, in position relative to the bluff and the unnumbered Cree squatting silent along the higher ridges of the Hills, motionless mounds, faceless against the Sunday morning sunlight edging between and over them down along the tree tips, down into the shadows of the bluff. Nothing moves. Beside the second gun the red-coated officer has flung a handful of grass into the motion-less air, almost to the rim of the red sun.

And there is a voice. It is an incredible voice that rises from among the young poplars ripped of their spring bark, from among the dead somewhere lying there, out of the arm-deep pit shorter than a man; a voice rises over the exploding smoke and thunder of guns that reel back in their positions, worked over, serviced by the grimed motionless men in bright coats and glinting buttons, a voice so high and clear, so unbelievably high and strong in its unending wordless cry.

The voice of "Gitchie-Manitou Wayo" — interpreted as "voice of the Great Spirit" — that is, The Almighty Voice. His death chant no less incredible in its beauty than in its incomprehensible happiness.

I say "wordless cry" because that is the way it sounds to me. I could be more accurate if I had a reliable inter-preter who would make a reliable interpretation. For I do not, of course, understand the Cree myself.

ALL ON THEIR KNEES

One

DOWN ON ONE KNEE he thrust his arms under, groping for a grip. It was curled, head and arms balled round to belly and knees. He fought the blizzard's weight and that unyielding curl, sweat bursting from his pores. For a long moment he curled over, around it, fumbling and hugging at its iron cold as if in love, then he got his arms locked and heaved erect. He staggered: the world wheeled over under the gritted snow and, incredible wonder, balanced on the sleigh track, a hard sure line for his feet.

Gradually a shadow bunched in the streaking white and he was floundering beside the sleigh. He tipped it in, felt for the reins; the horses moved as he clambered up. He tugged his robe over it and hunched behind the dash, heart violent in his chest.

Turn-off, make the turn-off, there's nothing beyond. Head down and mitt over his mouth, he breathed deeply once and again, then he stood up. No bush alongside; he could not even see the horses' heads now; only their rumps, occasionally bellies, remained, dark and heaving. My god if the tracks are drifted too much and they miss — in the wind — something — he thrust back his hood and the blizzard awakened his numb face. Nothing. He forced his lips to a whistle, the thin sound swallowed as it left his mouth, but suddenly a wild bark, and Roarer was plunging beside the sleigh. He yelled, "Hey, hey! Get up there!" reaching down. The dog sprang at his mitt and then vanished ahead.

The wind shifted to eddy and bush formed on the right. Once they turned, the blizzard's sweep was broken by poplar and spruce but the drifts were higher. The black was nearly finished, the reins told him this, and its momentary lag behind the bay in leaping at each new snow-ridge. The timing staggered so badly that once the black's haunch jammed the sleigh an instant before it leaped, the sleigh struck the drift at an angle and he had to hurl himself flat against the tilt. Something struck him behind the knees then and he crumpled across the dash. Rein pressure gone, the horses almost floundered but he jerked erect, screaming, slapping, and they plunged on. On the hard level between drifts, he shoved the balled shape away from his feet, back under the robes.

Mutt's barking welcomed them to the homestead clearing and the wilder storm. He snapped the icicles off the horses' nostrils and left them spent in their stall. At the sleigh again, he got one leg in, heaved it against himself and staggered to the door. Its very rigidity calmed him; like a heap of firewood he propped it up on his knee to lift the latch.

Where in the — well — he hooked a table leg and dragged the table from the wall. As his lamp caught the match flame, the dogs growled in the doorway. "Good fella! Good girl! But out now, come on, out." He eased them into the lean-to and pulled the door tight.

His glance slid around the little room — god what if — but his hesitation broke before it stopped his movement and he shrugged off his hooded sheepskin and was at the table, tugging, prying for a hold. Finally his hand found a doubled limb; he braced himself. Gelidly a knee rose, straightened; the other leg moved as hardly, but moved, and he could thrust up under the parka to feel a bare warmth seemingly hugged together there. He edged farther, searching, his fingers felt a frazzle, prodded roughness that suddenly slipped like grease. He jerked back, knowing before the light etched his bloody fingers.

Herman saw the red smudge, blackening, the familiar room opening into darkness. He shook his head; come on, blood is blood, everybody has it — but who expects a frozen lump — the tracks, maybe there were sleighs on the road just before — it was warm! Swiftly he unbent the arms and pulled back the head. An Indian, about his own age and, perhaps, alive — breathing, yes. He stretched for a dishcloth behind the stove, plunged it into the water pail and began wiping the dark face. No cut in the shaggy parka; maybe wounded inside a house. Maybe dropped for dead.

The man twitched. Suddenly his head jerked his cheek down against the table and his muscles knotted in spasms here and there; stomach, thigh, shoulder, ankle. Herman held him to the final long shudder, and the limbs relaxed. He got the bottle of whisky from the cupboard then and took one long swallow. Only the features remained contorted, the mouth hanging open a little.

Night had long since thickened the storm when Herman finished bedding his stock and returned to the house. On the hides beside the stove, the Indian had not moved. Unconscious; or dead? Sleeping. Thick hair in a jagged cut at the neck; skin almost transparent over sharp bones; he knew all the Cree on the reserve across the Wapiti River but this man — he looked starved. Perhaps he was no Cree.

Tossing off coat and mitts, Herman washed, then lifted the blanket to study the sprawl of dried blood gluing the shirt against the chest. There it couldn't be fatal and it wasn't bleeding now, no frostbite. The long fingers seemed all right, curled like that. He pried at the moccasins; stockings worn thin, and the skin blotchy to the ankle.

He was testing a basin of lukewarm water with his finger when his glance met the Indian's, eyes wide, staring. The pupils shone as strangely, intensely black and unblinking as two polished knobs on some wooden —

Herman shuddered. Then the broad nostrils flared in breathing and he said, "Hey! You're lucky I was crazy enough to try going to town. You okay?"

The eyes did not waver.

"I was crazy, yeah, and to stop too," Herman laughed, too loud in the little room and he turned to pull up a bench. "You'll have to be higher so I can try to fix those feet." He lined two chairs against the bench; the other shifted an arm feebly and Herman stooped, "Just easy with it, easy." He lifted him, holding his torso rigid, and eased him to the bench so that below the knee his legs hung to the floor. He got the basin and began bathing the icy feet.

When he had changed the dirty water twice the blotchiness seemed to be fading. An enormous hunger suddenly moved in him. He propped the Indian's legs so that his feet hung free in the water, then got out meat and bread. In the pan the meat spit, its aroma drifting through the smoked moose-hide smell, strange in this room. He offered him a piece of meat on a fork; he gnawed as if it would stick in his throat. Herman dipped some bread in milk.

When the Indian had eaten bread and, with his head supported, drunk some milk laced with whisky, Herman soaked away the shirts and the filthy scarf. A wide gash lay across the left lower ribs, glancing off one and then another. Blood welled in red beads here and there but, oddly, it seemed clean, inflamed only at the apex. He got his medicine box and fished out the needle and catgut boiling in a pot on the stove. Even for his stubby fingers the heavy gut fit the needle easily. "This is just for cattle, you know, but it works. Fixed my leg good, once, when a crazy boar ripped her from here to here."

He reached for the iodine, and the Indian's look flicked up at him, abruptly alive and blazing as the blizzard roared outside. But as swiftly his eyes closed, and he said no word. "Hey," Herman said, "you better have some whisky, straight."

After he cleaned up and sat down at the kitchen table, elbows spread wide. The bay shying and his own stupidity, as he thought it then, at getting out to see what it might be and the instant of terror, as totally violent, as totally strange to him after all the Saskatchewan blizzards he had outfaced, when the track vanished under his feet just before he saw the drift forming over the mound — he was not even sleepy, now. The storm whined about the cabin. In eight years no one but himself had ever slept in the bedroom until a half-dead — aw, he had done with those thoughts. No one visited him; that fact required no thinking. No more than the Mennonite deacon's remembered voice when, at Herman's persistence in marrying his daughter, he had named him the bastard of a woman long since dead and left him to stumble out, past the rigid face of the church minister, into that long ago summer night. His washbasin mirror had stared back at him and his face bloody with mosquitoes crushed in the trudge home.

He stirred. The things he had brought from town: he had ordered them long ago, carefully, and risked a dash to town before the storm for them, but now they could wait. He piled packages and mail on the table, and a magazine cover made him pause. "Christmas is coming," it stated. A doll lay among blankets: through the frosted window behind it a child's face stared in. Round eyes staring at the doll white as frosting. After a time he roused: the title was high enough, trim it and hang it up. He flipped the page; just a poem centred in a grey-outlined barn and he had already begun the tear when he saw the title and first line.

"The Oxen." "Christmas Eve and twelve of the clock." His glance slipped down the stanzas: he had never heard of Thomas Hardy. It was short so he read it deliberately. At the third stanza he was shaping the words under his breath,

> … Yet I feel
> If someone said on Christmas Eve,
> 'Come; see the oxen kneel
>
> 'In the lonely barton by yonder coomb
> Our children used to know,'
> I should go with him in the gloom,
> Hoping it might be so.

"Barton" and "coomb" were explained at the bottom of the page. He could not remember when he had last read a poem. And impossible too. Maybe when he was very small, the arms of whom he then believed his mother around his chest, her warm chin on his shoulder while what he then believed to be the flat German voice of his father murmured on about Jesus, yes, born in a barn on such a night, yes — maybe then. But his barn now, the two heifers, his yearling — old Brindy buckling to either heaven or hell! — he roared aloud before he remembered the Indian.

Almost eleven. The poem was as good as an evening verse. He got up, stretched, listening to the dark bedroom. Strange smell they always had, different from any white. Not just dirt; on the reserve Mrs. Labret was as clean as they come but you knew it walking in the door. A whiff of alcohol, a snore audible above the storm; strange too, here. He stripped to his underwear, flicked the hides straight and, rolling his sheepskin into a pillow, snubbed the lamp and lay down.

Firelight wavered against the ceiling. Shapes of Indians stumbling, sticking out legs and arms like sticks towards barns swaybacked under snow where cattle leaned, legs tucked under them, before cribs piled with hay. Strain as he would, there was a weight on his shoulder; he could not see what his tangled exhaustion seemed to insist. And, as the blizzard continued worrying at the house, his grimace faded to vacant sleep.

Two

Next morning the man's gaunt body shook in fever. After redressing the wound, Herman wallowed into the storm to feed his stock. The yearling nuzzled his sleeve and

while it ate mash he scratched its ears. The white mark-
ings lay on its broad curly face in perfect symmetry. To
hunt deer was impossible, and he no longer raised pigs.

Abruptly he untied the rope, tugged the pail away,
and led the big calf out. It plunged about in the wind's
bite, butting him playfully as he dug at the toolshed door.
In a surge of emotion he wrestled it a moment, its body
big and flinging, then he got his arms clenched around it
and tossed it bodily into a drift. When it gambolled up he
had the door free. Inside he put down the pail and, snorting, it reburied its nose in the mash. He reached for the
mallet on the shelf; just as the yearling began raising its
face to him, he struck down hard.

Three

Two days later noon sunlight blazed through the iced
window onto the table between them eating. The man
could sit and so there was no longer need for fresh beef
borscht. Herman watched him work at the heap of steak
and bannock. Like a hammer mill, but silent, without a
pause as if there would never be an end until there was
nothing. His wide mouth no longer pulled so gauntly
against his teeth and he limped without apparent pain.
But then he had never shown pain. And since that
momentary flicker of — what it had been Herman was
no longer sure; sometimes he wondered whether he had
not been hoodwinked in what he thought he saw that
night, threading the needle. Since the fever the man had

muttered perhaps ten words to necessary questions, face expressionless, black eyes blank beyond reach. Sometimes it seemed to Herman the man was not even there; he would come in and the house as silent, as empty as ever, and he would look into the bedroom: the man lay on the bed, face empty, staring nowhere. Well, the beef disappearing was proof! He grinned and said,

"You from the Cree, over the river? I don't think I ever saw you."

The other held a last piece of meat speared on his fork. "No."

"What's your band then?"

The pause stretched. "Chipeweyan."

"That's a long way north." Herman wiped bannock around in his plate. "Real cold too this winter, so early too. Hunting?"

"Yeh. No deer there."

Finality in his tone, almost like resentment. Herman pushed the dishes together. When he looked up the other's glance slid away.

"No deer," the man's voice repeated behind him.

"Yeah. And a family to feed too, eh?" But the other said nothing.

He was placing the last dish in the cupboard when the dogs barked outside and he went to the door. Two figures plodded over the blinding drifts. Herman squinted; the dogs were silent now, leaping about them. In the immense cold the world shone with a hard, implacable brilliance, lifeless in a sheer light with which the sun seemed to have little or nothing to do. It hung above the bush as if frozen on the sky.

No one was at the table when he turned, and it was a moment before he could make out the Chipeweyan standing in the bedroom door. His parka, which had padded the chair, he clutched to his chest. Herman said, "It's two men. I can't see who but —" and then he realized that the expression on the man's face was terror. Its very density seemed to hunch him together so that the shirt of Herman's he wore hung even more baggily, his body coiled to leap into flight. Herman said quietly, "From the dogs, one of them —" but stopped. In two and a half days the man had slept or accepted bandaging, spoonfeeding, washing of frozen feet, lying aloof and motionless as if waiting for his body to get over its weakness and catch up to wherever his will had long since been. No emotion; not even a twitch when iodine touched the sewn wound. Now, this, as they stood, hearing the approaching sounds. The unbalanced door scraped; the man was gone.

Feet stomped outside and he thrust open the outer door.

"Hello, Herman."

"Hey!" His breath caught in his throat. "Hello, Bill. Hello," to the other shape against the unbearable snow. "Come — come in, outa that."

"Thanks." They kicked off their snowshoes and the room was packed with them. Herman pushed forward two chairs.

"Sit down, warm up."

Bill was fumbling with buttons. "Christ that sun's awful. Even with the glasses I'm blind." His mackinaw opened to a vee of scarlet police tunic. "Herman, this's Constable Brazier, from Saskatoon."

The constable was tall, younger than the corporal and his blistered face drooped at a long, heavy jaw. "How do you do," he said in a strangely toneless voice.

Herman nodded. "You never hiked all the way from Hany?"

Bill groaned, "I bet. We had to leave the snow rig at the road, your drifts are damn well over the trees!"

"And it's quiet on foot." Herman laughed, "Except for the dogs!"

Bill's laugh bounced about the room. "Yeah, dammit, I guess I forgot them dogs!"

"They haven't forgot you — "

"Why are you so concerned about our coming quiet, Mr. Paetkau?" The dry voice was the constable's.

Herman glanced at him momentarily, shrugged. "Dunno. Guess we, Bill and me, try to joke sometimes." He turned to the stove. "Anyways, it's cold. I'll heat some borscht."

"By god that's what this god-forsaken cold needs — more people with a good pot of Mennonite borscht on the stove!" Bill got out of his coat entirely. "You might as well have some too."

There was a brief silence before the constable answered, "I'll check the barn in the meantime."

Bill said heavily, "Look, there's hardly — look, Herman, we're — "

"Sure," Herman swung around, poker in hand, "go ahead." Brazier, already at the door, stopped as Herman followed him.

"I won't need help."

"I wasn't coming — it's just the dogs." The growl that greeted the policeman faded at his: "Let him alone, you hear. Mutt!" The dogs sat down again, ears cocked at the black figure pushing into the glare.

Bill stood before the picture tacked by the bedroom door. "Nice," he cleared his throat gruffly. "Coming all right, hmm. December 24 and a cop hasn't even time for a Christmas picture."

Herman went to the cupboard. "I'd join you but I only got two bowls."

The corporal swung around. "Look, this Brazier and his — he's okay all right. It's just his first big job, just out of Regina and head crapfull of theory. You know." They had known each other since Bill Gent's first Treaty Day in Hany more than two years before when Herman, one of the few whites who spoke any Cree, helped quiet a brawl behind the livery barn.

"Sure. Who you looking for?"

"A Chip from west of Reindeer Lake, name of Carbeau. His sister's Joe Sturgeon's wife — you know, Tough Joe, on Stony Point. He came there the day the blizzard started, had a fight and Joe got killed and Carbeau got away on a stolen horse. They say he's cut pretty bad."

Herman stirred the soup. "What'd they fight about?"

"That's the funny part. It started when Carbeau got there, right away, but nobody'll say why. Yet. Maybe Joe was beating up his sister. She wouldn't say but she looked pretty bad. You ever hear of Indian men fighting about that?"

"Yeah."

"Yeah? Well, maybe them Chips up there learned real fast from the whites," Bill guffawed. "They steal about like them anyway. More likely Joe owed this Carbeau meat from last year. Reports are there's nothing of anything around Reindeer this winter, not even rabbits."

Out of the corner of his eye Herman saw Bill's bright scarlet move from the bedroom door; perhaps he was now looking at the bracket above the table, at the alarm clock there, or the faded gothic letters on the German Bible. But it was in the room like a presence, that abrupt unfathomable terror, seeping through, choking the room. Bill talked on,

"...relatives cut him off back north and they just about had him this side of Poplar Lake when the blizzard hit. We found the horse dead on the road this morning three miles west with a leg bust. He probably tried walking this way. You see any sign of the poor dev — "

A growl flared outside and Herman sprang to the door. "Mutt! Drop it!" Brazier was stooped at the door of the kennel, his gloved hand clamped rigid in the dog's jaws.

The constable straightened, face livid. "That's a vicious dog. Ought to be chained." He was rubbing his hand. "And that one followed me every step."

"They're not pets."

"Look, I'm no prowling Indian — "

Their looks met, held, and fury roiled in Herman. "You figure they should know your uniform?" Then he saw the constable's track around the house. "If you looked at tracks, you'da seen there was just dogs around the dog-house. It'd be pretty cold in there, through that storm."

Bill in the doorway was looking at him oddly; he had said too much. Too much? It was impossible. Even if he wanted to.

"The borscht's hot," he said, turning.

The two policemen ate quickly, silently, and in a few moments Bill pushed back. "Thanks Herman. That old touch is still right there!"

"Yes," Brazier said. "I've never tasted it before, but it is very good. Thank you."

Herman nodded. Take him and get.

Bill said into the awkward hush, buttoning his coat, "Yeah. As I was saying when the dogs caught Brazier — ah — " he snorted, "red-handed, you get home before the blizzard?"

"Huh-uh. It got me a couple miles south of the church."

"I figured. See any sign of Carbeau?"

So say it so they get. He opened his mouth and met the tall constable's look; cold, as if performing some drill of inhuman precision. He said to Bill, "I can't say nothing that would be enough for him."

The policemen glanced at each other. For a moment only the fire snapped in the stove. Bill jerked, "All right, take the bedroom, I'll get the cellar."

Staring down at the cabbage stuck to the rim of the borscht-pot, something turned over in Herman and he felt spent, filthy. When they came in the door he should have just said, "The bedroom. Sic 'em" to that long-jawed — Brazier had not come out. He twisted, peered into the bedroom. The constable was dropping the end of the cot, turning irresolute, eyes probing the tiny room. If he's got a nose, he can smell him! After a moment he came out leaving the door ajar. His glance circled, moved to the ceiling and Herman heard him catch his breath.

"Where's your ladder?"

"Huh?"

"Your ladder, for the attic." Herman stared at him and the policeman seemed almost to smile for the first time. He said, "I want the ladder to get into your attic. Understand?"

In his confusion Herman nearly laughed. "It's just a loft, a little — I don't — " The other's look was hardening. "Stand on a chair."

The constable jerked one around, stepped up and nudged the trapdoor with his hand. A shower of dust fell in his face; he started as if a current had struck him.

"That's enough." Bill stood on the cellar steps, pushing away his flashlight. "Nobody's been there." As the other two stood motionless he emerged entirely and pulled on his mitts. "You see no sign at all, eh, coming home?"

Herman lied, without comprehension, "No."

"I'm sorry, Herman," the corporal hesitated, his face mottled red. "It's my fault. The first thing you're supposed to know in this job is who to ask and who to search. One of the drivers ahead of you on the road remembered his horses shying somewhere after the church, but he hadn't thought much of it. We never found nothing; I knew you'd of stopped if your nags shied. All right! Thanks again for the borscht. So merry Christmas!"

Herman watched them slip on their snowshoes. His eyes followed them across the clearing until they were lost in the unrelenting light. There was no sense anywhere, neither his lies nor the nothing in the bedroom. Or the world with its sun and inhuman, mocking whiteness. He turned back at last into the black house and he did not know how long he stood, arms propped on the table, head hanging, before he knew Carbeau was watching him from the bedroom door.

"My god," he said, and sat down.

Carbeau limped to the other chair. "Never saw me behind the door."

They looked at each other; laughter burst from Herman, a roar that fluttered the cupboard curtains and hushed. The other smiled. Herman exclaimed suddenly, "They won't quit, what's the use of running? It'd be a year or two for manslaughter, at most. Why didn't you come out?"

Carbeau's lean finger poked along the edge of sunshine on the oilcloth. "Why didn't you say?"

Herman said, finally, "I dunno."

After a time Carbeau said, "I was getting to Labret's now." He nodded slowly.

"They won't come back — " but stopped. "You know Labrets?" he asked irrelevently.

"My uncle."

"Hey, I thought they're Cree. Didn't he say — "

Carbeau was looking away. "Yeh. My uncle."

"You know the way from here?"

"Yeh."

Herman stood up heavily. "You'd better sleep, and start when it's dark."

He put on his barn coat and went out. He cleaned the barn thoroughly for the first time since the storm and, as the sun set, did the chores. He returned to the house and heated the last of the borscht. When he went into the bedroom, Carbeau awoke and they ate supper.

Herman said, as they finished, "Even five miles with them stitches — well — if it don't open, take them out in two, three days. Mrs. Labret can do it." He pointed to the worn knapsack he had gotten from the bedroom. "There's some meat and bannock. Labrets don't have much either, this winter. Here, you'll need another shirt."

The other was staring at him and Herman continued, almost loud, "Hey, where's your gun? You run your deer down?"

Carbeau said slowly, "In the fight — I — "

"Sure sure," Herman got up and reached above the door to the gunrack. "I don't need these both. Some shells," he rummaged in a drawer, "here, you can bring it back when — when you don't need it."

Carbeau stood looking down at the little mound of things. "You better start," Herman said. "You ain't going fast."

When Carbeau was dressed at last, the knapsack on his back and the gun in his hand, Herman hooked his snowshoes off the nail in the lean-to. The other man could not seem to move; then he said almost inaudibly,

"No."

"Look, it's over five miles, belly-deep! I'm not going no — " but Carbeau jerked up to him, frost-blackened face contorted,

"Joe, I — I come jus' — jus' to ki — "

"Hey, hey!" Herman was shouting the words away, "you'll have time, to make yourself a pair! Leave these at Labret's! You hear me!"

Carbeau's face slowly hardened. He seemed to stoop forward, as if accepting a weight, then turned and limped heavily out on the porch. He stepped into the snowshoes. The two dogs sat at attention as in the gentle moonlight he moved into his stride. At the clearing's edge Herman thought his figure hesitated, but then it was gone.

When he became aware of the cold, he went in. He sat at the table a long time before he got up and took down the picture. He glanced at it, turned it over and, with lips moving, read the poem. Gradually his broad face softened, as if a fathomless serenity blossomed like child's laughter in him. He folded the paper carefully and put it in his shirt pocket. He again pulled the hides before the stove, stretched out face downward, and fell instantly asleep.

Four

He awoke, lifting his head from his arms. In the absolute stillness the lamp burned, sputtering on its wick. He pushed himself up and looked at the clock. Then he pulled on his barn coat, blew out the lamp after lighting the lantern, and stepped out into the silver, frozen world. The northern lights flamed a path down the endless sky. He could not have explained what he expected to see as his hands pulled the barn door open.

THE BEAUTIFUL SEWERS
OF PARIS, ALBERTA

The sewer is the conscience of the city. All things converge into it, and are confronted with one another. In this lurid place there is darkness, but there are no secrets.

— VICTOR HUGO, *Les Misérables*, 1862

ONE AUGUST DAY IN 1952, a few weeks before I entered my last year of high school, I bought Victor Hugo's massive novel, *Les Misérables*. The English edition, 1,222 pages long and published in 1931 by The Modern Library of the World's Best Books, the Giant Series, translated by Charles E. Wilbour. That same summer I worked on the construction crew that was laying the first water and sewer mains under the streets of my home town of Coaldale, Alberta. I was seventeen.

Coaldale, population 800, had no bookstore. Neither did nearby Lethbridge (population 22,000), but some time earlier I had discovered that the stationary store on Seventh Street South did offer a back corner with a few "world classics" — none of which had been written in Canada, of course. In December 1951 I had bought my first book there — *The Pickwick Papers* by Charles Dickens — and spent all of Christmas Day (except the compulsory morning church service) lying on the living-room couch laughing myself into fits until my mother, whose gift to me the book was, decided she had made a mistake in letting me choose it. She had had no choice. I wanted a book and she could not read English, but to waste an entire serious holiday laughing? Fortunately I was a fast reader, though enjoyment and coughing fits slowed me down on this one.

But *Les Misérables* is no novel of laughter and forgetting, not even in a brilliant, windy southern Alberta summer Sunday of the early fifties. Nor can the present world-touring musical version of the story make it that. As Hugo states in his 1862 preface, the book deals with "the degradation of man by poverty, the ruin of woman by starvation, and the dwarfing of childhood by physical and spiritual night."

Now the fact is that most modern Canadians like myself are immeasurably fortunate; not one of those conditions has ever really applied to us. Nevertheless, when I walk along the beautiful shaded streets of Coaldale, I remember the deep trenches that piled up the earth here in pyramidal rows forty years ago, the sewers that surely still lie where I helped place them. And I also think of the

hero of *Les Misérables*, Jean Valjean, carrying his unconscious enemy with such ineffable honour through the
immense, leviathan sewers of 1830 Paris.

To descend into the sewer is to enter the grave.

Anyone in their right mind knows that no prairie
town is a Paris, France. Such knowledge is particularly
obvious to those who year after year live in such a town.
The main irrigation ditch which still marks the southern
boundary of Coaldale, the ditch which in 1952 watered all
the gardens and small strawberry patches and corn and
beanfields, which filled every cistern (or the common open
reservoir where you could go, like Cosette, with a pail),
filled each cistern under or beside every tiny wooden
house through an intricate web of overgrown ditches
supposedly kept clear of weeds and wading, widdling children by the one hired town worker who was all at the
same time constable, volunteer fire chief, dogcatcher,
wooden sidewalk repairman and waterman, that ditch of
reversed tributaries was certainly no Seine River. The
glazed clay or much larger concrete sewer pipes which
the workers of Bennett and White Ltd., Edmonton,
nested in sand, fitted together and buried beneath the
streets in 1952 under contract with Mayor Russell Davis
and the Coaldale Town Council, were nothing at all like
the legendary architectured Paris sewers begun sometime
in the Middle Ages and which became both a grave and
an asylum for crime, intelligence, social protest, liberty of

conscience and every conceivable human debauchery, day and night. I know that most of the Coaldale sewers were too small even for a child to crawl into; not a single one was (then) large enough for a big man to walk in erect, leave alone carry another draped over his shoulder.

And I, at seventeen, was certainly no Bruneseau who in 1805 would be the one man in all of Napoleon's empire brave enough to enter the Paris sewers, and then spend seven years expanding their network. In fact, though I was hired on the first day of the project, in less than two months, before it was completed, I was fired.

Like everyone else Bennett and White hired in Coaldale, I was a labourer — a "grunt." Our work was mostly lifting and carrying things, digging them up or burying them in the places designated by the foreman and various bosses, who all came from somewhere else. A nice brainless business, being a grunt; you just do everything anyone orders because you're right down there with the sewer pipe, as low as you'll get without more digging. I, however, was a shade less grunty than most; for some reason (Because I could read and write? I cannot remember having to demonstrate that ability to anyone.) on the very first day the project engineer pointed at me and the foreman said,

"You, go with him."

So there I was frequently without a shovel, riding about town in the engineer's brown Model A Ford — a curiosity even then — the "rod and chain" man. While my fellow grunts heaved sand and gravel and cement into the grinding maw of a mixer, or backfilled around pipe deep in the trench, or muscled clay joints and concrete manhole sections off the trucks, I held a graduated stick motionless, or anchored what I at first supposed was an endless measuring tape — "Hold it right there, don't move it!" — but soon discovered was a "chain." A steel chain certainly but nothing at all like the one riveted around Jean Valjean's neck to march him to the prison galleys of Toulon.

If my life were a massive romance like *Les Misérables* where everyone (especially the villains) always and continuously return until all are either dead or married, I would by now have met that engineer again: perhaps five years older than I, a third-year civil engineering student at University of Alberta on his summer job, his blond, tough and compact body shorter than mine, his slightly lopsided grin with a tooth missing on the right side. But I cannot remember his name, nor will he remember the gangly kid he left to lounge in the shade of his Model A while the other grunts sweated and gasped in the burning sun and he argued with the foreman.

I didn't lounge often, for within two days I had learned a grunt's basic survival rules: 1) *never* sit down; 2) *never* stand with your hands in your pockets. But often the engineer did not need me and then I worked with the rest; that was when the others, who were never told to sit in the Model A, got their small revenges on me: the heavy ends of the pipes, the extra shovelling where there was room for only one to work, the deepest mud after a rain where the huge planks supporting the trench walls oozed, bulged ominously between their horizontal braces.

He was wading in the hideous muck of the city....
All dripping with slime, his soul filled with a strange
light.

The best trench workers quickly proved to be the older immigrant men who had somehow survived the war and had managed, with what was left of their families, to get into Canada. Those who were refugees — displaced persons, or DPS as they were called derisively, or "schmoes" after the sub-human critters in the very popular Li'l Abner comic strip — worked at anything without question. Their lack of English saved them from the precise details of racism, but it certainly did not save them from its pervasive, abusive tone.

That racism bothered me; mostly, to be honest about it now, for myself. After all, though born in Canada, I was of refugee parents myself; at home we had never spoken anything but an obscure German dialect, a language I used to explain the foreman's peremptory orders to my fellow Mennonite labourers. But tired muscles and common sweat soon push such attitudes in a workgang aside: work hard enough together and you get to deride a man not for his race but for his evasions, his laziness. It seems to me now, thinking back to 1952, that male concepts about women are much harder to change than concepts about race.

O, the summer girls walking by with their brief blouses knotted up under their breasts, their white shorts, their arms and legs week by week turning a deeper, more limpid golden brown under that libidinous sun.

Psychologists inform us that boys of fifteen to seventeen may well be the most sex-dominated creatures on earth. If I was that, I wanted to keep it strictly private. My horniness — I could not, then, have expressed it that way — was a burden I carried in absolute silence, an ogre to be wrestled with, and occasionally indulged somehow, loathed or loved, and fought with again, fought into and through guilt and then inevitably back into guilt again with remorse and inner rage.

Given that, to hear such tangled privacies brayed about the streets by the other young grunts in our workgang every time a beautiful girl — they were *all* beautiful, always! — became visible, embarrassed and humiliated me. Wolf whistles, cries of "Hubba! Hubba!", howls, obscene offers, brutal and violent gestures: the older immigrant men worked on, oblivious. After surviving both Stalin and Hitler, they must have found these endlessly repeated performances merely childish, banal. But I listened, I couldn't stop myself, though I mostly pretended to ignore them; as I tried to ignore the bragging about weekend conquests. And so I came to prefer the depths of the trench. From below, at least they sounded indistinct, merely animals yowling.

The young engineer spoke very little; he never said a word when a woman passed us. Sometimes he would smile, but he kept on working. One of his main jobs was to make certain the sewer was laid absolutely on gradient, and that's where his arguments with the foreman started. Time and again, to prove his point about the violation of benchmarks he had set, I'd have to slide down into the cool, sweet earth and work my extended measuring rod, as directed, from one joint to another along those inter-laced pipes. And then he'd be expostulating again:

"You put in a 'little bump,' like you say, when you lay the pipe and you cut capacity — look, almost a third!"

Diagrams, formulas, circled numbers racing left-handed across his spiral notebook from that ever-sharp, precise draftsman's pen.

A sewer is a cynic. It tells all.

The longest, biggest line cut down Main Street, which was also Alberta Number 3 Highway between Medicine Hat and Lethbridge — just recently paved, of course, so we really sliced it up, wide and mountainous along the north side and a smaller branch at right angles into every house or business. After carving up the residential streets with feeder lines, we had begun very deep (eighteen feet?) on east Main, and as August lengthened and the huge trencher steadily chewed us up towards the town hotel near the western end of the business section, the arguments got louder.

"You do that, you've got to lay twice the diameter! It's supposed to handle *all* this town's shit!"

Throughout the summer I had wondered how whoever-it-was had decided on the various pipe sizes anyway. Had they interviewed every homeowner and business about length of residence and then gone into each outhouse and measured it for hole capacity and percentage filled?

"Besides all the other crap that always gets shoved down sewers," the engineer muttered grimly to me, who could have no opinion but at dislocated moments might provide an ear. Shit, apparently, was the least of it.

Why in this sewer summer of 1952 (at 82 cents an hour it was the most I'd ever earned) did I begin with Hugo rather than any of the other Modern Library giants ($2.95 each) I bought later — Cervantes, Dos Passos, Pushkin, Joyce, Tolstoy? Perhaps because of its giant intestine, the "cloaca" which, as Hugo explains, "has been the disease of Paris" throughout history. In part five of *Les Misérables* he describes it for fifteen pages, and then devotes another twenty-three pages to getting Jean Valjean, with Marius on his shoulder, out of it. Well, why?

Perhaps, to be blunt about it, I was wondering how one dealt with shit. Clearly the world, including me, was full of it, and here on the apparently open prairie there were neither enough bushes nor even spaces — as it seemed to me there had always been in homestead Saskatchewan where I lived the first twelve years of my life — for it to be voided properly unseen, and thereafter to be permitted the privacy of its individual disintegration. In sunny southern Alberta it seemed necessary to rip up the landscape and yell about it in the streets.

Holding this immense novel in my hand now, I am suddenly certain that I bought it originally because of the sewer. For I had read the story much earlier, in Saskatchewan when I was twelve: a simplified version by a certain Solomon Cleaver that, from somewhere, contained pictures. In that one-room Speedwell School I am reading *Jean Val Jean*, leaning against the warm galvanized guard of the heater which is two gas barrels welded together; on the temporary stage across one end of the room five girls are practising "Good King Wenceslas" for the Christmas concert. The black-and-white picture, when I turn the page, is captioned: "Jean carries the wounded Marius to safety through the filthy sewers of Paris." Jean is a lank-haired old man, face contorted, submerged to above his waist in what looks like molten lead. Behind him the gleaming maw of the sewer twists away into darkness.

"Carried to safety." When I go to find *Jean Val Jean* in the university library, I discover it in the Canadian Literature section! It seems Solomon Cleaver was "a young minister in Winnipeg [who] decided to tell the story in his own words…he repeated it more than 800 times to over 100,000 people, and was obliged to reject one invitation in every four which crowded upon him." So, the publishers' foreword continues, he was "prevailed upon to have it published": first in 1935 and then, after ten reprintings, Clarke Irwin of Toronto brought it out as a true *Canadian Classic*.

And the pictures: fourteen in all from an early thirties French movie. Cosette leaning over a dying Jean looks like Greta Garbo in golden ringlets.

And the sewer? Surely every young lover deserves to be carried from the fallen barricades of His Revolution to safety through a filthy sewer.

How could Solomon Cleaver squeeze Victor Hugo's gigantic story onto 119 small pages? Jean Valjean's passage through the sewers shrinks from 39 pages to 627 words; the final two chapters become a verse from a Scottish Covenanters' hymn. How truly classic Canadian.

Well, Paris, France, is a place, but Coaldale, Alberta, is most certainly a place also. In late August 1952 the trench had reached the western end of town, and my fellow grunt and I were hand tunnelling a small branch of it under the sidewalk in front of the hotel, directly beneath the Ladies and Escorts sign. We took turns, one lying on his back, loosening and pulling back a short spadeful of earth while the other used a long-handled shovel to throw it up onto street level. At the moment of crisis I could see at my feet only his head, sprinkled with red clay and talking, talking Low German as he had all afternoon, me intense with listening.

"Holy ssshit, you buggersh! How'll we ever get this fuckin' job done at that ssspeed!"

The foreman! His bulging red face tilted down at us, maybe about to topple in. But I was somewhere far away, in 1944, watching refugees push their carts through the

frozen mud of Stalin's oppression, surrounded by the
German army's disastrous retreat across the endless, devastating vistas of the Ukrainian steppes.

"Shit yourself," I yelled up. "You workin' so hard in
the hotel every day, gettin' drunk!"

After that we had nothing to do but drop our shovels
right there, get out of that ditch and hoof it to the office
portable and pick up our last cheque. The foreman drove
his pickup there to tell the bookkeeper, but he sure as hell
wasn't givin' no smartass bastards a lift. So we walked
east the length of Main Street all cut up with bumpy
trenches, and I felt stupid because my big mouth had gotten Pete fired. He just laughed; he was two years older
than I, but his father had vanished long ago in Stalin's
Siberia and he and his mother and younger siblings were
true refugees, working at anything to make a living. He
laughed and said school started in a week anyway; he was
going to school and learn to be a good Canadian. Like me.

A prairie town, uniquely its own place in the dazzling
summer sun. Spread across the wide land, dark trees and
roofs surrounded by the white spray of irrigation sprin-
klers moving steadily across, around fields. No more men
in gumboots leaning on shovels over openings in little
ditches — "Welcome to Coaldale, Gem of the West,
Population 5,280." Here and there among the bungalows
the small, old houses sit well below street level; the green
rushes grow in the seepage along the Main Ditch, the
giant cottonwoods still lean over its surprisingly clear

water. Pouring over falls between the same old timbers that might, just might, still record the scars of my boyhood knife. Beautiful, pastoral, the air bright to the line of snow on Big Chief, that always distant, holy mountain. No revolutionary barricades ever anywhere in the streets; so it is perhaps necessary to seek that strange light for one's soul in the treacherous, filthy, safety of sewers.

At present the sewer almost realizes the ideal of what is understood in England by the word "respectable".... The filth comports itself decently.

THE NAMING OF
ALBERT JOHNSON

1. *The Eagle River, Yukon*
   Wednesday, February 17, 1932
   Tuesday, February 16, 1932

THERE IS ARCTIC SILENCE at last, after the long snarl of rifles. As if all the stubby trees within earshot had finished splitting in the cold. Then the sound of the airplane almost around the river's bend begins to return, turning as tight a spiral as it may up over bank and trees and back down, over the man crumpled on the bedroll, over the frantic staked dog teams, spluttering, down, glancing down off the wind-ridged river. Tail leaping, almost cartwheeling over its desperate roar for skis, immense sound rocketing from that bouncing black dot on the level glare but stopped finally, its prop whirl staggering out motionless just behind the man moving inevitably forward on snowshoes, not looking back, step by step up the river with his rifle ready. Hesitates, lifts one foot, then the other, stops, and moves forward again to the splotch in the vast whiteness before him.

The pack is too huge, and apparently worried by rats with very long, fine teeth. Behind it a twisted body. Unbelievably small. One outflung hand still clutching a rifle, but no motion, nothing, the airplane dead and only the distant sounds of dogs somewhere, of men moving at the banks of the river. The police rifle points down, steadily extending the police arm until it can lever the body, already stiffening, up. A red crater for hip. As if one small part of that incredible toughness had rebelled at last, exploded red out of itself, splattering itself with itself when everything but itself was at last unreachable. But the face is turning up. Rime, and clots of snow ground into whiskers, the fur hat hurled somewhere by bullets perhaps and the whipped cowlick already a mat frozen above half-open eyes showing only white, nostrils flared, the concrete face wiped clean of everything but snarl. Freezing snarl and teeth. As if the long clenched jaws had tightened down beyond some ultimate cog and openly locked their teeth into their own torn lips in one final wordlessly silent scream.

The pilot blunders up, gasping. "By god, we got the son, of a bitch!" stumbles across the back of the snowshoes and recovers beside the policeman. Gagging a little, "My g — " All that sudden colour propped up by the rifle barrel on the otherwise white snow. And the terrible face.

The one necessary bullet, in the spine where its small
entry cannot be seen at this moment, and was never felt as
six others were, knocked the man face down in the snow.
Though that would never loosen his grip on his rifle. The
man had been working himself over on his side, not concerned as it seemed for the bullets singing to him from the
level drifts in front of him or the trees on either bank.
With his left hand he was reaching into his coat pocket to
reload his Savage .30-30, almost warm on the inside of his
other bare hand, and he knew as every good hunter must
that he had exactly thirty-nine bullets left besides the one
hidden under the rifle's butt plate. If they moved in any
closer he also had the Winchester .22 with sixty-four bullets, and closer still there will be the sawed-off shotgun,
though he had only a few shells left, he could not now be
certain exactly how many. He had stuffed snow tight into
the hole where one or perhaps even two shells had
exploded in his opposite hip pocket. A man could lose his
blood in a minute from a hole that size but the snow was
still white and icy the instant he had to glance at it, pack-
ing it in. If they had got him there before forcing him
down behind his pack in the middle of the river, he could
not have moved enough to pull out of the pack straps,
leave alone get behind it for protection. Bullets twitch it,
whine about his tea tin like his axe handle snapping once
at his legs as he ran from the eastern riverbank too steep
to clamber up, a very bad mistake to have to discover after
spending several minutes and a hundred yards of strength
running his snowshoes towards it. Not a single rock, steep

and bare like polished planks. But he had gained a little on them, he saw that as he curved without stopping towards the centre of the river and the line of trees beyond it. That bank is easily climbed, he knows because he climbed it that morning, but all the dogs and men so suddenly around the hairpin turn surprised him towards the nearest bank, and he sees the teams spreading to out-flank him, three towards the low west bank. And two of them bending over the one army radioman he got.

Instantly the man knew it was the river that had betrayed him. He had outlegged their dogs and lost the plane time and again on glare-ice and in fog and brush and between the endless trails of caribou herds, but the sluggish loops of this river doubling back on itself have betrayed him. It is his own best move, forward and then back, circle forward and further back, backwards, so the ones following his separate tracks will suddenly confront each other in cursing bewilderment. But this river, it cannot be named the Porcupine, has out-doubled him. For the dogs leaping towards him around the bend, the roaring radioman heaving at his sled, scrabbling for his rifle, this is clearly what he saw when he climbed the tree on the far bank; one of the teams he saw then across a wide tongue of land already ahead of him, as it seemed, and he started back to get further behind them before he followed and picked them off singly in whatever tracks of his they thought they were following. These dogs and this driver rounding to face him as he walks so carefully backwards in his snowshoes on the curve of his own tracks.

Whatever this river has done spiralling back into the Yukon hills, his rifle will not betray him. Words are bellowing out of the racket of teams hurtling around the bend. His rifle speaks easily, wordlessly to the army radioman kneeling, sharpshooter position, left elbow propped on left knee. The sights glided together certain and deadly, and long before the sound had returned that one kneeling was already flung back clean as frozen wood bursting at his axe.

He has not eaten, he believes it must be two days, and the rabbit tracks are so old they give no hope for his snares. The squirrel burrow may be better. He is scraping curls from tiny spruce twigs, watching them tighten against the lard pail, watching the flames as it seems there licking the tin blacker with their gold tongues. The fire lives with him, and he will soon examine the tinfoil of matches in his pocket, and the tinfoil bundle in his pack and also the other two paper-wrapped packages. That must be done daily, if possible. The pack, unopened, with the .22 laced to its side is between his left shoulder and the snow hollow; the moose hides spread under and behind him; the snowshoes stuck erect into the snow on the right, the long axe lying there and the rifle also, in its cloth cover but on the moose-hide pouch. He has already worked carefully on his feet, kneading as much of the frost out of one and then the other as he can before the fire, though two toes on the left are black and the heel of the right is rubbed raw. Bad lacing when he walked backwards, and too numb for him to notice. The one toe can only be kept another day, perhaps, but he has only a gun-oily rag for his heel. Gun oil? Spruce gum? Wait. His feet wrapped and ready to move instantly and he sits watching warmth curl around the pail. Leans his face down into it. Then he puts the knife away in his clothes and pulls out a tiny paper. His hard fingers unfold it carefully, he studies the crystals a moment, and then as the flames tighten the blackened spirals of spruce he pours that into the steaming pail. He studies the paper, the brownness of it; the suggestion of a word beginning, or perhaps ending, that shines through its substance. He lowers it steadily then until it darkens, smiling as a spot of deep brown breaks through the possible name and curls back a black empty circle towards his fingers. He lets it go, feeling warmth like a massage in its final flare and dying. There is nothing left but a smaller fold of pepper and a bag of salt so when he drinks it is very slowly, letting each mouthful move for every part of his tongue to hold a moment this last faint sweetness.

He sits in the small yellow globe created by fire. Drinking. The wind breathes through the small spruce, his body rests motionlessly; knowing that dug into the snow with drifts and spruce tips above him they could see his smokeless fire only if they flew directly over him. And the plane cannot fly at night. They are somewhere very close now, and their plane less than a few minutes behind. It has flown straight in an hour, again and again, all he had overlaid with tangled tracks in five weeks, but the silent land is what it is. He is now resting motionlessly. And waiting.

And the whisky-jacks are suddenly there. He had not known them before to come after dark, but grey and white tipped with black they fluffed themselves at the grey edge of his light, watching, and then one hopped two hops. Sideways. The first living thing he had seen since the caribou. But he reaches for the bits of babiche he had cut and rubbed in salt, laid ready on the cloth of the rifle-butt. He throws, the draggle-tail is gone but the other watches, head cocked, then jumps so easily the long space his stiff throw had managed, and the bit is gone. He does not move his body, tosses another bit, and another, closer, closer, and then draggle-tail is there scrabbling for the bit, and he twitches the white string lying beside the bits of babiche left by the rifle, sees the bigger piece tug from the snow and draggle-tail leap to it. Gulp. He tugs, feels the slight weight as the thread lifts from the snow in the fire-light, and now the other is gone while draggle-tail comes towards him inevitably, string pulling the beak sound-lessly agape, wings desperate in snow, dragged between rifle and fire into the waiting claw of his hand. He felt the bird's blood beat against his palm, the legs and tail and wings thud an instant, shuddering and then limp between his relentless fingers.

Wings. Noiselessly he felt the beautiful muscles shift, slip over bones delicate as twigs. He could lope circles around any dogs they set on his trail but that beast labelled in letters combing the clouds, staring everywhere until its roar suddenly blundered up out of a canyon or over a ridge, laying its relentless shadow like words on the world:

he would have dragged every tree in the Yukon together
to build a fire and boil that. Steel pipes and canvas and
wires and name, that stinking noise. In the silence under
the spruce he skims the tiny fat bubbles from the darkening soup; watches them coagulate yellow on the shavings.
Better than gun oil, or gum. He began to unwrap his feet
again but listening, always listening. The delicate furrow
of the bird pointed towards him in the snow.

2. *The Richardson Mountains, N.W.T.*
            Tuesday, February 9, 1932
            Saturday, January 30, 1932

Though it means moving two and three miles to their one,
the best trail to confuse them in the foothill ravines was a
spiral zigzag. West of the mountains he has not seen them;
he has outrun them so far in crossing the Richardson
Mountains during the blizzard that when he reaches a
river he thought it must be the Porcupine because he seems
at last to be inside something that is completely alone. But
the creeks draining east lay in seemingly parallel but eventually converging canyons with tundra plateaus glazed
under wind between them, and when he paused on one leg
of his zag he sometimes saw them, across one plateau or in
a canyon, labouring with their dogs and sleds as it seems
ahead of him. In the white scream of the mountain pass
where no human being has ever ventured in winter he
does not dare pause to sleep for two days and the long

night between them, one toe and perhaps another frozen beyond saving and parts of his face dead, but in the east he had seen the trackers up close, once been above them and watched them coming along his trails towards each other unawares out of two converging canyons with their sleds and drivers trailing, and suddenly round the cliff to face each other in cursing amazement. He was far enough not to hear their words as they heated water for tea, wasting daylight minutes, beating their hands to keep warm.

The police drive the dog teams now, and the Indians sometimes; the ones who can track him on the glazed snow, through zags and bends, always wary of ambush, are the two army radiomen. One of the sleds is loaded with batteries when it should be food, but they sniff silently along his tracks, loping giant circles ahead of the heaving dogs and swinging arms like semaphores when they find a trail leading as it seems directly back towards the sleds they have just left. He would not have thought them so relentless at unravelling his trails, these two who every morning tried to raise the police on their frozen radio, and when he was convinced they would follow him as certainly as Millen and the plane roared up, dropping supplies, it was time to accept the rising blizzard over the mountains and find at last, for certain, the Porcupine River.

It is certainly Millen who brought the plane north just before the blizzard, and it was Millen who saw his smoke and heard him coughing, whistling in that canyon camp hidden in trees under a cliff so steep he has to chop handholds in the frozen rock to get out of there. Without dynamite again, or bombs, they could not dig him out; even in his unending alert his heart jerks at the sound of what was a foot slipping against a frozen tree up the ridge facing him. His rifle is out of its sheath, the shell racking home in the cold like precise steel biting. There is nothing more; an animal? A tree bursting? He crouches motionless, for if they are there they should be all around him, perhaps above on the cliff, and he will not move until he knows. Only the wind worrying spruce and snow, whining wordlessly. There, twenty yards away a shadow moves, Millen certainly, and his shot snaps as his rifle swings up, as he drops. Bullets snick from everywhere, their sound booming back and forth along the canyon. He has only fired once and is down, completely aware, on the wrong side of his fire and he shoots carefully again to draw their shots and they come, four harmlessly high and nicely spaced out: there are two — Millen and another — below him in the canyon and two a bit higher on the right ridge, one of them that slipped. Nothing up the canyon or above on the cliff. With that knowledge he gathered himself and leaped over the fire against the cliff and one on the ridge made a good shot that cut his jacket and he could fall as if gut-shot in the hollow or deadfall. Until the fire died, he was almost comfortable.

In the growing dusk he watches the big Swede, who drove dogs very well, crawl towards Millen stretched out, face down. He watches him tie Millen's legs together with the laces of his mukluks and drag him backwards, ploughing a long furrow and leaving the rifle sunk in the snow. He wastes no shot at their steady firing, and when they stop there are Millen's words still

You're surrounded. King isn't dead. Will you give

waiting, frozen in the canyon. He lay absolutely motionless behind the deadfall against the cliff, as if he were dead, knowing they would have to move finally. He flexed his feet continuously, and his fingers as he shifted the rifle no more quickly than a clock hand, moving into the position it would have to be when they charged him. They almost outwait him; it is really a question between the coming darkness and his freezing despite his invisible motions, but before darkness Millen had to move. Two of them were coming and he shifted his rifle slightly on the log to cover the left one — it must have been the long cold that made him mistake that for Millen — who dived out of sight, his shot thundering along the canyon, but Millen did not drop behind anything. Simply down on one knee, firing. Once, twice, bullets tore the log and then he had his head up with those eyes staring straight down his sights and he fired two shots so fast the roar in the canyon sounded as one and Millen stood up, the whole length over him, whirled in that silent unmistakable way and crashed face down in the snow. He hears them dragging and chopping trees for a stage cache to keep the body, and in the darkness he chops handholds up the face of the cliff, step by step as he hoists himself and his pack out of another good shelter. As he has had to leave others.

3. *The Rat River, N.W.T.*

> Saturday, January 10, 1932
> Thursday, December 31, 1931
> Tuesday, July 28, 1931

In his regular round of each loophole he peers down the promontory towards their fires glaring up from behind the riverbank. They surround him on three sides, nine of them with no more than forty dogs, which in this cold means they already need more supplies than they can have brought with them. They will be making plans for something, suddenly, beyond bullets against his logs and guns and it will have to come soon. In the long darkness, and he can wait far easier than they. Dynamite. If they have any more to thaw out very carefully after blowing open the roof and stovepipe as darkness settled, a hole hardly big enough for one of them — a Norwegian, they were everywhere with their long noses — to fill it an instant, staring down at him gathering himself from the corner out of roof-sod and pipes and snow: the cabin barely stuck above the drifts but that one was gigantic to lean in like that, staring until he lifted his rifle and the long face vanished an instant before his bullet passed through that space. But the hole was large enough for the cold to slide down along the wall and work itself into his trench, which would be all that saved him when they used the last of their dynamite. He began to feel what they had stalked him with all day: cold tightening steadily as steel around toes, face, around fingers.

In the clearing still nothing stirs. There is only the penumbra of light along the circle of the bank as if they had laid a trench-fire to thaw the entire promontory and were soundlessly burrowing in under him. Their flares were long dead, the sky across the river flickering with orange lights to vanish down into spruce and willows again, like the shadow blotting a notch in the eastern bank, and he thrust his rifle through the chink and had almost got a shot away when a projectile arced against the sky and he jerked the gun out, diving, into the trench deep under the wall among the moose hides that could not protect him from the roof and walls tearing apart so loud it seemed most of himself had been blasted to the farthest granules of sweet, silent earth. The sods and foot-thick logs he had built together where the river curled were gone and he would climb out and walk away as he always had, but first he pulled himself up and out between the splinters, still holding the rifle, just in time to see yellow light humpling through the snow towards him and he fired three times so fast it sounded in his ears as though his cabin was continuing to explode. The shadows around the light dance in one spot an instant but come on in a straight black line, lengthening down, faster, and the light cuts straight across his eyes and he gets away the fourth shot and the light tears itself into bits. He might have been lying on his back staring up into night and had the stars explode into existence above him. And whatever darkness is left before him then blunders

away, desperately ploughing away from him through the
snow like the first one who came twice with a voice repeating at his door

I am Constable Alfred King, are you in there?

fist thudding the door the second time with a paper
creaking louder than his voice so thin in the cold silence

*I have a search warrant now, we have had complaints
and if you don't open*

and then ploughing away in a long desperate scrabble
through the sun-shot snow while the three others at the
riverbank thumped their bullets hopelessly high into the
logs but shattering the window again and again until they
dragged King and each other head first over the bank
while he placed lead carefully over them, snapping willow bits on top of them and still seeing, strangely, the tiny
hole that had materialized up into his door when he
flexed the trigger, still hearing the grunt that had wormed
in through the slivers of the board he had whipsawn himself. Legs and feet wrapped in moose hide lay a moment
across his window, level in the snow, jerking as if barely
attached to a body knocked over helpless, a face somewhere twisted in gradually developing pain that had first
leaned against his door, fist banging while that other one
held the dogs at the edge of the clearing, waiting

Hallo? Hallo? This is Constable Alfred King of the
Royal Canadian Mounted Police. I want to talk to
you. Constable Millen

and they looked into each other's eyes, once, through his
tiny window. The eyes peering down into his — could he
be seen from out of the blinding sun? — squinted blue
from a boy's round face with a bulging nose bridged over
pale with cold. King, of the Royal Mounted. Like a silly
book title, or the funny papers. He didn't look it as much
as Spike Millen, main snooper and tracker at Arctic Red
River who baked pies and danced, everybody said, better
than any man in the north. Let them dance hipped in snow,
get themselves dragged away under spruce and dangling
traps, asking, laying words on him, naming things

Yukon, you come across from the Yukon? You got a
trapper's licence? The Loucheaux trap the Rat, up
towards the Richardson Mountains. You'll need a
licence, why not

Words. Dropping out of nothing into advice. Maybe he
wanted a kicker to move that new canoe against the Rat
River? Loaded down as it is. The Rat drops fast, you have
to hand-line the portage anyway to get past Destruction
City where those would-be Klondikers wintered in '98.
He looked up at the trader above him on the wedge of
gravel. He had expected at least silence. From a trader
standing with the bulge of seven hundred dollars in his

pocket; in the south a man could feed himself with that for two years. Mouths always full of words, pushing, every mouth falling open and dropping words from nothing into meaning. The trader's eyes shifted finally, perhaps to the junction of the rivers behind them, south and west, the united river clicking under the canoe. As he raised his paddle. The new rifle oiled and ready with its butt almost touching his knees as he kneels, ready to pull the canoe around.

4. *Above Fort McPherson, N.W.T.*
        Tuesday, July 7, 1931

The Porcupine River, as he thought it was then, chuckled between the three logs of his raft. He could hear that below him, under the mosquitoes probing the mesh about his head, and see the gold lengthen up the river like the canoe that would come towards him from the north where the sun just refused to open the spiky horizon. Gilded, hammered out slowly, soundlessly towards him the thick gold. He sat almost without breathing, watching it come like silence. And then imperceptibly the black spired riverbend grew pointed, stretched itself in a thin straight line double-bumped, gradually spreading a straight wedge below the sun through the golden river. When he had gathered that slowly into anger it was already too late to choke his fire; the vee had abruptly bent towards him, the bowman already raised his paddle;

hailed. Almost it seemed as if a name had been blundered into the silence, but he did not move in his fury. The river chuckled again.

"...O-o-o-o..." the point of the wedge almost under him now. And the sound of a name, that was so clear he could almost distinguish it. Perhaps he already knew what it was, had long since lived this in that endlessly enraged chamber of himself, even to the strange Indian accent mounded below him in the canoe bow where the black hump of the stern partner moved them straight towards him out of the fanned ripples, crumpling gold. To the humps of his raft below on the gravel waiting to anchor them.

"What d'ya want."

"You Albert Johnson?"

It could have been the sternman who named him. The sun like hatchet-strokes across slanted eyes, the gaunt noses below him there holding the canoe against the current, their paddles hooked in the logs of his raft. Two Loucheaux half-faces, black and red kneeling in the roiled gold of the river, the words thudding softly in his ears.

You Albert Johnson?

One midnight above the Arctic Circle to hear again the inevitability of name. He has not heard it in four years, it could be to the very day since that Vancouver garden, staring into the evening sun and hearing this quiet sound from these motionless — perhaps they are men kneeling there, perhaps waiting for him to accept again what has now been laid inevitably upon him, the name come to meet him in his journey north, come out of the north around the bend and against the current of the Peel River, as they name that too, to confront him on a river he thought another and aloud where he would have found after all his years, at long last, only nameless silence.

You Albert Johnson?

"Yes," he said finally.

And out of his rage he begins to gather words together. Slowly, every word he can locate, as heavily as he would gather stones on a Saskatchewan field, to hold them for one violent moment against himself between his two hands before he heaves them up and hurls them — but they are gone. The ripples of their passing may have been smoothing out as he stares at where they should have been had they been there. Only the briefly golden river lies before him, whatever its name may be since it must have one, bending back somewhere beyond that land, curling back upon itself in its giant, relentless spirals down to the implacable, and ice-choked, arctic sea.

THE ANGEL OF THE TAR SANDS

SPRING HAD MOST CERTAINLY, finally, come. The morning drive to the plant from Fort McMurray was so dazzling with fresh green against the heavy spruce, the air so unearthly bright that it swallowed the smoke from the candy-striped chimneys as if it did not exist. Which is just lovely, the superintendent thought, cut out all the visible crud, shut up the environmentalists, and he went into his neat office (with the river view with islands) humming, "Alberta blue, Alberta blue, the taste keeps — " but did not get his tan golfing jacket off before he was interrupted. Not by the radio-telephone, by Tak the day operator on Number Two Bucket in person, walking past the secretary without stopping.

"What the hell?" the superintendent said, quickly annoyed.

"I ain't reporting this on no radio," Tak's imperturbable Japanese-Canadian face was tense, "if them reporters hear about this one they're gonna — "

"You scrape out *another* buffalo skeleton, for god's sake?"

"No, it's maybe a dinosaur this time, one of them real old — "

But the superintendent, swearing, was already out the door yelling for Bertha who was always on stand-by now with her spade. If one of the three nine-storey-high bucket-wheels stopped turning for an hour the plant dropped capacity, but another archaeological leak could stop every bit of production for a month while bifocalled professors stuck their noses...the jeep leaped along the track beside the conveyor belt running a third empty already and in three minutes he had Bertha with her long-handled spade busy on the face of the fifty-foot cliff that Number Two had been gnawing out. A shape emerged, quickly.

"What the..." staring, the superintendent could not find his ritual words, "...is that?"

"When the bucket hit the corner of it," Tak said, "I figured hey, that's the bones of a — "

"That's not just bone, it's...skin and...." The superintendent could not say the word.

"Wings," Bertha said it for him, digging her spade in with steady care. "That's wings, like you'd expect on a angel."

For that's what it was, plain as the day now, tucked tight into the oozing black cliff, an angel. Tak had seen only a corner of bones sheared clean but now that Bertha had it more uncovered they saw the manlike head through one folded-over pair of wings and the manlike legs, feet through another pair, very gaunt, the film of feathers and perhaps skin so thin and engrained with tarry sand that at first it was impossible to notice anything except the white bones inside them. The third pair of wings was pressed flat by the sand at a very awkward — it must have been a most painful —

"The middle two," Bertha said, trying to brush the sticky sand aside with her hand, carefully, "is what it flies with."

"Wouldn't it…he…fly with all six…six.…" The superintendent stopped, overwhelmed by the unscientific shape uncovered there so blatantly.

"You can look it up," Bertha said with a sideways glance at his ignorance, "Isaiah, chapter six."

But then she gagged too for the angel had moved. Not one of them was touching it, that was certain, but it had moved irrefutably. As they watched, stunned, the wings unfolded bottom and top, a head emerged, turned, and they saw the fierce hoary lineaments of an ancient man. His mouth all encrusted with tar pulled open and out came a sound. A long, throat-clearing streak of sound. They staggered back, fell; the superintendent found himself on his knees, staring up at the shape which wasn't really very tall, it just seemed immensely broad and overwhelming, the three sets of wings now sweeping back and forth as if loosening up in some seraphic 5BX plan. The voice rumbled like thunder, steadily on.

"Well," muttered Tak, "whatever it is, it sure ain't talking Japanese."

The superintendent suddenly saw himself as an altar boy, the angel suspended above him there and bits of words rose to his lips: *"Pax vobis...cem...cum,"* he ventured, but the connections were lost in the years. *"Magnifi...cat...ave Mar...."*

The obsidian eyes of the angel glared directly at him and it roared something, dreadfully. Bertha laughed aloud.

"Forget the popish stuff," she said. "It's talking Hutterite, Hutterite German."

"Wha...." The superintendent had lost all words; he was down to syllables only.

"I left the colony, years ago I...." But then she was too busy listening. The angel kept on speaking, non-stop as if words had been plugged up inside for eons, and its hands (it had only two of them, in the usual place at the ends of two arms) brushed double over its bucket-damaged shoulder and that appeared restored, whole just like the other, while it brushed the soil and tarry sand from its wings, flexing the middle ones again and again because they obviously had suffered much from their position.

"Ber...Ber..." the superintendent said. Finally he looked at Tak, pleading for a voice.

"What's it saying," Tak asked her, "Bertha, please? Bertha?"

She was listening with overwhelming intensity; there was nothing in this world but to hear. Tak touched her shoulder, shook her, but she did not notice. Suddenly the angel stopped speaking; it was studying her.

"I...I can't...." Bertha confessed to it at last, "I can understand every word you...every word, but I can't say, I've forgotten...."

In its silence the angel looked at her; slowly its expression changed. It might have been showing pity, though of course that is really difficult to tell with angels. Then it folded its lower wings over its feet, its upper wings over its face, and with an ineffable movement of its giant middle wings it rose, straight upward into the blue sky. They bent back staring after it, and in a moment it had vanished in light.

"O dear God," Bertha murmured after a time. "Our Elder always said they spoke Hutterite in heaven."

They three contemplated each other and they saw in each other's eyes the dread, the abrupt tearing sensation of doubt. Had they seen...and as one they looked at the sand cliff still oozing tar, the spade leaning against it. Beside the hole where Bertha had dug: the shape of the angel, indelible. Bertha was the first to get up.

"I quit," she said. "Right this minute."

"Of course, I understand." The superintendent was on his feet. "Tak, run your bucket through there, get it going quick."

"Okay," Tak said heavily. "You're the boss."

"It doesn't matter how fast you do it," Bertha said to the superintendent but she was watching Tak trudge into the shadow of the giant wheel. "It was there, we saw it."

And at her words the superintendent had a vision. He saw like an opened book the immense curves of the Athabasca River swinging through wilderness down from the glacial pinnacles of the Rocky Mountains and across Alberta and joined by the Berland and the McLeod and the Pembina and the Pelican and the Christina and the Clearwater and the Firebag rivers, and all the surface of the earth was gone, the Tertiary and the Lower Cretaceous layers of strata had been ripped away and the thousands of square miles of black bituminous sand were exposed, laid open, slanting down into the molten centre of the earth, *O miserere, miserere*, the words sang in his head and he felt their meaning though he could not have explained them, much less remembered Psalm 51, and after a time he could open his eyes and lift his head. The huge plant, he knew every bolt and pipe, still sprawled between him and the river; the brilliant air still swallowed the smoke from all the red-striped chimneys as if it did not exist, and he knew that through a thousand secret openings the oil ran there, gurgling in each precisely numbered pipe and jointure, sweet and clear like golden brown honey.

Tak was beside the steel ladder, about to start the long climb into the machine. Bertha touched his shoulder and they both looked up.

"Next time you'll recognize it," she said happily. "And then it'll talk Japanese."

DID JESUS EVER LAUGH?

AROUND THIS APARTMENT at least they haven't stuck in trees for birds to sit on and try to sing. Just bushes to keep you off the patch of grass too small for a gopher and then up blank like a north-end coulee in fall, twenty stories cement straight up and down, maybe seventeen apartments on each, say around twelve or thirteen hundred in all; you know, a grey slab box with metal windows. In twelve or thirteen hundred, a place like this, there should be one. One at least.

You'd think so, wouldn't you, but you can't count on it; I've tried a few. Football and hockey games aren't worth the snot you blow waiting and the late movie's absolutely blank. Nothing. There's too much of this people coming out now trying to jack themselves down after some man's north end been flipping through the sheets. It's just nothing like it was.

You'd think a place the size of Edmonton (over seven hundred thousand friendly people says the sign on the

Calgary Trail), it's amazing with that number of people and all that preaching flushing through their heads how few there really are in the whole city. At least the few I've seen, and I spend my time looking. I'm never not looking and I know; there are but few. Bars and nightclubs have always been like you know, hopeless. The biggest encouragement I ever had about Edmonton was I found two within four feet of each other at the Willingman Brothers Evangelistic Revival Incorporated last year when they come out at the Gardens. In broad daylight! By the time I could move they had both disappeared and I nearly lost them, both. They say Billy Graham could be coming next fall, but it's probably too much to pray for.

So that's why I was on apartment blocks now, in broad daylight. Waiting actually isn't too bad there sometimes, with the clouds down and November wind prying in where the liner's torn away on the old Lincoln's doors. It's a beautiful car yet, better every year. I can see it black, from here. I work it over with hard wax at least once a week, you know really sweat it with elbow grease like I always did. All the soft parts in it are about gone and I've got these nice hard boards shoved under the seat covers where I sit. On days like that I can sit, watching and waiting, wherever I've parked and I'll get numb slowly till there's no feeling in me at all and I'm just sunk down, eyes along the bright black edge of the hood, watching. Not feeling a thing, just eyes, waiting.

But this fall's been bad; the summer was cold and rainy but now in October the sun shines as if it's gone mad and

Edmonton was prairie. The leaves come gliding off the trees and it's warm and people walking around without coats. It gets so you — I — can't sit at all; all of a sudden I have to get out even when I have a good parking space and the meter doesn't have to get fed. I just have to get out, walk around in the sunshine if you can imagine that, I have to rub behind my knees where the edge of the board cuts. It's terrible; I stand there feeling my blood move. The warm air washing over my face. It's so bad then I even forget the words.

But today, no sunshine. I could sit in the car easy just off the corner where this poured slab was sticking up, holding the concrete clouds. A few dozen had gone by, in and out, but they were no good. One glance will always tell me, I never need more. You're watching and waiting; it seems like all my life now I've spent like this, watching and waiting and there always being so few, so few, for weeks it's hanging in your mind there aren't any left anywhere in the world and then it happens like it always has who knows how it's almost past before you suddenly know and you wonder how many you maybe missed just like that because you were hopeless even while you're sitting up, slowly, careful, feeling it, letting it soak into you again as you're looking and moving, always like the first time at that circus and dead-white up high against the canvas the white leg starts out, feeling slowly along something you can't see but it must be there while the drum rolls and you tighten, slowly, and then so sudden you haven't seen the move she's standing complete, alone,

white arms crossed out, standing up there above everything on nothing. Though you know there has to be a
wire. I was on the sidewalk, standing, and walking then.
Not fast, just enough to stay behind, feeling the tightness
work me like a beautiful dull ache towards the grey block,
under the grey porch, and the tune was there, the words
and tune too right there as if I was soaked with it,

> Leave the dance with me sweet Sally,
> Come with me just

walking just fast enough to stay behind because a woman
with a heavy bag of groceries will not, of course, walk
very fast.

With only one bag the outer door was no trouble; she
swung that easily and I was slowing down so I wouldn't
come up and show I had no key by not offering to open
the inner one (wear a tie and always move calm, that's all)
but it was all fine, of course, just fine as it always is if
you've been able to wait long enough: a man all in black
pushed out that minute and held the door, she didn't
have to bother with a key. I went in fast and caught the
door as it started to shut after her. I nodded but the man
was past and didn't even grunt; he went past without a
look at his best deed for the day. When I see him again, I'll
thank him.

Two steps up to three closed elevator doors; there was
a rubber rug on the floor, and the little lobby off the front
door had three bile-green couches and a coffee table with

a comic book ripped like some kids had been tearing their hair out there. A blown-up kodachrome saved wallpaper on one wall. Mountain lakes! I can't stand them. Where we waited for the elevator was a trough of dark broad plants with flowers stuck in sandpails. The flowers were big as my fist and cold, just beautiful.

The middle elevator thumped and five people came out, one a woman with a wiener-dog on a string and two girls. Their stockings were mottled white so their legs looked like dead birch sticking in a puddle, but the rest of them — ugh — they were ugly, so smooth and round-faced with long straight hair the way you see them now wherever you look in the world. And tight skirts so short when they sit they'd show to the crotch, their boobs sticking out, it was obscene,

O look it's grey out.

I said bring your coat.

This lipstick doesn't match it.

O look it's so grey.

I said bring your coat.

But my ear-rings....

their stick legs tapping along the rubber rug, twitching each bandage of a skirt.

She had pushed her floor and I leaned over the panel to push the same one, just in case she was looking. But she wasn't, of course. Why should anybody look at me? They never do, especially in elevators where there are more than two people; even when there are only two. People in cities don't look at each other; their glances slide over, like the man standing beside me with a face as if he'd slept maybe two minutes in some can last night and nicotine all over his cigarette fingers, letting the smoke curl at me. That's just the way it is, always, somebody's cancer poking at your face, you can count on it like the sun rising

> *...with me just once more.*
> *Follow me tonight, we'll take the boat from shore.*
> *I will keep you warm, sweet Sally,*
> *In your dan*

the door was open and she going, I almost hummed it away. But of course I was moving (even if I'd lost my arm in the door), following like a gentleman, and turned left as she turned right, the hall carpet under my feet and one glance at a door number as she walked down the lighted hall — 1808 — and wheeling after her, only three strides behind when she stopped by a door, fumbling in her shoulder purse, and just beside her as the top of the grocery bag split from her tilt and movement, split so I can stick out my hand for the box of Tide sliding out, grab the whole grocery bag, like a gentleman, just perfect, it is absolutely just perfect.

"Oh — " then softer, "oh — thanks, that — yes, thank you," reaching.

I might as well hold it now, you open up.

"Oh, yes, of course," the key is out as she hesitates, "I usually," and in the lock, "I should have put it down," turning, "but usually I manage," the door clicks and she looks up from its little movement, her hands coming up to take the bag and she'd have touched my hands doing it if I hadn't jerked away, my shoulder swinging the door in — don't for God's sake don't not yet — so I can hardly get my mouth open,

I — I m-might as well — as well c-carry it in....

Her glance flickers up at me in the dim hall light and I step in fast — don't give her a chance not a chance — 1815 — and in the little hall with the usual white plaster walls and the kitchen straight ahead my heart slows, settling back even as I hesitate with my back to her still somewhere in the doorway, or maybe the hall,

Where would you like it, please?

like a gentleman delivery boy. The hesitation is all I need, just a little pause you see, little things always will happen but you cut through them with calm direct action and they're no problem. Then just take a deep breath and away you go.

"Anywhere I — on the kitchen counter — my mother-in-law, you needn't — "

No trouble at all, I might as well, and among the dirty dishes I thrust the bag, I might as well, careful with two egg-marked plates, turning to her in perfect calm and look. Now. The big move left. It's starting to roll and a man in black goes past in the hall behind her but doesn't so much as glance, it's starting as I start to the door. Her face loosens like she pulled a cord. She shifts sort of sideways, smile and words start slow, then burst as she opens just a little in relief,

"That was — oh, very kind, of you, I was downstairs washing and the detergent ran out so I hopped down to the grocery while my mother-in-law was..." — ooo lady you've got a long way to go — I'm hearing her, I guess, where she stands aside against the coat closet in the grey apartment hall, talking, shifting as I move so there's thirty inches between us, steady, as I reach for the door and she is back between the kitchen's dutch doors, separating them, the light (a momentary break of sunshine outside?) from the window like bullets spraying from her black solid lovely shape as I turn from closing the door and slipping up the door chain without so much as a small rattle, can lean back then against that closed door; and look. The song really rolling now

> *... Sally*
> *In your dancing gown,*
> *Warm as the tropic sea*
> *Far from the lights of t*

rolling so I have to wrench myself erect or right then and there I'll be already into the chorus!

She is making a sound; I don't hear quite and her face is in shadow as the light fades again, but her hands go slowly up to her throat, first one and then the other. I'm standing solid now, weight even on my two feet and everything back under control; I always have to watch that, when the first stage ends. Once after too long I got rolling so strong I — well, spilt milk.

Excuse me, I move to see the lashes on her eye. You talking to me? She's now against the kitchen counter and her hands drop. Just my right height for a woman, five foot six. Her voice, well, there've been better, but not bad. With other things, the voice is fringe benefit.

"...the — no idea who you are. I thanked you for your," her arms lift a little; she has nice motion that way; "and now, go."

Of course not.

She hasn't a touch of make-up and her eyes dead grey, as they have to be. Not a speck of colour in her eyes. Her face going like stone, she turns, very nice, and walks past the table off the kitchen and around the partition into the living room and while she is still far enough away not to get hurt by something flying I put a bullet through the telephone. The silencer cost me but it's the best you can get; the shot is no louder than a kid falling on its head out of a high chair; the noise is the telephone flying apart on the bookshelf, what's left of it crashing to the hardwood. The bell clangs as it hits, something sizzles

We are all alone, sweet

but I can cut that one easy. Her move rushed me a little and I'm already in the second verse. That's not so good.

You shouldn't of made me do that. Take this out so quick. I put it away. Rushing don't help a thing.

Her back is like you pulled a lever and turned her to rock, half-tilted against the bookshelf. After a while her little finger starts to jerk back and forth a little on the spine of a book lying there; it looks like a Bible, lying with bits of black telephone on its black cover.

Where's Mother-in-law?

Her finger stops; after a while she whispers, not turning. "Mother-in-law?"

Yeah. When we come in. Where's she?

"She — she lives in Vauxhall, three hundred miles — "

That's okay, I was born in Alberta, I know enough about Vauxhall. All right. Would you kindly show me around, you know.

"Show you...."

Just take it easy, around the apartment I mean, that's all.

She wheels so fast I think she's ready for something and look up from her tight ankles quick, but she's just on the edge of crying. That's no good at all; is she the wrong —

"Please, oh please, for the love of — "

Don't do that! and she stops very fast. You know how I can't hold my hand with a voice like that and I have to talk fast. Just don't do that, talk like that. Just business, like you wanted to sell something, okay, and I was buying? Now show me the apartment.

She's looking at me and her face hardens again — I knew it, she's the cream the real solid kind who pick it up fast — slowly hardens out of her other expression. She walks ahead of me, voice stripped like she's selling the place.

"You — saw the kitchen, dining area, living room. This is the hall closet."

That's handy, right by the door. I'm standing back a bit, looking forward mostly to be polite; hall closets don't do much for me.

"Each apartment has them there" — atta girl edge in your voice edge — "and this is the storage area, small but conven..." she's got the door open and with a twist before I start to see it she's half inside and I've got to grab her, get both my hands out and actually grab her! Yank her before she's inside and the door slammed behind her and who knows what they've got in

all alone, sweet Sally,
Far from the dance on shore,
Where your lovers wait to

that far into the second verse and not ten minutes with her. She's rushing me, that's all I can say, she's a good one, the best maybe but she's rushing me and I can't say anything at all when I break myself out of it and get my face and hands more or less calmed down again (sometimes I've never had to use my hands at all, you know that) and she's staring at me from where she's spread against the dim wall in the hallway, staring up till I can finally get my face quiet and my hands down. My jaw unlocked.

It's that door, that one. Don't you make one move.

It was her fault, that TV trick with the storage room, and she knows it. I have the one closed bedroom door open without taking my eyes off her, bent back, hands still spread where she caught herself, back against the wall. The shades are drawn, it's even nicer dark in there, but I've got to see sharp right now so I reach in with my left hand and flick on the light. An instant is enough; a grey bun of hair on the bed facing the other way and a quilt over the shoulders. The quilt helps. There's hardly a twitch and it's done in a flick, no different from putting two into the dummy out on the range so fast and tight the sergeant can't yell a thing because if he's got two bits to his name he can cover both holes. The song and tune holding it right on

> *lovers wait to hold you close once more.*
> *But you'll dance again sweet Sally,*
> *As you glide on down,*
> *Down, down in the sea far*

though I'm still a little mad she pushed me so fast. It's not really right and when I think about it later it'll be such a waste, so fast now. You really should have time to think about it all, step by step. Appreciate. Well — I've put it away, and my hands are free again. The door's shut.

Into the living room, you can sit on a chair, okay?

I knew she was right. She gets herself straightened up, it takes time but she does and she walks quite steadily into the living room and makes it fine to the armchair beside the bookshelf. The couch across the room for me. Just fine. Beautiful in fact.

You understand of course it's never happened this fast before, so much and so fast. I would never have dreamed to find anyone who could handle it the way she does, that would have been out of the question to imagine seeing I had such terrible waits even finding anyone. Oh, the waiting I've done, sitting, my body going dead sitting, or sometimes walking a little, waiting outside all those buildings in a place the size of Edmonton, seven hundred thousand friendly souls and how can it be I couldn't, didn't find anyone, no one after you, and you — ah-h-h — just sitting here across from her with her slim legs decently together and skirt over her knees even when everything has exploded as it were in her usual life, to sit there and face me again with a dark solid face like rock and I don't have to begin anything. She will keep facing me I know without a word and her face set until I'm good and ready to start. When I'm ready.

There is, of course, no reason in the world why a human being should laugh.

I stop there like usual; I'm so sure now I don't have to bother at all timing it, that she'll butt in. She sits, her arms down along her thighs but she is not slumped. She does not blink and I am sitting right where her eyes seem to meet, although they don't seem quite to see me. She's alive and perfectly inert the way one can only dream and even then knowing you'll wake up before you can taste it all but there's no waking here, not now

Down, down in the sea
Far from the lights of town, Michael row

but that's trouble, the last verse starts like the chorus and if I don't watch that — you remember don't you — I'll be on in the chorus at last before the last verse because the first words are the same, and then it's all been wasted. All! But now I sense it of course right away, the second word in the last verse is "weep" and I pull up. With someone like this I can probably keep this going — well I can try again can't I — the complete song, every verse, she looking like she is, so I can cut the song and continue. At my leisure.

The problem with laughing is it makes you forget. You relax, and the bad you've done you begin to forget it. Right away. That's wrong, you see. Don't you. You shouldn't just be able to forget about what you've done wrong. You should have it right there in front of your thinking all the time, know every wrinkle of it. Not wash it away with a laugh or a grin or a big-laugh and slap on the back. You gotta keep it in front of you all the time and that's the biggest thing that's wrong with laughing because it washes it out, you relax and it's gone, right out of sight and out of mind and that shouldn't happen like that outa sight and outa mind which is where laughing gets you because people should just hafta see and keep on seeing and staring right in the face every bit of everything and they've done ever done....

Her expression has changed, and it's just as well because it breaks up my talk. Maybe she said something? I know, I was stumbling already, repeating myself. That's another thing that usually happens when it's so long. I repeat and then I'm going in circles. I know that, you don't have to — it's hard to stop, like some other things, unless you get help and here again she's got it. Just the look is enough and I can get stopped. No problem; start again.

You know these men nowadays call themselves theologians and call others to a new morality and call God dead? No doubt you've heard all about that, you can't get away from it hardly unless you plug yourself up, eyes, ears, nose, everything — well, God is dead for them, sure, because they've laughed him to death. There's just nothing left sacred and serious but somebody cuts it up laughing. Can you think of anything they don't laugh at now? I could give you ten minutes and you couldn't think of nothing, bright as I know you are. The Devil in the Snake got Eve to eat the apple by cracking a joke about God and the Devil's been laughing ever since. You laugh and you don't keep the proper things down no more — you get rid of them, right. The stuff's got to be kept down, down where it belongs and not laugh it away, and whatever you do you've got to be able to face it, square face to face and face it right out, and not once do you laugh it away easy. You do every bit you do dead sober, you live a godly, righteous and sober life like the Bible says, right. A righteous and sober life, facing everything you do without....

She may have been saying something again. I can't be sure of course, because I was explaining something to her, but she may have been saying something because I see now that her mouth is moving and it may have been moving and it may have been probably moving for some time. Her hand has definitely moved; she has the Bible in her hand now and is brushing the bits of black telephone off, holding it clutched in front of her with her eyes closed like sleep, but her lips move.

Right like the Bible says. I know you're a Bible reader, and I believe what the Bible says too. I don't always do right, I know that, and I've been punished, don't think I haven't, but I'm never getting punished because I don't know and didn't care I was doing wrong. I'll know it before anybody else. The trouble with the world that walks past every day is they don't know they're doing wrong and they don't care if they did because they're so busy laughing it all away. Everything's laughed at. People are always looking around, hoping to see something they shouldn't see, something to laugh at. Women wear clothes — not you but there's plenty right in this building with you, you've seen them, showing things God never meant to be shown and people look and look and laugh to cover up the evil grinding in their heads when they look. Smiling everywhere, just notice it sometime. It isn't right and I've got the proof for it. You know the final proof?

I wait, like I always can afford to wait and I know from this one I'll get response. But I'm so relaxed, and the verse comes

Michael weep for dear sweet Sally
Down in the deep blue sea,
Hang your head and cry down by the gallows tr

thanks heavenly God she's been saying something again, though I haven't heard it, and her staring mouth moving helps me cut across to her and hear her saying, aloud,

"…ever done, what have I ever done to anybody that you — "

Hey hey now, I've got to jump in here fast. I can't have overestimated her, but dear God! Now that is no question for us sitting here like this. Don't do that, don't do that at all.

And she stopped, of course. She sits there motionless again, holding the Bible, her fingers dead white along the edges. The darkness has come in more from outside and someone I know is walking down the hall. You can hear him even with the thin rug there. This place was really built on the cheap, and maybe I should have figured that more before. I guess I did but I didn't think of all the possible implications of that, though by now you'd think I'd know better. Mistakes; I keep doing wrong and one of these — cut that!

You've got the proof right there, in your hand. The Bible. The Book of Jesus. You ever read that Jesus laughed?

She doesn't say a word that I can hear. Her eyes are wide, looking, her face rigid and her lips moving but I can't hear a word so I carry right on or I'll be through all that last verse and then there's nothing left but the chorus.

No. You never. You'll never read that we know right now, both of us, Jesus never done it. He healed the blind and wiped off the sores of lepers and threw out devils and whipped moneychangers and told Pharisees they were just so many sonsabitches and he gave the hungry food sometimes. But when did he ever laugh? Eh? You ever catch Jesus laughing? Nosir.

"...talking of Jesus after the unspeakable things you've..." she goes on talking, her face still rigid like it's been cast forever but her hand gesturing down the apartment hall.

The old woman now, right, and she went in sleep. She never knew a thing of it. We should all pray for that. She could have lived to ninety-five, here and in Vaux — the — the medicine, they have, now, and her teeth falling out and not able to control herself and you always wiping up her mess. Oh, I know, Jesus raised some from the dead, about three the Bible says, and some relatives thanked him for it but you never read nothing from the ones that was raised, do you? Not a thank you, not from one of them. He never done it for the dead ones, let me tell you, it was the living, just some of them, nagging him. Anyway, if he did it for the dead, why didn't he do it more? Tell me that. There must have been plenty dead with Jesus walking the country, and he just raised three. Nosir, There's nothing to worry about the dead. They never laugh. Not even when they come back.

I must have been talking a long time. My mouth feels dry and she has pulled herself back in her chair, as if she were trying to push back as far as she could. Has she been saying something? Perhaps. Maybe that's why for a minute the sun coming in through the slatted window, the big one in the living room where we sit, my body coming back now a bit and relaxing on what once was a good foam-rubber couch but now worn thin and thread-bare, though it's really clean, I seem to have lost where I was. Even the — no —

> *Down in the deep —*
> *Hang your — head and — cry down by the gall*

No, that's there okay. But it's so far gone. I must have been wasting it somewhere, and she's talking too; I can hear her, so I have to talk more.

I've heard it all before, yeah, he raised three and loved them all. So in all them hundreds of years since, how many you think he killed?

That's everybody's mistake about Jesus. He had a lot more things in his mouth than love. That's the forgotten Jesus. Like hanging stones around your neck and into the sea with you, down down, or calling a woman that isn't a Jew like him a dog, just like a lot of other Jews do now, just walk down the pawn street and you'll hear. Or that about the sheep and the goats. Everybody lined up, all the nations, great and small it says right here in your Bible, Matthew, chapter 25, and the big finger coming out and the voice, "You sheep right," and "You goat left." That's judgement, and sheep and goats sliding right and left without so much as a snicker anywhere. Dead sober, dead, and the goats knowing dead sure why they're going. They know why. Because compared to a sheep a goat's a LAUGHER

Sheep   the range flat grey powdered rock dusted in hollows to grey chewed root   sheep-like clouds, white on grey-green, white in the streaky blue   the horizon so far and straight the hills turning on a shimmer of griddle heat   sheep like clouds, sheep whitish pancakes fuzzing grey in the heat, frying flat, speckled under the specks of hawks stuck on the blue for gophers   above hawks and sheep and flat grey to the horizon end in sky hang vultures, flat, sailing like dead ashes hooked on the heat over the impossible level of sage and stubble gnawed grey by sheep and gophers and the unending sun   soft at the flat edge of it, almost gentle but slowly hoisting itself higher and higher to burn over the gaunt woolly sheep panting against each other, sides thumping in the heat till their backs merge in the shimmer of flat earth sweating greyness and light under the ash of vultures endlessly turning turning   sheep. The goat standing in the one patch of shade   beside the sleeping-wagon   alone in a herd of sheep   no female to chase in a small surge through the flat backs and a momentary lunging elevation   a female of his kind   always erect already in whatever shade, on whatever elevation, a sweat-spot beside the wagon or any stone large enough for two hooves   head erect, horns curled back chewing   standing and chewing endless under the ash   chewing with a twist to his mouth, head

turning from the panting sheep smeared flat over the land
facing ahead, a twist in his mouth   the flat blazing earth
flimmering   in heat

   ...where's the girl?

   She stops what she has been saying to me; whatever it
all was. Her mouth just stops and she is looking.

   "Excuse me?" she says finally. "Please!"

   Your girl? She at school now I guess? She just stares.
Over there, the picture. I see everything. How old is she?

   "It was, just last, fall, before she started school, just
last, we got that picture...." She's staring at me now and
the expression on her face is changing again. She is looking at her wristwatch and her expression is changing as I
watch, her fingers slowly kneading the smooth leather of
the Bible.

   In the dark northern lights come and go   washing
out the stars in colour with their slow twitch   alone in a
world bending flat backwards   the goat's white tail flickers   you can step off into stars   his black head nodding.
He coughs.

   "...finally dressed, it was such a hurry. And like I
said when we finally got there, after all the fuss of the
accident right in the underpass, it wouldn't have really
caused any trouble if it hadn't happened right in the
underpass, we almost cancelled everything, but Jake said
it couldn't be helped, it wasn't his fault and Mama had
come from Vauxhall to see her start school so why go
through it all again but we were all so upset it came out
stiff upset by the accident she's usually such a happy little

girl the photographer tried everything and even got out his jack-in-the-box but she didn't want to laugh. He tried everything and Jake almost choked but she just couldn't seem...."

down by the gallows

her mouth stops. And her face breaks. Breaks like when a hammer hits a dried-out clod of southern Alberta gumbo

tree
Michael weep for

She is screaming. Sitting perfectly motionless holding the Bible in front of her, staring at her wristwatch, screaming.

"God my god my god, that horrible song, stop it! STOP IT!"

I told you she was the right one. The song is in my head of course, I've of course never sung it out loud again and I wouldn't, you know that, even with her, but she knows. She's that kind

dear sweet

she's on her feet, screaming, moving *her dancing* coming towards me, her hands set like claws *drifting in the tide* too fast! It's too fast, she's coming too fast, reaching *the lights of town Michael row the* but it's too fast! I can't finish! I just can't jam it all in so FA-A-A-A

The blanket from the shelf in the hall closet covers her easily. Even the Bible lying there, splattered out. I shouldn't have counted on her that much. Depended so much. Sitting so still, talking so long and perfectly normal — weren't you talking about your life, all those growing up things, don't you remember? — I should have expected she'd break and got it finished. But it was so comfortable, at last. That was my mistake, I know, but we have to have time or it doesn't do any good. You taught me that too. And this almost worked, you can't really say it didn't till you had to spoil it but it worked — well, it's a minute to four — all afternoon? She was better than anyone, since. In a place the size of Edmonton, to find so few! But there's still the little girl. Is there?

I'm sitting erect on the windowsill eighteen floors up. There's no balcony, this place is too cheap, and there's not even a screen but my head is very steady on heights so it is not dangerous at all. Though it has never been this high before. The black bridge, beautiful with black heavy steel, reaches over the valley, low water glinting here and there under the sodden clouds. Apartment blocks stick up all over but the black level line is the best thing about the best thing about the valley, a line straight across the green hollow, though now in late fall the leaves are finally gone there is mostly grey left. They are gone. The valley, the river, the road and the spidered trees, the sidewalk and the parking lot approach below. All variations on grey.

Four o'clock so it must be very close to time. The sun pretty well gone. A black spot of someone comes out from under the porch and cuts across the grey, passing behind my black Lincoln. I sit. She'll be coming soon. Has there been pounding on the door? I listen but then, how can you tell? The song hanging there, waiting, still waiting to be finished finally. Flat Vauxhall. Is someone pounding? Is there?

Or is it a knock?

AFTER THIRTY YEARS
OF MARRIAGE

AFTER THIRTY YEARS of marriage and six children, Papa and my total worldly wealth was a mortgaged house in Rockford, Illinois, and a plot in the Rockford cemetery where little John Wesley had been lying for sixteen years. Land in Illinois cost a hundred dollars an acre; we cleared a thousand dollars from the sale of our house and on March 20, 1906, Papa and our second youngest son, Jolson, boarded the train for Red Deer, Alberta. With three men over eighteen left in the family, we could file on 480 acres of free land; a few years of hard work on that much land and we believed we would return to the States with enough money so our three youngest sons, Ethan, Jolson and Billings (still too young to file, unfortunately), could go to school and Papa and me retire in some comfort.

There was, of course, no land available near Red Deer. Actually, of the thirty-six sections in any Alberta township, sixteen are already owned by the CPR, one by the Hudson's Bay Company, and two reserved for schools, so that only seventeen widely scattered sections, the even-numbered ones, can ever be homesteaded on. When Ethan and Billings and I arrived in Alberta near the end of June, we travelled to the railhead which was then at Stettler. There we found Papa and Jolson shingling, their lips purple with nails, and after many colourful kisses they told us they had filed sight-unseen on land seventy miles east and our first problem would be to get there. I had a migraine headache from sitting up four days and nights on trains but I managed to cook my first Canadian meal to hugged and kissed acclaim.

I had been able to borrow an extra two hundred dollars in Illinois. That was not nearly enough for a team of horses, but together with what Papa and Jolson had earned building in Stettler, we purchased two oxen. One was a blotchy red, the other coal black, and both had great extended ears that waved in time with their majestic pace. They were immediately christened Tom and Bruce, good short names for yelling, Papa said, and when we harnessed them, put bits in their mouths, and hitched them to the wagon, we found them as fundamentally opposed to motion as any mountain, but ever faithful and above all patient. That compensated for almost everything. How often I leaned against Tom's powerful shoulder and cried until I had no tears left, and he would turn his flat, triangular head towards me, his eyes so steady and unchanging. We had them both as long as we were in Alberta.

Papa and Jolson had taken a hunting knife and shot-gun with them, and Ethan (not to be outdone) bought a .30-30 for eighteen dollars. It seemed a very large amount of money to me, but it proved its value the second day out from Stettler. There were ducks on the sloughs (as they call the ponds here) everywhere, but far too wary for a shotgun so when we saw a lovely goose stretching its neck at us out of the bullrushes, Ethan got out his big gun. Papa laughed, "You'll blow it to pieces!" And sure enough, when Ethan leaned on the wagon and fired, the goose vanished as the ducks rose in a frightful clatter. Billings waded out and discovered the bullet had slit its jugular vein! Ethan never fired that gun again — we never saw an animal around the homestead that needed it — so his marksmanship became a family legend, and though the goose was excellent, I always thought it too dear at eighteen dollars plus a bullet. Later that summer Jolson stacked hay; by saving every single penny, he brought home twenty dollars for a month's work.

When we found the iron peg with four square holes dug around it that marked the corner of one of our quarter sections, we all went a little daffy. We had been travelling for five days at ox-pace over open land the colour of burnt bread, land which none of us could have ever imagined. We would see a settler's sod house or board shanty four hours before we passed it, and at most we saw three a day. Papa jumped from the wagon, "I want to enter first," and Ethan said, "I'm with you," and then all three boys had jumped off, even young Billings, and with their hands on Papa's shoulders they walked onto the promised land together while I watched them over the backs of the oxen. Then we oriented ourselves to the sun and by the end of the day had found our other two quarters. There was one homesteader near us, three miles southwest, and Ethan got a pail of water from his barrel and with the wood we had carried with us we made camp. That Mr. Williams, who had been a Union soldier during the Civil War, brought us luck: when Papa and the boys began digging a well beside our tent the next morning, they struck cold fresh water nine feet down; the land looked so featureless, slightly rolling and covered with buffalo grass, that the only reason we camped there was because I felt I had to be in sight of Williams' cabin.

Though it was barely July, all the things that had to be done before winter almost made us dizzy, just to list them. When our eyes grew accustomed to distance, we discovered other homesteaders about us: almost all of them from the States, but no one had time for a July 4 celebration that year. We had a well, a very great blessing, but we had to buy a cow and chickens, fence, put up hay, and above all build a house and barns for ourselves and our animals. Besides that, we had to find wood to burn and also break land so that next spring we could seed and grow our first cash crop. In the meantime, we had to live on our resources, such as they were, and so instead of all the boys being able to help Papa steadily, both Ethan and Jolson hired out to neighbouring ranchers and settlers for fencing, haying, any kind of heavy work that could be got. We needed the cash to buy food and clothing for the hard winter that everyone who had lived in the country for a year took great joy in assuring us was certainly ahead. If I had known then that the winter of 1906-07 would be the worst in the living memory of anyone on the Canadian prairies, I know I would have despaired. But I did not know, and I suppose that was for the better.

Actually, the summer was very pleasant, and at first I was not really afraid of the endless space all around. The mosquitoes were more or less over after about two weeks, though not completely gone till September, and Papa discovered that there were wooded hills southwest of us, enormous numbers of gnarled and dead aspen so we could haul as much firewood as we pleased. I refused to live in a sod shanty; I knew it was cheap and warm but I also knew it was like a tent — quite impossible to keep clean — and though the trees were too short to build a conventional house of horizontal logs, they gave me an idea. I sketched it on the back of a milk-can label and within a week Jolson had dug a trench for the foundation of the house twenty-eight by eighteen feet. Its walls were to be made of two rows of vertical poles with the space between them filled with mud from the lake. There was not another house like it in the entire country, and after we had spent the winter in it we knew why. But it seemed fine at the time, though it required nine loads of logs and forty tons (as the boys estimated) of mud just for the walls. We moved out of the tent into it on Saturday, October 20, 1906. The roof had not been completed and that night I was as cold as I had ever been in my life. The wind howled so dreadfully I did not know how I would have endured it in the tent hammering, jerking on its ropes. That is perhaps the worst of living on the Alberta prairie: the wind. There is not a bush anywhere, and it gets a two-hundred-mile clean run at you from the mountains.

But that was the coming of winter. Summer was beautiful, and I had never seen such skies or light. From the wooded hills the prairie spread east like water falling away, wind brushing the grass and the small sloughs everywhere dark green and blue and indigo and the horizon merging with the sky in a bluish dust. On the CPR section beside us lay the perfect circle of a pond surrounded by willows, the water so sweet it must have been fed by springs, and the paths of the buffalo radiated from it like the spokes of a wheel cut two and three feet into the ground; in the long evenings when the light settled down like a slow blanket, you could so easily imagine those huge black shapes coming single file from all directions towards the last bright centre of water, silent, moving lower and lower into the earth cut by their paths. Then suddenly the ducks would begin talking: gossipy old women among the rushes so loud I could hear them a mile away in the tent complaining, comparing children, and bang! Billings' shotgun would explode, bang again as the ducks splattered up and away, and soon I would be plucking — hopefully mallards because they were the largest and always the fattest for some reason — and at sunset Papa and Ethan and Jolson would have meat to fill their stomachs, empty from all day cutting and stacking hay: they each wanted half a duck at least or a whole prairie chicken.

The Alberta sunsets were beyond description. Such burning reds I never saw anywhere again, either in nature or art. It seemed to me then that if this world is finally to be judged by fire, surely that fire has been kindled already.

Cooking? How did I cook. Like a squaw at an open fire mostly, bending there until I was more smoked than my meal cooked. I had few enough cooking worries; there came a time when eating potatoes and oatmeal was nearly as monotonous as cooking them. Until our stove arrived from Illinois — in September — I had to walk to Williams' every other day with my dough and an armful of wood to bake four loaves in their stove. Often, on that endless walk with my arms numb with those seemingly light things I was carrying, I found a rock or badger mound to sit on and cry. An especially good place for this was "Buffalo Rock," a huge stone in a hollow worn out by hooves of buffalo itching themselves. I sat there, my head against the rock rubbed smooth as marble, but when Billings came with me, we two swinging the dough pan between us and both of us with half an armful of wood, then we stopped there to rest only, to drink some water and laugh at the gophers chasing each other so easily across the prairie. How handy to live in the ground, he said once, to have a smooth pointed body that could whistle in and out of narrow tunnels. No tent to clutch desperately in wind or thunderstorm, and covered with fur against both flies and mosquitoes.

That was best about outdoor cooking: the soaring pests disliked smoke. Of course we had smudges in the evening, but the tent could not be tied up tight in the hot nights and no one can sleep in a cloud of smoke, so we really had no protection. Sometimes towards evening the oxen were neither red nor black, simply grey with mosquitoes. As Papa said one late supper, "It's a great comfort to eat in the dark. You don't know what all you're eating."

Every time I was down with my two- or three-day headaches, I felt these terrible insects would finish me, whining, crawling, burrowing everywhere. Actually there were homesteaders who gave up their claims because of them. Perhaps the women did it. The men had hard daily drudgery to weary them so they slept through insects and storms too; above all, they had visible results of a house wall or an acre of ploughing to prove themselves, but women have to keep at the same few things over and over and wait for their men to come from wherever they are. I could never see my men haying because, though it appears flat, the prairie is filled with slopes and hollows; wherever I looked there was simply the endless horizon. For days then I saw no living, moving things from the tent, and I never dared venture from it for fear I would be lost — I never did lose myself, but I always had the numb ache that I would. When I finally saw a distant moving wagon, or a herd of cattle filing at noon towards the sweet pond to drink, I felt a relief, a companionship I rarely knew in Rockford when my neighbours came for afternoon tea.

I have never been one to complain, and I won't begin now, but pioneering is work for very strong people, or a group of people like ourselves who have various strengths between them. Many people came to Alberta not knowing that. For someone alone, or if Papa had had only me, we could not have lasted a month. But our boys were unbelievable; I never knew my oldest three children, grown up and happily married in Illinois, the way I now knew these last three, the way they tackled problems that would have turned an old person grey, worked for months on ranches or on railway crews where gambling and loose living destroyed many married men while our boys brought home every penny they earned, laughing and telling us endless stories. I remember one terrible day when the heat and flies had literally hammered me flat and my migraine had built to such a pressure that I knew the plates of my skull were bouncing, grinding together in agony, and then towards evening I heard Billings come home singing at the top of his voice, "Back, back, back to Baltimore!" his high boyish sound floating as if it came from everywhere around me and I struggled to my feet and came out of the tent and the sun was low and mellow beyond the horizon like a burning town; I just hugged him all sweaty and he gave me a fast squeeze, not seeing my tears. "There are so many flowers," he said, pushing back, "it's too bad we have to tear them up with the plough."

And the people. The best thing about homesteading is that everyone begins at the same place, really with nothing but themselves on the empty land. That's true no matter how many "things" you bring with you: you struggle with the mosquitoes, the water, the wood, the loneliness, the space and distance all around; that is, the land. After a year this begins to change, and by the end of the second summer when the hail had smashed some of our crops into our new ploughing and others got fifty bushels to the acre, the pioneering oneness clearly began to go, go forever. But the first year: I used the Williams' stove, they came to our good well for drinking water; Papa used Erik Olsen's haymower while he ploughed with our plough. If you had something a neighbour needed, or ate a meal when a neighbour came by, you shared. That was the strange, human effect the first year with a new land had on all of us, and for some it was so strong that it did not vanish, Billings told me later, to the end of their lives.

The prairie fire of May 12, 1907, had the entire country fighting it, together. Though we had seen a few distant fires in the late fall, the worst season is early spring just before the green grass comes. The fire travels on the wind, and with its own terrible heat creates such a draft that often no running horse can stay ahead of it; the only protection is a slough or ploughed land or a backfire — anything which deprives it of fuel — and if these barriers are too narrow the headfire will simply leap over them. That day a father six miles south of us had gone to the timber — why he would leave when the smoke had been visible all day before and the smell of burning on the evening air, I don't know — and left a girl alone with an invalid mother and three little children. The house was poorly fireguarded, and the girl led the children to the ploughed field and told them to sit there together and not to move or look anywhere while she went back for the mother. But the children must have been terrified: they started back towards home and so when the father returned home, driving furiously from the hills when he noticed the fire, he found his house and stacks and barns in ashes and himself the only survivor of his entire family.

We saw the high smoke when we got up that morning, and the wind was from the southeast. Ethan rode south (we had a pony by then) to the ridges while Papa and Jolson ploughed a wider fireguard and Billings and I laid out sacks and set pails of water. Soon Ethan returned as fast as his horse could gallop, but by that time we could already see the flames and smoke driving across the hills only three miles away. The men quickly began setting a line of small fires farther and farther south, very carefully: if you set too wide a backfire, you can create a prairie fire of your own. A family north of us started a backfire two miles from their house, just to be sure, and burned down their homestead before the wildfire even reached them. But despite the black wedge of prairie on two sides of us, the approach of that fire was awesome. The men went forward with the neighbours to see if they could turn the headfire; but Billings and I had to stay at the house with sacks and pails: if the fire got past the men and jumped the guard, we would have to scream for help and try to control it until help came.

The fire burns in a wedge. The headfire at its point creates such a flaming whirlwind that it rushes ahead as if it were following a trail of gunpowder. Nothing can stop a headfire in May prairie grass on a windy day. The boys fought towards it with sacks soaked with water, the smoke suffocating, and then suddenly the smoke lifted in the wind and they saw a wall of flames driving towards them and they ran, desperately, and if the freshwater pond had not been within twenty yards of them, they and the horse would have burned alive. Ethan rode, Jolson jumped right into the water, and the flames passed them like a giant locomotive roaring through a station.

"Maybe it caught Papa!" Ethan gasped. "On the other side."

Jolson was already pulling himself out of the muck. "Come on!" he shouted and ran across the smoking grass leaping with scattered patches of fire. Ethan had a longer struggle to get the frightened horse across.

But Papa was all right; he and the neighbours had stopped the western sidefires so when Jolson sprinted up their only concern was us and the homestead. I saw that headfire approaching, and with Billings beside me felt so totally helpless, a puny human nailed to the ground with a wet sack in her hands and that inhuman scourge roaring...the backfire and guards made it hesitate, just for an instant, and Billings screamed, "It'll stop, Mama, see, see!" but it would not have, I know, that momentary hesitation was nothing to that horrible furnace driving at us but then like a breath from heaven a westerly crosswind wafted over us, unbelievably, and perhaps all the people in the country were praying with me and Billings and Papa and Ethan and Jolson. For like a startled animal that headfire leaned, suddenly leaped sideways and roared around us along the east side of our guard, northward. When the men ran up, scorched and gasping, Billings and I were slapping out the last bits of flame on the haystack and the house roof. Papa kissed me, right in front of everyone, and then they ran off north and east after the slowly spreading sidefires. The headfire didn't die until it ran into the big lake seven miles north of us.

Such a black smoking world you cannot imagine. We were a grey island in the deepest corner of hell. Wherever you stepped your feet burned, smoke sprang at you. But a day later it rained, a warm, soft, penetrating rain and the glory of grass and flowers that grew out of those ashes within a week I cannot describe. The wonders of the world are endless, how out of the greatest terror God surprises us again and again with more beauty and goodness than we ever had before.

That was our first spring, after we had come through the winter of 1906-07. We had lived it in our unique house, of course, and that was a mixed blessing too. The house was clean enough after the tent: once, during the summer I had gotten out my broom and leaned it against the front of the tent, not with the intention of sweeping anything (after all not even I, as Ethan pointed out, could clean up the whole prairie) but just to remind me of a future hope; however, the house was cold. Indescribably. The wall of lake-mud dried, cracked, and we could not fill the cracks carefully enough. I put on my heaviest clothes for bed, and in the morning granules of snow were sifted over me, my breath frozen into ice on my pillow. I have never been so cold, and during my headaches the house became worse than Hades. The men could not, of course, stay all day with me during my sickness, not even Billings, because there was so much work to do and I did not want them to stay: I preferred my agony alone, to their restless impatience, but how often I prayed for the understanding hand of a woman. Very few homesteaders wintered on their claims; they returned East or moved into town, but since so much of our summer energy had gone into building the disastrous house at my insistence, we could not afford that. However, one of our absent neighbours had a little organ which they permitted us to use for the winter, and I do believe it saved my sanity. I would play, pumping furiously, singing every song I knew and pieces I made up so loudly that Ethan swore he heard it all the way to Mr. Mason's store and post office, three miles above the howling wind. I told him he'd freeze his ears if he didn't keep them covered.

But one day in February not even the organ helped. Both Ethan and Jolson were working away at the time and Papa and Billings had been fixing the barn against the hard storms; I was the second day into a migraine and about three o'clock Papa said he should go to Mason's as there had been no blizzard and probably the mail had come in. Billings looked at me so longingly that I said he should go along, but please, come home quickly. So they trudged off into the snow, and I waited.

Five hours! I made supper for six o'clock, as usual, but nothing. I wanted to rush out, search, but of course there were two of them and besides I was terrified of the winter prairie. My head hammered; my feet were blue with cold no matter how much wood I banged into the stove. And outside lay that vast motionless stillness which comes only before the worst storms, a night where the moonlight turns the endless waves of snow into rigid, frozen steel. And when those two men finally came in, with no mail, they said they'd been choring in the barn for half an hour, just so they could save putting on their mackinaws again and oh they were sorry they hadn't bothered to tell me they were back!

I got out of bed, thrust my feet into my old slippers, and started for the door in my nightgown.

"Sara," Papa said, "where are you going?"

"Outside. To stand on my head in a snowdrift."

Papa and Billings sank back into their chairs, their arms hanging down limp, the most marvellous expression of helplessness on their faces.

"Why Sar," Papa said finally, "I believe you're crazy."

"I *know* it," and I got the door wrenched open and marched around to the west side of the house where the drifts were the deepest. I broke the crust, knelt down and stuck my head into the snow as deeply as I could without smothering and I held it there until it felt quite frozen and all the rest of me too. Then I picked up a big piece of snow and went back into the house. The men sat there, looking at me, not having moved a muscle. I wrapped the snow in a towel and lay down on it like a pillow and I slept without waking or dreaming and in the morning my headache had vanished and so had my temper.

We stayed five years in Alberta, and we stayed that long because of Billings. Our first crop was smashed by hail so we couldn't sell out or leave that year, but then the crops were steadily better as we ploughed more land and also bought cattle so that in three years Ethan could enrol in the winter session at the University of Chicago and Jolson was taking correspondence courses from there too. They both studied until they finished their Ph.D.'s and became professors, thanks to our Alberta homestead, but Billings returned to Alberta after a year of high school in Illinois and he refused to go back. We could not talk him out of it. So we stayed for five years: he was nineteen then and he bought Ethan's and Jolson's quarters with money he borrowed against our quarter, which we gave him outright, and he stayed on to become one of the old-timers of the district. He even became a Canadian citizen and celebrated the first of July instead of the fourth. Papa and I returned to Illinois, more bent and no richer, but we had been able to give our last three sons a good start in life, though one life was very different from the way we had foreseen it.

OOLULIK

I N THE STOREROOM is where I am that afternoon, getting ready two sled loads of supplies when the dogs
began to howl outside. From their tone a team must be
approaching so I climb out, up on the drifts that cover all
but the roofs of Tyrel Bay post. The short February afternoon is grey over the snow and the wind rising in a falling
temperature. Paliayak and several of his people are
already beside the mounds of their houses, looking west.

In that direction we still hope. The fall caribou must
have gone south there, for only stragglers came down the
usual eastern branch of migration and Paliayak's camp,
which hunts east and south, just made Tyrel Bay the week
before. With three of nineteen people lost to the long
January hunger. Squinting against the gloom, I finally
make out the dot moving where the curve of the bay
would have been except for the level drifts. The figure
seems barely to move; there can be only two, at most
three, dogs on the sled. I shout to John on the blue roof of

the store, swept bare by the wind, "Take the light sled and four dogs." In a few moments he is gone, dogs running madly. I go down into the store to brew tea and stir the beans. Beans. Eight hundred pounds of uncooked beans neatly labelled "Emergency Rations" for a land without a natural fuel supply. And the one government plane that came in just before the darkness hasn't returned to correct what may be mix-up, may be stupidity. Even after soaking six hours, it takes a rolling three-hour boil to cook a potful.

Beside the stove two of the four children staying in my room because of their frostbite play intently with a ball of string. I watch them rolling the ball back and forth, the string running out like a track over the floor and then rolling up again. They are warm and full of food; the aroma of beans drifts through the store. The children play without a sound.

When the barking approaches, I go out. It is bitterly cold now with the wind still rising, but all the people are standing by the two houses watching the approach. In a few moments John draws up; he has picked up the driver, two dogs and little sled without bothering to unhitch anything. The dogs are barely skeletons. They lie motionless on the sled, and when the man lifts his face to us for a long moment I can see only starvation; then I recognize Keluah, Ikpuck's younger brother. We lift him from the sled and into the store. The little children look up as we come in, then run quickly to their mothers who are in the group that follows.

After he has drunk three mugs of tea I ask Keluah in the language of the people, "You come from Ikpuck?" He nods. "Does his family have meat and fuel?"

His mouth moves, reluctantly, "No."

The circle of brown faces stirs but no one says a word. I ask, "Where is the camp?"

"On Dubawnt Lake, with the others."

"Turatuk. Vukarsee. Nakown. Lootevek." He speaks as if behind his closed eyelids he sees the grouped humps of snow houses on the long shore of the lake. It is at least ninety miles from Tyrel Bay, and there is no need to ask whether the others had food.

"Why did you all camp at the lake?"

Keluah lies on the blankets against the counter; it takes a long time for him to speak. "Some deer came last fall, but not much. We hunted, shooting stragglers and here and there a small herd. But there were not enough for caches, we always ate everything we killed. A little after the twilight came Ikpuck found a good herd at Dubawnt Lake. We killed them all, and we could again lick the blood from our hands and our bellies were full. But the others had found nothing for many days, and they camped at Dubawnt one by one when they had no food. We fished. But we have no meat since the middle of the darkness."

Incredibly, not one clear hint of this has reached the post. But there has been no movement this winter: the weather unbelievably bad and the foxes at low ebb. If the reconnaissance plane had only come after I sent John to Baker Lake in early January — but it did not and that thought is useless. Three weeks without food during the darkness. Forty-five people in six camps traded west last fall — and then I remember. "Keluah," I say quickly, "where is the camp of Itooi?" The largest of the western camps, it contains ten people, the families of Itooi and his brother-in-law Ukwa.

The man lifts his gaunt face from the cup of broth John is giving him. "Itooi would not stay at the lake when the deer were gone. He said the few fish would give out too and we would all die in one place. He and Ukwa went south to the Front River, they said."

"Have the fish given out at Dubawnt?"

"Yes."

"Have some of the people died?"

Keluah is slowly drinking the soup, the muscles of his cheek working to control himself before his hunger. Finally he pulls back and lifts seven fingers. "I left so long ago, with the last dogs. But some had died." There is no need to say he was the strongest man left in the camp. Ninety miles in seven days, with a blizzard only two days before.

Paliayak is looking at Keluah, reading every hour of that fight in the frost-black face. I say to him carefully, "Can you make up two teams from your dogs? Are there three men who can travel?"

He nods his huge head. "We can."

"I wanted us to rest at least another day, but now we cannot. One could take four of my best dogs and the small sled to Baker Lake. If the weather holds, perhaps in three days. I could send a message to take to the Mounted Police, to fly out with food. Two could come with me, with loads for Dubawnt."

Paliayak says heavily, "It will blizzard soon — two, three hours."

"Will it be too bad to travel?"

"Perhaps." He shrugs.

I look at them all standing in a circle around Keluah who is almost slumped down, his mouth hanging slack as in sleep. They are the people of this land and they know better than I what is ahead on this trail, but I do not have to ask them if they will. "The blizzard will have to take care of itself; we have no time to wait for it." A fleeting smile touches the faces of the people. Then we move quickly to complete our preparations.

Though the wind continues to rise from the north and the ground-drift whirls about our legs and over the dogs, especially in the hollows of the land, it does not snow and the sky remains clear. We have the moon and the trail at first needs no breaking. As I jog along this seems an ordinary dead-of-winter trip, where the only matters to watch for are frostbite and over-fatigue. Ordinarily, if I did not have to keep sharp eye on my two companions to make sure they keep up even though my sled is too heavy for six dogs. And if, above all, I did not know that waiting for us were the people and that even an hour longer could make all the difference for some of them. That Paliayak's son Atchuk will get through to Baker Lake is as sure as anything can be; next to his father he is the best man in the band and with the light sled and fresh dogs he cannot fail. Except for the unexpected. But Itooi early taught me that the margin of safety on the barrens is so narrow that if the dangerous unexpected comes it is almost inevitably fatal; therefore it can be disregarded. Do your best and if it fails you will not likely have another chance. Atchuk: a hundred and fifty miles in about the time we make ninety. If the weather is even barely flyable the plane will be in Dubawnt within two hours from Baker Lake; arriving perhaps as quickly as we. They will fly immediately, beyond doubt; emergency sloughs bureaucracy aside, thank god. But verified emergencies are often already too late. That too is a fact of the Arctic barrens. For the whole matter depends on the plane. With no more dogs left in the camp, we cannot hope to get all the people out with our three sleds. Besides, the bigger the loads we haul in, the more dogs we need and the more food for them we need and if we are held by a blizzard even for a few days — and in this season we cannot expect to get away without one — then it is a question whether the food and fuel oil we are pulling down the trail now against the side-blast of the wind will be of any help at all to the thirty-five persons at Dubawnt, except to slightly prolong their pain. And as for Itooi's camp —

I stop thinking about it. If the people are to be saved at all it will have to be the plane; if it comes the loads we are now hauling will make a difference. What we need now is a mug-up. I whistle to the dogs.

My oil-stove is already warm under the tea-pail when Paliayak and Nukak pull up out of the darkness. We slump in the lee of my sled, faces near the meagre warmth. Presently Paliayak says, "Maybe the blizzard won't come. See, the lights." They have emerged as we went, out of the east and northern sky: a great white-frozen band tinged pink that flimmers and shifts over the endless level of the land. There are still no clouds, and now perhaps there will be none for a little. Under the lights the winter darkness softens and the land spreads blank around us to a horizonless silver. Once when we rested on the trail Itooi told me that the lights were the souls of unborn children playing with their umbilical cords. Even after years between this land and sky, the lights can touch terror. I look at the other two and they smile grimly. "It is good," I say. "We will move until the weather turns."

We cannot do quite that. Eighteen hours later we are two-thirds of the way to Dubawnt and we must make a sleep-stop. The weather has held, fiercely cold but steady; for five hours I have been pulling with the dogs. Quickly we build a snow house, feed the dogs, gnaw some frozen meat washed down by tea and crawl into the robes. In ten hours we are on our way again, not rested but moving. And the weather holds, the temperature about fifty below. I pull with the dogs immediately as do the others but we are moving across the coarser grain of the land now and we make less than twenty miles in eight hours. In the last two the snow begins to sting head-on. We are almost to the lake-ice then and still perhaps ten miles from the camp, but we have to stop and risk the storm getting worse. We waste no fifteen minutes on a house but simply pull the sleds into a triangle and huddle in the robes in that shelter. Exhausted, we sleep. When I next look at my wristwatch in the darkness of the robe it is four hours later. Nearly noon. I cannot feel my left foot and I pull off mukluks and socks, massaging, until the pain comes back. Then I push half-erect. The wind shrieks but it is not yet full blizzard.

The wind shifts to the northeast after we take to the trail, which is lucky because the dogs could not have faced it for ten miles. Nor we. The lake, at least, has no eskers. There is still a trace of daylight left when we corner the last headland and see the mounds of the people's snow houses. The dogs rouse their last efforts and break into a trot at my urging. My leader even raises his head and howls, to be echoed feebly by some of the other dogs, but no answering sound comes from the camp. No figure emerges from the scattered houses even when I halloo as loudly as I can, running.

I stop at the first circle of houses and halloo again. Entrances blocked, I cannot see any tracks from one house to the next. I dig out my flashlight as Paliayak and Nukak pull up. Their faces are gaunt with exhaustion and without a sound the dogs drop in their traces. We trudge together to the nearest tunnel entrance. Paliayak pulls the block of snow aside; I bend to crawl, calling as cheerily as I can, "Someone from far has come for a visit," following the beam of my light down the long entrance.

The tunnel opens up into the house and when I get to the end I raise my head with the light. The beam flashes around the domed roof and against the worn caribou of the figure crouching almost at my face beside the entrance. My heart thuds as I struggle erect, the two behind me in the passage, "Hello! We've come from Tyrel Bay!" But the figure does not move, it is hunched forward over the stove, its hands palm-out to the heat and even as I lean forward I comprehend the house is dead cold. Paliayak's face emerges out of the entrance hole as I touch the shoulder. It topples like a stone; Turatuk, frozen rigid.

We stare at the face fallen over in the dirt against the empty oil can, the body visible here and there through tatters of fur. No sound at all in the house, not even our breathing, and then I remember the sleeping bench along the back. Only a bumpy robe; I jerk it back and there lie Turatuk's wife and his seven-year-old son and baby daughter, in a row, as they slept.

Paliayak and Nukak have not moved out of the entrance. I fling the beam of light around the small house, but there is only the useless tin stove, dog skulls, bones, the empty oil drum, a few scattered pots, and the bodies. They have eaten everything — extra clothes, hides, the very dog bones are split for marrow. Someone has chewed the leather braided handle of Turatuk's dog whip. I say, "The other houses — there must be some still," and Nukak plunges out of sight with Paliayak behind him.

We go the round of the death encampment. In some houses weak voices answer when I call at the entrance and we crawl in. We empty one of the larger houses and Paliayak and Nukak help or carry the living to it, setting up stoves and melting snow and heating meat while I run on, from house to house. I find several where the people, though alive, cannot answer my call so each must be searched. The darkness has long come when I have finished all the houses I can find. Of thirty-five people who should be here, we have found seventeen alive. Of the men only Ikpuck and Nakown remain; the hunters inevitably go first. I squat beside Ikpuck and in his face I cannot see the brightness of the isymatah, the leader of his people. He says, in my silence, "We sent Nayak to you in the middle of the great darkness. Then at last we sent also Keluah."

"Yes. Keluah told us. But Nayak never came."

"Ahhh," it is a sound deep in his throat.

"Ikpuck, we have searched all the houses here, three in this group and four to the west, where you were. Are there others here? And have you heard of Itooi and Ukwa?"

Beyond Ikpuck, where Paliayak is doing woman's work, the fragrance of thawing meat fills the snow house with warmth and strength. Ikpuck does not move as he speaks, "One has not heard from Itooi. They were going back to camp on Front River, but one has not heard of them since the darkness."

"Yes," I say in his silence. "When the plane comes we will find them. Perhaps they have found the deer. Are there others here?"

After a moment he says, "Long ago Lootevek and his oldest son went on the hunt, but they did not come back.

His wife — and his other children — are in their house beyond the others, over the little creek."

"So far away? If she is alone, why — " I stop.

Ikpuck says heavily, "She was asked to come here, several times. But she would not." As I move quickly to go Ikpuck looks up, fleetingly. "It would perhaps be well if two men went to that house."

I look at him an instant, at a loss to decipher his tone. "How many children?"

"Three."

Impossible. Outside I find Nukak unloading the last from my sled, and in a moment we are beating west along the shore. Under the overcast the wind drives like needles across the lake; it must be clear tomorrow if we are to expect the plane from Baker. One or two of the seventeen may not recover, but the rest surely will. And if Itooi's band has escaped with only one or two deaths and if Lootevek's wife and two children, or perhaps even three, remain, why out of the forty-five that had traded west at Tyrel Bay last fall twenty-seven or even twenty-eight are alive to — but I cannot face the thought at the moment: nor the fact that in ninety miles of travel we saw only two rabbits, no owls or fox tracks; nor that as far as I know only two men and three teen-age boys are left to this group of the people. I think rather of the people as they were last summer, friendly, laughing together with their friends in the sunshine on the bay when the land briefly burst open with flowers. I rub the frostbite on my cheek. It seems very long ago since I heard their laughter.

"There," says Nukak as the lead dog barks, then all howl in chorus. A small mound barely pokes out of a drift. We drive up, the dogs hushing. Lootevek always was a loner and his wife, a large strong woman, hardly even smiled, but in the camps he seemed to lose some of the moroseness which fell on him when he lived near the store. I brace myself and push aside the entrance block. "Hallo! We have come from Tyrel Bay," I call, bending down into the tunnel.

And suddenly out of that black tunnel rises laughter.

The sound echoing in the narrowness is beyond measure more horrible than the silence we fear. I stop and Nukak's scramble behind me ceases. I cannot unravel thought; I can only shout, "We are coming," and lunge forward, Nukak at my heels. The house is dark but I fling the light-beam up before me and we are inside. It is as cold as the other houses, but on the sleeping bench Lootevek's wife sits erect, wearing her outside parka, her eyes glaring through matted hair, her mouth still hanging slack from the sound which greeted us. We stare at her. I move the light, but she is obviously the only person in the house.

"Where are the chil — " I begin but Nukak jogs my arm, gesturing to the floor. There are so many split bones lying about that I stumbled coming in. As I blink down at them now suddenly the woman laughs again. And in that shriek I understand.

There is no way to get her from the house but tie her in the sleeping robe and kick through the wall to the sled. We bring her to main camp and put her in a house by herself where her laughter will not terrify the rest of the people. Then, after several hours of feeding broth to those who cannot sit erect, I crawl into my sleeping bag.

Paliayak rouses me after eight hours; we go out, and clearly the blizzard that has been holding off is moving in over the lake from the north and east — the direction of Baker Lake. No plane on earth can get aloft in that. There is nothing to say, so we go back in and heat food. As we eat I explain a plan. He shakes his head, but helps load the sled. He stands looking after me as I urge the rested dogs out on the lake. Perhaps, with a light sled and rested dogs, I can cover the twenty-odd miles somewhere along which Itooi's Front River camp may be before the weight of the storm hits. And if forced to stop I can wait out the blizzard as well on the trail as in this dreadful camp. So we run.

When the blue shadow that precedes dawn comes up over the long white land breaking trail for the dogs is no easier for the wind rises inevitably, nagging loose snow, and the bank of cloud more clearly rolls higher behind me. About dawn I make out the ridges on the lakeshore between which the Front River breaks to the lake and I turn south. Once on the twisting river I cannot lose my way: I simply follow until I reach the camp. If Itooi has left the river — well, it is useless to think of that.

The diffuse sun-blob is as high as it will rise when between the van lashes of the storm I think I hear the echo of a plane. I am chewing meat as I run, not daring to stop for tea, but at that I stop and tear back my hood.

There it is again! I stare around, the blood pounding in my head, searching for direction from the wind-torn sound. The dogs prick up their ears, and then I see the flash of it, between tags of drift, coming up over the esker from the southeast. I jerk the covering from the sled, clamber up a rock ridge and wave frantically. The snow swirls around me and the plane noses on obliviously west and north. Then, suddenly, it banks towards me. A red and silver Norseman; they must have radioed from Baker to Churchill and they risked a try into the storm. The plane roars over and I wave northeast towards the lake. It circles right, red lights flashing. Don't be so stupid! And you know there's no place to land on the riverbed or on the ridges! He passes over again, very low, so slowly the stall warning must be roaring in his ears. He dips and I see his face: Jimmy Hughes of Churchill. Swinging the tarp towards the lake, I scream at him though he cannot hear me, and he lifts up again into the wind. The wings waggle. He understands; and knows as well as I he's daring the face of the storm to try and unload, take on some of the people and get out before he's grounded. In a few moments he will be over the camp from which I've been struggling four hours. If the storm had held off we could have searched — but there is no need for such thought, and I clamber down to the team.

Two hours later it is impossible. The blizzard has been upon us in full fury for over an hour and only because it is behind us could we still trek. In its blindness now I realize I could go within twenty feet of the camp never knowing. And I have to stop while I have enough strength to build a snow house. Suddenly the dogs whine behind me. I stop, look back at them and then ahead. There is nothing except the streaking snow. I get my mitt on my leader's collar. "Okay, c'mon."

We move ahead slowly, and then abruptly the snow darkens and a shape is floundering towards me. "Hallo!" I reach for the shoulder and head bent into the white wind. The figure jerks and straightens. I am staring into the sunken frostbitten face of Oolulik, wife of Itooi.

I hold her by the shoulders then, for when she recognizes me she seems almost to crumple. After a moment I can ask, "Are you breaking trail for the others? Are they behind you?" I brush the ice from her face and she shakes her head with a shudder. "Where are they? Can we get to them before the storm is highest?"

She says through frost-broken lips, "They are in the camp by the Lake of Little Men." Somewhere beyond — perhaps five, perhaps eight miles, where the Front River runs out of the lake, where the deer cross and where for generations the people have hunted them by setting up inukshuk, rows of rock mounds that at a distance look like short men, to channel the deer into the river for easier spearing. Three years before Itooi took me there for the fall kill; there were full meat caches that winter. I stare at his wife now, trying for a moment not to think what her being out in this storm alone means, trying not to understand the small bump on her back under the parka. She murmurs, "They are without breath in the snow houses, Itooi also. Only the baby."

For a moment we hunch there, our backs to the storm. "Come," I say finally, "we must find a drift for a snow house."

There is little time to look, and the house we manage to build is tiny. But it is shelter, and when I get the oil-stove and the food inside from the sled there is warmth. I melt snow for water and give Oolulik the soup to drink from around thawing meat. She soaks a bit of hide in it and gives it to the baby to suck, but he seems almost beyond that. I should have remembered milk but she looks at me and murmurs, "Tomorrow one will have milk for him." I crawl out to feed the dogs; the storm is so intense now that I cannot see my feet. I check the dogs' chains, pull the sleeping robe off the sled and struggle back into the house. Oolulik is holding her child to her under the parka, bending back and forth over the little stove as if rocking in sleep. I rouse her. "The storm will be long, and we must save the oil. Here." I spread my heavy robe on the sleeping bench; she looks at it. She herself sewed it for me three winters before. "I know," I say at her look, "you could carry nothing but the child. But we must stay warm." I squat by the stove.

She lays the naked boy in the robe, then pulls off her own worn, frost-hardened clothes, spreads them out on the floor and gets into the robe. I blow out the stove and in the darkness I quickly undress and I lay out my clothes to freeze. Then I crawl into the robe also. It is just large enough. I can feel the ice of her emaciated body against mine but I know that together we will soon be warm, and as she hunches closer the wind's whine over the house is already dying in my ear.

For the first three days of the storm we do little but sleep. Oolulik eats what she can and cares for the child. He is her only concern and as she grows stronger she has milk for him but he does not improve. She rocks him gently, holding him to her under the parka, and in the long hours she tells, in snatches, the story of what had happened at the camp by the Lake of Little Men. If we were not alone in the cramped snow house and her strong handsome face haggard as I have never seen it, I could almost think we were in the hunting camp as we have been so often and that any moment my friend Itooi will crawl through the door and lift his laughing face to us and shout, "Telling old stories again? No one bothers with them now, only a few women! Ha! But just now a deer happened to run under the guns. Perhaps it will be enough for supper!" But no deer will ever again just happen to run under Itooi's unerring rifle. He lies where he has fallen over the fish hole in the ice, Ukwa's knife-wounds in his back. For Ukwa, big simple childlike man who could not hunt very well, and did not have to as long as his brother-in-law cared for him and his family, broke mentally under the long hunger. In his madness he may have believed Itooi was deceiving him in dividing the few fish on which the two families subsisted, so he — who knows — the fact was he went to Itooi jigging for fish, stabbed him, then went to his brother-in-law's house and before Oolulik knew what was happening had already stabbed the oldest girl as she lay beside her brother. Oolulik, strong in terror, succeeded in wrestling him down and tying him because he kept crawling back to the sleeping bench, insanely intent on the ten-year-old boy, Mala. Then, the baby on her back, she went out to get Itooi to do what had to be done with the madman. She found her husband face down in the ice hole. There was only one law left her: survival. She returned to her house, pulled a thong taut around Ukwa's neck, dressed Mala in what hides were left and, with the baby still on her back, leaving her dead and Ukwa's wife — her sister — and children she could not know in what condition, with time only for one desperate effort for her two sons, she began the trek for Dubawnt Lake under the threat of the storm. But Mala was too weak; in an hour he collapsed. She waited beside the boy until his panting stopped, then covered him with snow and turned again to the storm. Some hours later I found her.

We are safe now; we have food and shelter. But it is too late for the baby and on the third day he dies.

On the fourth day she gives me the body and I take it out. Finding my marker, I dig out the sled and lay the body under it where the dogs cannot reach. The blizzard howls without cease. There is no way to help Ukwa's family even if they are alive. The storm roars over me for a time, then I return into the house. Oolulik is sitting as I left her and I begin to melt snow to make tea. We have said nothing since the child died, and I cannot endure the silence. But how to break it? We have known each other since I came to Tyrel Bay and though we are about the same age, she is my mother as Itooi has been my father in the north. Now I can only make her tea.

She drinks a little. Eyes closed, she squats on the sleeping bench, swaying silently. I drink tea, listening to the storm, and presently I sense her singing beside me. It is not a Christian hymn such as the people love to sing together when the missionary comes to Tyrel twice a year and which they sing together when they hold their daily morning prayers. It is the old song of the people that I heard only once or twice during my earliest days in the north, a song as I have long since not been able to beg from Oolulik. Like the singers of the people long ago, she is composing as she sings, and it is her own song:

> *Where have gone the deer,*
> *The animals on which we live?*
> *Who gave us meat and blood soup to drink,*
> *Our dogs strength to run over the snow?*
> *Once their strong sinews sewed our clothes,*
> *And their bones gave the sweet-brown marrow;*
> *Then our houses were warm with the fire of their fat*
> *And our cheeks smeared with their juices.*
> *Eyaya — eya.*
>
> *And when they would not come,*
> *Long ago,*

The angakok would send his soul beneath the lake
Where lives the mighty spirit Pinga
And there sing a charm for her that would soothe her
And the deer would come
In great herds that covered the land
And the birds that follow them hide the autumn sun.
We would hunt them at the sacred crossings
Where the little men stand guard,
And the angakoks would sing their songs,
And the people would keep strictly to the taboos
And not offend Pinga,
And in the winter the storm would wail about the
      house,
The dogs roll up, their snouts under their tails,
On the ledge the sleeping boy would lie
On his back, breathing through his open mouth,
His little stomach bulging round.
Eyaya — eya.

Were it not Oolulik, the wisest woman among the
western people who is singing, and were her song not so
terrible in beauty, I would think her mind has given way.
For though she is the daughter of a great angakok and it
was whispered among the people that even as a child she
had already shown some of his power, she gave her name
to the missionary as a young girl and all her life she has
been a fervent Christian. She told me the legends of the
people only after much persuading. Itooi was the church
catechist for the band, leading the services during the long

months the missionary could not visit them. Like all the people, they were profoundly devotional. The two times I was with them at Baker Lake they attended church services every day six days of the week. The angakok to them had long ago been declared the power of Satanasi, the devil. And now Oolulik sings on:

> When all the people came safely from the hunt
> Then we knew our amulets were strong,
> And the angakok who had gained his strength
> In the lonely way of the barrens
> Would sing of Sila, the great spirit
> That holds up the world and the people
> And speaks in no words
> But in the storm and snow and rain
> And sometimes through unknowing children
>   at play,
> Who hear a soft gentle voice,
> And the angakok knows
> That peril threatens.
> When all is well Sila sends no messages.
> He remains solitary, silent.
> And there is meat in the camp, and the drum dance
> Calls the people for dance and laughter and song.
> The women lie in the arms of the song-cousins of
>   their husbands;
> And the angakok speaks through the fire of the
>   seance.

She has stopped, her face tilts back towards the low roof of the house, her eyes closed. Her song in its short endlessly repeating melody has grown loud, but now it drops away:

Eyaya — eya
Where have gone the deer,
And the people of the deer?
Eyaya — eya.

When I can bear to look at her again she is motionless on the sleeping bench, looking at me with bright dry eyes. Suddenly she says, "When the white man came to the people with guns and oil for heating, it was almost as if we no longer needed shamans or taboo for we could hunt the deer wherever we wished, from far. Then the missionary came and told us of Jesus and we listened and soon our old beliefs seemed of little use for us to live. We have lived this way most of my life, and every year the deer have been less. And our prayers to God do not bring them back. In the old days the shaman did."

Finally I can say something. "Oolulik, you do not believe that. The shaman could not bring the deer if there were none."

"There always were deer."

"Yes, but they have been over-hunted, here, in the north, in the south."

"Because men have guns."

"Partly, but also — "

"And they no longer keep the taboo of not killing more than can be eaten. The missionaries tell us that we must believe other things, and the white men do not even believe what the white missionary says. We have seen them in Baker Lake; many never go to church, and yet they are fat and warm and never hungry. We believed and prayed, and see — " she gestures about the tiny house. "There is nothing left to believe. The deer and the people are gone."

"The people are not all gone. There are many left in the eastern bands, and to the north, and the deer will come back in a few years. The government is beginning to make surveys and soon we will know why the deer — "

She is looking at me with a gentle smile and I cannot continue. "Abramesi," she says. "You are a good man. But you did not go with us to church. You do not believe either."

Finally I can murmur, "But you have believed for many years, long before you met me. And you still believe."

She does not look at me but stares against the wall of the house as if studying the storm that howls beyond. She says at last, "The deer are gone and the people of the deer are gone. I also wish to go away."

There is nothing to be said. Later I crawl out and feed the dogs; there is only one skimpy feeding left, but from the sound of the storm it may break tomorrow. I go in and prepare food for us. Oolulik eats little, squatting silently on the floor. She will remain that way all night, swaying back and forth, singing softly to herself. I undress, crawl into the robe, and pull it tight over my ears.

I awake to the smell of food. Oolulik is at the stove and there is no sound of wind outside. I dress quickly and crawl out. Stars sparkle in the fierce calm cold; when the sun comes up the world will blaze white. In a few moments we have eaten, loaded, and are on our way. Oolulik rides the sled with the body of the child. She leads us unerringly to the spot; we find the body of her other son and take it with us also. Travelling is fast on the wind-hard drifts. In an hour we are at the camp, and even as I clear the entrance of Ukwa's house I hear the plane coming from the north. It will spot the dog team so I concern myself no further with it for the moment but scramble into the house. Amazingly, Ukwa's wife and two of the three children are still, if barely, alive. They know nothing; only that Ukwa has not returned. I start the stove, put on frozen meat and crawl out. The plane is landing on the ice of the lake and with a jolt I see it is the RCMP craft from Baker. A little luck now would have been too much to expect.

Corporal Blake must, of course, examine all the bodies. Oolulik has brought all hers to the sled, and after he crawls into what was her house and examines Ukwa. There is no way of concealing the way he died and I translate while the policeman questions her. Nothing can be done: she has killed the man and she must be arrested. It seems we will have to take the bodies of the two men with us for medical examination, but then it leaps in me and I curse him, long, completely. When I can control myself he says only, "Yes, it would be too much for the plane." And he permits Oolulik and me to take what is left of her family out on the wind-swept hill overlooking the lake. There is, of course, no way to dig a grave. We do what the Eskimos did long ago: lay them on the ground, cover them with the few wind-cleared rocks we can pry loose, and leave them to the elements and the wild animals. In the house I had found Itooi's prayer book and now I hand it to Oolulik to read a prayer over the four graves. But she takes it from my hand and, without opening it, thrusts it under the rocks. Then, squinting against the blazing sun on the snow, we drive down the hill. Blake has helped Ukwa's family to the plane, and when we arrive the two sisters look silently at each other, one knowing, one unknowing though without hope. We climb in; four adults, two children and five muzzled dogs make an awkward load but soon we are airborne. We circle over the hill with its patch black against the snow, and head for Tyrel Bay.

Two days later when the plane comes in from Baker again to evacuate the last of the people from Dubawnt Lake, the pilot tells me that the first night Oolulik spent in jail she hanged herself. She too had gone away.

BEAR SPIRIT IN A
STRANGE LAND

"A BEAR IS NOT A BEAR," said the prairie Cree who once knew the giant plains grizzly, now extinct. "A bear is a four-legged Person, he is spirit. That spirit dwells in every bear you can see, but mostly it is on high. There are many bear spirit powers, and over them all is the great one that can never be seen, the Great Parent of Bear."

On a New York subway a man is leaning over me, left hand hooked on the bar above, the right gesturing down the car. With each lateral lunge of the train his mouth swings almost against my ear. He is an official trying to explain how I must get off to find the American Museum of Natural History, but there seem to be too many trains at too many levels steel-screaming beside and over and under us through the Manhattan rock; no matter how close he swings he cannot quite bellow loud enough for me to understand him. But he keeps on repeating the same words, I understand that, and gradually something emerges in the unbelievable noise that is so shrill and unending it already seems to be no sound at all except my head breaking: "...this express, catch the local...back..."

When the train finally stops he gets me through the hissing doors, pointing, a friendly uniformed man whose face smiles between the large pads clamped like earphones to his head. Somewhere under there he may be wired for Mozart. The train shrieks away, taking most of the oily air with it, but above me, or perhaps below, another is coming. Up the moving stairs I run, wait in another grimed green tunnel where for an instant nothing moves. The father of a Cree girl I know has, she thinks, a power thing with worms; there may be one in his bundle which her mother no longer puts up with in the house. If I told him about these immense steel worms, I believe he would never again catch so much as an accidental gopher in his traps.

So what am I doing here? I'm on the trail of a man buried on a cold January in Saskatchewan in 1888, but who for me is far from dead. His name is Big Bear. For several years I have tried to follow him wherever he once lived: from his birthplace near Jackfish Lake, Saskatchewan, to Frog Lake, Alberta, in the north, to the Missouri River, Montana, in the south: to find traces of him, to see what is left of what he saw in that long lifetime before 1885 when he and the Plains Cree who followed him rode over the prairie wherever their spirit moved them.

On March 24, 1879, the Saskatchewan *Herald* explained who Big Bear was: "All the tribes — that is the Sioux [of Sitting Bull], Blackfoot [of Crowfoot], Bloods, Sarcees, Assiniboines, Stoneys, Cree and Saulteaux — all now form but one party, having the same mind. Big Bear, up to this time, cannot be accused of uttering a single objectionable word, but the fact of his being the head and soul of all our Canadian plain Indians leaves room for conjecture." The *Herald* was quoting a man who knew: Father Lestanc, O.M.I., veteran priest of the Saskatchewan Métis who were out on the plains that dreadful winter of 1878-79 because the buffalo no longer came within two hundred miles of Batoche. The Métis, led by Gabriel Dumont, were wintering with Big Bear's People at The Forks of the Red Deer and South Saskatchewan rivers.

For by the spring of 1879 it was finally becoming clear even to government officials that the buffalo was on the brink of annihilation; that the 15,000 prairie Indians, already decimated by smallpox, were actually dying of malnutrition. Several thousand had wintered with Big Bear at The Forks because there were still some buffalo there and because he alone of all the ancient and traditional chiefs (in contrast to Hudson's Bay and government sanctioned chiefs) had never yet signed any treaty, surrendered anything to the white man. Clearly, if the prairie Indians were to get a better treaty than the present one which was, as Governor Morris explained so carefully in 1876, "offered as a gift since they had still their old mode of living," Big Bear was the leader to get it. Without the buffalo there was no "mode of living" on the plains — they needed far more than "gifts."

Big Bear in New York? Not voluntarily, of course, but the tunnels around me here don't actually seem that much different from the limestone-and-steel corridors of Stony Mountain Penitentiary high above the Manitoba plain where I followed him a year ago. Except for the noise and dirt. White men are very resourceful; once they have forced you to give up the land, there isn't very much they cannot legally arrange to do with you, one way or another. And this new violence must be the approaching local.

When I emerge from underground, the first-of-June air along Central Park West smells almost of leafy trees, of grass; but immediately more of diesel, and sausages roasting on a brazier wheeled against the iron fence. A man turns them occasionally as I pass. Inside the Theodore Roosevelt Memorial Entrance the air is cleaner — cleaned, I guess — a probably-steel statue of the Roughrider President presiding. The stone hall is immense, people echo here like whispers moving in caves, and then at the information booth I discover that I have come across the continent and somewhere mislaid the letter I need to get myself beyond the public display to the guardians of the museum vaults. I search myself again: there's a list of numbers I want, but no letter. I must have a name to call, I ask for the museum directory — I'll probably recognize the name — and am handed a fifty-page book in double columns. Confound it, if I can find an arrowhead in a six-centuries-old buffalo kill I can find a woman in a New York building! Or was it a man? Eventually I soothe the boothed lady into letting me within arm's length of a telephone, I discover "Department of Anthropology," dial again, and again, talking fast. Yes, there are people there; yes, I can get a pass. The man controlling the barrier points: "Voluntary Admission Fee." I hand him a bill and push at the turnstile.

"What's this?" the man says.

"Huh? It's — five dollars!"

"This don't mean nothing here," he says, and I stare in disbelief. New York is New York, okay, but don't they even recognize anything under — and then I recognize the Queen's face.

"Sorry!" I give him two colourless American dollars and get through.

The Plains Indians artifacts are not underground, and I'm happy about that following Dr. Philip Gifford up stone steps and iron steps, through fire doors and up to a small door which, unlocked, breathes asthmatically of air conditioning. There can be no window here and when the light clicks on it is as if out of the darkness an entire culture had exploded: the tiny room is crammed, stuffed tight. Gifford is working his way in but I stop in the doorway; mostly what I see is buffalo robes folded hide out in heaps on the floor and on the metal shelves, and then gradually there are beaded buckskin suits and drums and stone axes and rattles and incredible bladed clubs and horsebridles and black copper kettles and whips and beaded saddles and saddlebags and parfleches and bowl-shaped shields and buckskin gun cases crusted with unbelievable porcupine-quill embroidery.

Gifford is opening drawers and drawers. "The Mandelbaum smaller stuff is here, somewhere," he says. "It's all numbered very simply and in order." The tanned side of the buffalo skins seems tensile as nylon and on the other side the curly hair is almost coarse, but in deeper your fingers can feel — what is it? — delicacy, softness opening, warmth as if the animal were still alive beneath you there, breathing. "Yeah, this must be it. This what you wanted to see? Mr. Wiebe?"

I hear him then. He is holding a small grey stick towards me, grey canvas I see, weathered and pitted with holes very much like the binder canvas I remember from our bush farm in Saskatchewan. I stare so long he says, "It's the numbers all right, here," and he's about to pull out what's inside the sack and I step forward and take it from him quickly.

Just holding it I should — well, I've been trained to think logically; I can't defy classification. I've come over four thousand miles by jet and bus and subway and only about half a mile on my own feet and not once has my sole actually touched the ground, so I check the numbers on the little tags dangling from the open end of the sack. 50.2-3739 A-M. Yes. I am holding in my hands the sacred bundle of Big Bear.

Wrapped in this canvas is that spirit gift which gave Big Bear his name and his wisdom and his power, which hung around his neck when he rode on a raid or danced his vows to the Thunderbird in the Thirst Dance.

The vision for the bundle was given him at The Forks of the Red Deer and the South Saskatchewan rivers. It was fitting that his Cree should be wintering there in 1878-79, the last winter the buffalo would ever come north into Canada, because all his life that place had been the centre of the world for Big Bear. Whenever he mentioned it he would rotate the stem of a smoking pipe to the four directions and then point it towards The Forks because sometime before 1840 the Great Parent of Bear came to him there and gave him the vision that shaped his life.

Perhaps very early one morning his father Black Powder walked with the lad (no one knows what his name was, then) to the top of Bull's Forehead Hill. Together they erected the stick frameworks and hung cloth offerings on them, they placed the buffalo skull under their shelter, spread the bearskin. Then his father offered up a pipe, and left him. He saw Sun come over the knobby line of the Sand Hills and he kept his face facing Him all day, praying for vision, crying out and raising his arms in agony when it seemed he could no longer stand upright in the terrible light of the endless summer day. Stripped to his breechclout, his feet on the bear fur, he looked into the sun over the plains and the straight deep valley of the South Saskatchewan and the hills folded down to the point like old blankets until Sun finally vanished black into the wide bloody loops of the Red Deer and he could collapse.

On the second day he did not stand, or move. He was not hungry: it was thirst that wanted to break his concentration. He did not look even at the point where the rivers imperceptibly joined grey water and bent north and then east together. He wept and prayed, and at night the spirits began to come. Not one, many, but he refused; bear spirits came but he would not listen to them either. He fasted and prayed until finally out of his accepted suffering the overlord of all bear spirits came: the Great Parent of Bear. On that cactus-studded hill Bear scooped up wet clay and clawed it over his face, taught him his song and the words of it —

> *My teeth are my knives*
> *My claws are my knives*

— and told him how to make "that which is kept in a clean place": his sacred bundle. All his life it would be his sign that he was chosen; that, under the Creator, the most powerful spirit known to his people had come, and would come again, to assist him.

More than a hundred and thirty years later in a small room on the sixth floor of the American Museum of Natural History in New York City, I hold this sacred bundle. I tell anthropologist Gifford that this is it, yes, and he tells me I'm welcome to look around and take any pictures I want and finally he leaves. Even up in the centre of the building the walls and floor shiver with a kind of roar;

perhaps the subway burrows directly below here. I pull the bundle out of its battered sack.

It is a soft rectangle of greyed-mauve plaid cotton two feet long, ten inches wide and four thick; at one end the cloth is folded in but the other hangs free. The whole is tied together, not with leather thongs, but with binder-twine. I guess that, like everything else, is symbolic too.

There are proper ceremonies for opening this bundle, I know, and there are enough pipes here (carefully labelled in drawers) and the ransacked riches of prairie People undoubtedly already provide the proper circle of belief — but I am no proper person. The bundle was to be opened only when its core was to be worn either in battle or in ceremonial dance, but here there is no wet clay to claw over my face even if I had the faintest notion in which direction to turn towards The Forks, even if I knew one single word, had either song or prayer. Though I do intend to go into battle: against all the variegated and clotted ignorance of myself and my people about our past. Having held this story in my hand.

At each opening a new cloth was added inside as a thank offering, so the oldest is outside and the ten layers of printed cotton gradually brighten through shades and patterns of trader cloth to an innermost wrapping of red, yellow and blue stylized flowers on cream background crisp with newness. As I touch that I should feel something: something for this having been dragged across a continent to an up-and-down world that cannot be oriented in the cardinal directions because here there is no sun or earth or believable air; something for my own apprehension of wanting to see this, to somehow *have* this like any white who never has enough, of anything, as if it were even possible to actually have enough of anything except within your self; something of a prayer to the Great Spirit who Big Bear, and I also, believe shaped the universe as He did for no other reason than that apparently He wanted to; some prayer.

So then I unfolded the newest cloth.

The core of the bundle is "Chief's Son's Hand." It is a bear paw skinned out but with its five enormous claws still attached, tanned and supple, sewn on to red stroud shaped like a bib. The Cree believe that a person's soul comes to him at birth and resides along the back of the neck, and so wearing this Big Bear felt the weight of the Hand against his soul: he was in the assured, perfect relationship with the Great Bear Spirit.

The soul lives in the base of the neck: on September 13, 1876, Big Bear refuses the treaty by asking the Governor "to save me from what I most dread — hanging; it is not given to us to have the rope about our necks." And Governor Morris interprets that to mean Big Bear is a criminal and afraid of literal hanging! A logical enough thought, I guess, for a white man to whom language is always only proposition, and never parable.

In the nest of cloth with Chief's Son's Hand there is a short twist of tobacco and six inches of braided sweetgrass. The tobacco is dead but when I lift the sweetgrass I smell prairie. "When the sun rises on this land," Big Bear once said, "the shadow I cast is longer than any river."

I stayed in New York two days, and when the museum was open I was up in that small room. Gifford was helpful and sympathetic. David Mandelbaum was simply a good anthropologist: he found a group of natives no one in Canada had any interest in, got himself sponsored by the American Museum and spent several summers after 1933 living on the Battle River reserves, writing his doctoral thesis and collecting whatever Plains Cree artifacts he could. The thesis was published (available in any good library), and it certainly did preserve much invaluable information on early plains life. Gifford understood that, to a Canadian now, the bundle was a priceless historical item. I said I believed that to the Cree it was perhaps not so much *historical* as *sacred*. Perhaps so, he said, but a museum is "great" because it becomes an impersonal repository and never gives up anything it has once ransacked the world to acquire. Even if it really needed money badly, as the American Museum did; even if, by keeping this bundle locked in vaults, never displayed, it deprived a people of some historical and spiritual heritage they wanted badly to recover. All perfectly reasonable and of course unchangeable.

It was only two days, and it's hard to say what I did when the museum was closed. I certainly saw no Broadway play nor was lifted to the top of the Empire State Building. One night I know I walked around Times Square where, as John Mills wrote in *Life*, "every week are reported 15 robberies, 20 felonious assaults, 20 burglaries, 320 larcenies, 2 rapes, and more acts of prostitution, perversion and extortion than anyone has ever tried to count." Beyond the lights was violet sky, but everything on more or less the concrete level seemed like a machine set on "destruct," hammering me into pavement. I found an empty phone booth under a marquee spastic with *The Godfather* and in about a minute I was talking to Tena in British Columbia. She said the kids were all sleeping.

Mostly I think I lay on the saggy bed in a room on West 45th Street. Thinking about the unchanged panorama of The Forks, the long rivers joining. About the riverbank cemetery on the Poundmaker reservation, where Big Bear is buried on the spot where he gave his last Thirst Dance, June 16 to 19, 1884. His last free summer as chief of the Cree River People. When he felt the weight of Chief's Son's Hand against his soul for the last time.

THE YEAR WE GAVE
AWAY THE LAND

I REMEMBER EACH YEAR OF my long life as easily as I finger a string of beads; each bead is one particular thing that happened. But no Blackfoot can forget the year the whites count 1877. That was the year we gave away the land. I will tell you how it was.

Sunday, September 16

The Queen's white commissioner came with eighty Mounted Police and forty wagons over the round hills of the Bow River at the Crossing. Up on the prairie we had seen their dust curl all day, but still their white helmets and red coats shone in the sun, a long stiff worm of red and white and gleaming horses coming down into the valley with a white-fisted drummer rattling them ahead as they rode. Two of the wagons had those guns so big you can stick your fist into the barrels.

But at Blackfoot Crossing there were only Old Sun's and Crowfoot's bands of the Siksikas to watch them, and the Stoneys camped across the river running together to stare. Not a single Peigan or Sarcee had come, and I and my forty young men were the only Bloods. Without women or children, we could have been on a raid. We sat on our horses, watching. They came across the river flat, straight like whites do everything, straight, one wagon with a square canvas to keep the sun off the commissioner's blotchy face. They came bumping under the flags, straight to where the trees open on the Crossing. There Colonel Macleod lifted his hand and everything stopped. The police swung down and after a minute the blotchy man unbent himself, long and bony, out of his wagon.

"Tall Man," someone behind me named him.

And we laughed a little. I had a better name for him later, though I never said it; he was too strong for me. But he did not seem so then, just long and thin, and we stopped watching him because there were more police on the south hills. They were trying to chase grey cattle into the valley.

"There come the presents," someone said, and a few of us laughed again.

Monday, September 17

A little after noon they fired the guns. The sound rumbled down the valley and sent children and dogs running for shelter. Then all the chiefs went to see Macleod and Tall Man under the canvas inside the squares of police tents,

Bear's Paw and his Stoney councillors riding their best horses through the river. But no more people had come in. Old Sun would not open his mouth and Crowfoot said they would have to wait two days, maybe four. Macleod said to me,

"Medicine Calf, do you think Red Crow and Rainy Chief will be here with your people in two days?"

For a minute I looked at Jerry Potts, the guide and interpreter. His mother was a Blood killed in a whisky brawl before the police came and stopped that; he got paid well by Macleod, and when they had it he got quite a lot of confiscated whisky too, though he always wanted more.

"Why doesn't he ask Crowfoot again?" I said.

Potts swore, carefully under his hand. "He never understands, he still thinks the Blackfoot nation has one big head chief."

"That one," I nodded at Crowfoot, "doesn't mind pretending we do." Though if we had, it would have been my chief, Red Crow of the South Bloods. But Red Crow never wanted to talk to whites, so how could they know how powerful he was?

"What does he say?" Macleod asked Potts.

"He doesn't know," Potts said.

Tall Man was talking. The Mounted Police would give us food, the things piled inside the square and the bony cattle if we needed them, and Bear's Paw stood up and said he wanted everything, yes. But Crowfoot was studying Tall Man, whom none of us had ever seen before.

"We still have buffalo," was all Crowfoot said. And his tone meant what Big Bear had said three years before about treaties: "When we set a fox trap, we scatter meat all around, but when the fox is in the trap we knock him on the head. We want no bait, let your chiefs come like men and talk to us." I fought Big Bear four times. He was a Cree, our enemy, but that time he spoke true.

Macleod and Tall Man looked at each other when Potts translated Crowfoot's four words; they understood meanings. Then Old Sun stood up, and every Blackfoot stood up with him.

Tuesday, September 18

We rode east before dawn along the prairie above the river, and there we ran buffalo as the sun came up blood red. O, the land and the sky. When we returned dragging our travois heavy with meat, Sitting on an Eagle Tail with all his Peigans was at the Crossing, about nine hundred of them. And so were the traders from Fort Macleod and Edmonton, chopping down trees for walls to protect their goods. Many were Montana men. They carried their Winchesters naked on the saddle across their knees. We surrounded them, all bloody from hunting, and told them no treaty had been made and they would not chop down one more tree at this sacred place. So they went to the Mounted Police and Macleod said we were right. While we sat on our horses watching them they stacked their goods back inside their tents.

We danced and ate meat all night with the Peigans. Eiyan-nah, the stories and the singing!

Wednesday, September 19

When we came to the tent inside the police square the whites were already there, including six white women, more than any of us had ever seen. After the long, hot summer their faces were still like snow under their wide hats, their bright dresses pulled in so tight around the tops of their bodies. My young men stared and stared, such dry women looking shamelessly back at us, but laughing and whispering to each other like Blackfoot women.

We chiefs sat down in a half-circle in front of Tall Man and Macleod, and behind us our prairie people gathered, several thousand now though Red Crow and the Bloods had not come. Tall Man began in a high singsong, and after a moment he stopped, waited. But Jerry Potts could say nothing. Such speech was impossible for him, he never translated more than five words, no matter how long the original statement. Finally an old white man who had lived with the Peigans for years, he was called Bird, stepped forward. He could talk like a medicine man and Tall Man started again.

"The Great Spirit has made all things, it is by that Spirit that the Queen rules over this great country. She loves all her children, both white and red alike, but she hates wickedness. And that is why she sent the police to punish the bad men who robbed you with whisky."

"Did your father ever tell you a woman had our country?" Eagle Ribs asked me. He was war leader of the Siksikas as I was of the Bloods; we would have to explain all this to our warriors.

On his left Eagle Calf, leader of the Many Children band, said, "The whites are coming anyway, like in Montana. We should at least get some of those presents for our land."

"Twenty years ago," I told them, "I signed the Blood treaty with the Americans in Montana. And now you can't ride anywhere there without a white watching you. Treaties mean nothing."

"But look, this is Macleod," Eagle Calf said. "He talks for the Great Mother, he's different."

"He's just white too," Eagle Ribs said staring at the pale smiling women, their hands folded in their flowered laps.

"Last year," Tall Man was saying, "we made treaty with the Crees, and now we come to make treaty with the Blackfeet. In a few years the buffalo will all be destroyed and for this reason the Queen wishes you to live in some other way. She wishes you to allow her white children to come and live on your land, raise cattle, grow grain, and she will assist you to do the same."

"There are so many whites along the Oldman's River already," Eagle Ribs said, "they have ruined the hunting."

"She will also pay you," Tall Man shouted, "money every year, money as a gift so you cannot be cheated. Twenty-five dollars for each chief, twelve dollars each for signing, and five dollars every year after that, forever."

Forever is a long time.

"How can we give away land?" Eagle Ribs muttered.

"Maybe we can't give it," Eagle Calf said, "but those whites can sure take it. We better take their presents."

Eagle Ribs was looking at me. "What's 'money'?"

"Sometimes it's metal, sometimes a piece of paper with a picture. If you have enough of it, the traders give you a gun."

"Or a dipperful of whisky," Eagle Calf laughed.

"If you sign the treaty," Tall Man shouted, "a reserve of land will be set aside for you and your children forever, for every five persons you will have one square mile of land set aside. Cattle will be given to you, and potatoes like those grown at Fort Macleod. And we will send teachers so your children will learn to read books like this one...."

Tall Man was holding up a black missionary book, and Macleod just sat, nodding his heavy head. But I was hearing the mutter of young men behind me. That blotchy man had said that soon the buffalo would be destroyed. There were so few left now, and the Crees from the north and Sioux from the south were hunting those few also, I knew he was right. Eagle Ribs beside me was thinking my thoughts: the land and the buffalo, how else can prairie people live?

That evening I rode up to the prairie. Bull Head and the Sarcees had come in, they were raising their lodges in the circles of the valley. But Red Crow and Rainy Chief, my wives and children with them, had not come. The sun was gone behind the white teeth of the mountains, and a wind — as if the earth were breathing…hissss uhhh… hisssss uhhh — cold and hard, I could smell winter, I could smell dying. Like the terrible year of the Rotting Sickness when we scraped ourselves bloody against the traders' gateposts, trying to rub off the disease that killed us piece by piece, to give it back to the whites who gave it to us but themselves never suffered from it. The moon bulged up, white and blotchy, out of the land. Who had ever asked for them to come, if we could just kill them all, who would not pray a lifetime if only they could be wiped away like dirt in a sweat lodge?

My horse grazed a little in the dry circle of my reins. The earth under me was hard, warm; it moved so certainly with my breathing. But the police had stopped the whisky trading, the terrible drunkenness that killed us as surely as disease. And now Macleod said, "Sign." But how will we live? How can we live with them? Forever is a long time.

When the moon was down, I stood up. And prayed. After a time it came to me that war, raid and defence, which were my life with my people, these were not enough. Words had to be made here. And then Pemmican came to me in my prayer, the old medicine man of my people.

"The buffalo make you strong," were his words. "But what you eat from this money will bury our people all over the hills. You will be tied down, whites will take your land and fill it."

When I opened my eyes, I saw that the long light that comes before dawn had spread my shadow wide, grey across the prairie. A thin grey stick pointing west.

Thursday, September 20

After the guns fired, Crowfoot and Old Sun and Sitting on an Eagle Tail and Bull Head all said they would speak tomorrow. Then I stood up.

"My chief, Red Crow, is not here, but it is time now for defence so I will speak. The Spirit, not the Queen, gave us this land. The Queen sent Macleod with the police to stop the whisky. At that time I could not sleep, any sound might be my drunken brother coming to kill me or my children in his drunkenness. Now I can sleep, without being afraid. But there is still the land."

While Bird translated, Crowfoot watched me with his hard, beaked face. He understood whites better than anyone, he had thought about them for years.

"The Great Spirit," I said loudly, but really to Crowfoot, "it is hard to understand, but He must have sent the whites here to do what He wants. We Bloods signed a treaty with the Americans twenty years ago, and the first year they gave us large bags of flour and many blankets, the second year only half as much, and now it is nothing but a handful of flour and a rag. The Queen must give us fifty dollars for each chief, thirty dollars for every man, woman and child. Every year. We must be paid for all the trees the police and the whites have already cut, for there will soon be no firewood left for us. The land...the land is too much to give away for so little."

And Tall Man was laughing. "If our police have driven away the whisky traders," he said, "surely you cannot expect us to pay for the timber they used. For helping you so much, by rights you should pay us!"

And I burst out laughing, and all our people with me. Tall Man and Macleod and the police laughed too; but for a different reason, I think.

Crowfoot, however, did not laugh. And that night Red Crow and Rainy Chief with almost two thousand Bloods rode in. The whole valley was now filled with lodges, with the laughter of people and the running of horses. That was the last free gathering of the Blackfoot nation for though we talked all night in Crowfoot's lodge, though I said again and again that the treaty was too little, and though the North Peigans and Eagle Ribs wanted to wipe out every policeman and the commissioner at dawn and then ride east to the buffalo, nevertheless Red Crow stated he would agree with Crowfoot. And Crowfoot said, "The whites are coming. The Americans make treaties and then their army kills people like rabbits. Macleod treats every white and every Indian exactly the same. What can we do? We have to trust Macleod."

I walked to my lodge and saw the faces of my wives and children. But I did not sleep. At dawn Pemmican came to me again. "The whites will lead you by a halter," he said. "That is why I say, don't sign. But my life is old, over. Sign if you want to. Sign." I could hardly hear his voice, it was so old and broken.

Friday, September 21

All the tribes of the Blackfoot nation, Siksika, Blood and Peigan, and our allies the Sarcees, gathered with the Stoneys at the Crossing. And Crowfoot made the long speech the Queen's commissioners had sat up stiff all week to hear.

"Take pity on us with regard to our country, the prairies, the forests and the waters, the animals that live in them. Do not take them from us forever. We are the children of the plains, and the buffalo have been our food always. I hope you look upon the Blackfoot as your children now. If the police had not come, where would we all be? Bad men and whisky were killing us so fast, but the police have protected us as the feathers of the bird protect it from the frosts of winter. I am satisfied. I will sign the treaty."

And Red Crow spoke also.

"Three years ago, I first shook hands with Macleod at Oldman's River. Since that time he has made me many promises. He kept them all — not one has ever been broken. I trust him entirely, I will sign with Crowfoot."

They all said that, and finally I had to stand.

"I cannot be alone. I must say what my people say. I will sign."

And then Macleod opened his square, bearded mouth. "I am gratified to hear your kind words. I told you when

I came that nothing would be taken from you without your consent, and every promise we make to you here will be kept as certainly as the sun now shines upon us."

So on Saturday, September 22, 1877, we touched the pen and "did thereby cede, release, surrender and yield up forever" fifty thousand square miles — as much land as the Queen's entire country — for five dollars per year and a medal and a new suit of clothing for each chief every three years. Oh, there was a great deal of eating and hand-shaking, and four hundred of our warriors dressed their horses as for war and charged down the hills to circle the square tents of the police, shooting and screaming their war cries. But it meant nothing. The life we had lived since before the memories of our oldest fathers was gone. Four thousand three hundred and ninety-two of us had been paid off.

That winter three of our chiefs died. Crowfoot had to go to a white doctor to be cured of an illness. No snow fell on the prairies, and no buffalo came toward the foothills. Instead, prairie fires burned the earth black. And in two years there was not a single buffalo left on the land we had given away; in three, we had only flour "not quite unfit for food" to eat; and in four, one thousand five hundred of us were dead.

I touched the pen. My *X* is on the treaty. It is there following Crowfoot and Old Sun and Bull Head and Red Crow, the fifth of fifty-one chiefs and councillors.

I knew about money then, but I did not know what the treaty meant by "reserves to allow one square mile for each family of five persons." I know now, since I have lived on this "small place, land set aside." I and my children will live here, remembering; forever.

But there is still the land.

LOUIS RIEL: THE MAN
THEY COULDN'T HANG

T<small>HE PRAIRIE GRASS</small> between Regina and the North West Mounted Police barracks glittered with hoarfrost on the morning of November 16, 1885. Nicholas Flood Davin, the owner, editor and only reporter of the *Regina Leader* was driving Percy Sherwood, chief of the Dominion Police, in his buggy west to the barracks where gallows had been erected behind the guardroom. Sherwood had arrived by train from Ottawa the day before with the final warrant for the execution, and now Davin had in his pocket a personal pass from the sheriff of Regina so that he might witness, as he wrote later, "the closing act — the last event — in the not uneventful life of Louis Riel."

The French-Canadian sheriff S. E. Chapleau refused, however, to officiate at this event so longed for by English Canadians. It was the deputy sheriff, an English Canadian named Gibson, who unlocked Riel's cell door that morning. "A few minutes later," Davin writes: "[we] walked the length of the prison and there at the doorway knelt Riel, his profile showing clear against the light.... [He] was pale, deadly pale — and his face looked almost intellectual."

The evening before Davin had interviewed Riel for the last time. In order to get past the NWMP guard, in whose custody Riel had been at Regina since May 23, Davin disguised himself as a priest complete with "soutane, fake beard, broad-brimmed wide awake [hat?]" and Irish-brogue French about which the monolingual English policemen "made no difficulties." Surprised at prayer in his cell by this odd apparition, Riel apparently believed that a Conservative newspaperman in an age of vicious political news competition had actually come to "give his last message to the world.... He looked," Davin wrote, "in his peculiar way and said in French: 'Death comes directly to meet one. She does not conceal herself: I have only to look straight before me in order to see her clearly. I march to the end of my days. Formerly I saw her far away, but it seems to me now that she no longer walks slowly, no, she runs, she hurls herself upon me...oh my God, stop her....'"

Just as suddenly it seems, Riel breaks off and he is dictating final messages to his political friends and enemies, a long and prestigious Canadian list. Since Riel has himself always voted Conservative — indeed has been a Conservative M.P., the list includes the prime minister:

"Sir John Macdonald, I send you a message. I do not have the honour to know you personally.

Permit me nevertheless to address you a useful word.... Do not leave yourself be completely carried away by the glories of power. In the midst of your great and noble occupations take every day a few moments at least for devotion and prayer, and prepare yourself for death."

(Macdonald outlived Riel by six years. It is hard to say whether he accepted this advice, though no doubt it was sincerely offered.) Suddenly Riel pauses in his long statement. The reporter in false beard, ever voracious for copy with possible sensation, urges "Is that all? Have you no more to say?" Riel looks at him, one Catholic facing another: "'I have made my confession,' he says. 'I have taken the sacraments. I am prepared. But still the Spirit tells me, told me last night I should yet rule a vast country with power derived directly from heaven, look!' and he pointed to the vein in his left arm, 'there the Spirit speaks: "Riel will not die" until he has accomplished his mission....'"

"I left him," Davin writes, "with no little sadness."
And next morning he stands at the foot of the gallows and looks up as Riel continues the accomplishment of that mission:

He now stood on the drop. The cord is put on his neck. He said, "Courage, mon père."

Père André in subdued tones, "Courage,
courage." They shook hands with him as did Dr.
Jukes [the NWMP medical officer], and Riel preserving to the last that politeness which was so
characteristic of him and which was remarked
throughout his imprisonment....

After some further prayers, Deputy Sheriff Gibson
states officially: "Louis Riel, have you anything to say why
sentence of death should not be carried out on you?"
(The ceremony seems very much like a nineteenth
century wedding, where even at the last minute impedi-
ments could officially be raised; to perhaps prevent the
intended ceremony.)

Riel glancing where Père André stood about to
[de]scend the staircase anxious evidently to leave
the painful scene, said in French: "Shall I say
something?"
Père André: "No."
Riel (in French): "Then I should like to pray a lit-
    tle more."
Père André: "He asks to pray a little more."
Deputy Sheriff Gibson (looking at his watch):
    "Two minutes."
Father McWilliams: "Say 'Our Father,'" and
    addressing Mr. Gibson: "When he comes to
    'deliver us from evil,' tell him, then."

Mr. Gibson gave the directions to the hangman, who now put on Riel's head the white hood. Riel and Father Williams together: "Our Father who art in heaven, hallowed be Thy name, Thy Kingdom come, thy will be done on earth as it is in Heaven, give us this day our daily bread and deliver us — "

The hangman pulled the crank, and Riel fell a drop of nine feet.

Drs. Dodd and Cotton were below. The knot in the fall had slipped round from under the poll. The body quivered and swayed slightly to and fro. Dr. Dodd felt the pulse.

Leader Reporter: "How is his pulse, Doctor?"

Dr. Dodd: "It beats yet — slightly."

Leader Reporter, addressing Dr. Cotton: "I hope he is without pain."

Dr. Cotton: "O quite. All sensation is gone."

The body ceased to sway. It hung without a quiver. Dr. Dodd looking at his watch and feeling the pulse of what was Riel: "He is dead. Dead in two minutes." Dr. Cotton put his ear to where that restless heart beat:

"Dead," he said.

On that gallows they gave Riel the quick benefit of the long drop: nine feet. A short drop could create a truly brutal spectacle for the delectation of a public that wanted to see some real and violent punishment: there are plenty of seventeenth and eighteenth century descriptions of such spectacle — the body heaving, legs frantic in spasms, dreadful sounds of choking, the hangman lumbering down, grappling with, finally wrapping his arms around the contorted body and jerking down with all his strength to break the neck. But Riel was a substantial man, heavy, and nine feet was quite sufficient. I have in my novel, *The Scorched-Wood People*, described that instant of the fall, what Riel's awareness touched in that fraction of a second before the rope struck, but regarding outward physical matters, as Davin is at pains to point out, everything was more or less as scientifically proper and quick as it could be.

When they cut the body down and removed the hood, he concludes: "The once fiery eyes [were] closed forever as if in sleep, the strongly marked features and massive high brow looking peaceful."

Riel's "fiery, piercing eyes"... in the novel by Sheila Watson, *The Double Hook*, Coyote calls out over the ashes of dead Greta, calls "so that the walls of the valley magnify its voice and send it echoing back." Coyote calls out:

> *Happy are the dead,*
>   *for their eyes see no more.*

An Indian and Christian beatitude indeed: one which would be appropriate for a Roman Catholic French Métis, one would hope and pray:

Happy (blessed) are the dead,
for their eyes see no more.

But I doubt that Riel experienced this benediction. Davin admits that "some present wore a careless, thoughtless smile as they removed locks of hair from the dead man's brow," but then he quickly asserts "all seemed to think kindly of the dead." However, I am not really thinking of how others — we who live after Riel — have treated him. I am thinking of Riel himself, what he saw, what he sees for all time.

Perhaps this question of what Riel saw (or sees) can be approached by another question. Why was Louis Riel in Regina? Why was he available to be hanged at all? He certainly needn't have been. He was an American citizen, his wife and children were Americans, why wasn't he with his closest confidant and friend, the man who had gone a year before to get him from the United States, why wasn't he in Montana with Gabriel Dumont? Gabriel, according to his own probably not exaggerated account, killed at least thirty Canadians and died a quiet, private and peaceful death, of heart attack perhaps, in his bed on the afternoon of May 19, 1906; he had spent that spring morning hunting as he always did. In 1885 Gabriel organized and did almost all the killing of the war; Riel walked about with papers in his hands; a crucifix; raised his arm in prayer all day during the battles. Why was their ultimate fate so astonishingly different?

To phrase it another way, why do we mark November 16 — the death of Louis Riel — and not May 19, that of Gabriel Dumont?

For some time I have been thinking about the North West Rebellion as a *war*; the German General Carl von Clausewitz, the most formidable of nineteenth century war theorists, writes: "War is an act of force to compel our enemy to do our will...the principles of the art of war are in themselves extremely simple and quite within the reach of sound common sense....Extensive knowledge and deep learning are by no means necessary, nor are extraordinary intellectual faculties. A special mental quality [is convenient], a cunning or shrewdness."

Gabriel Dumont certainly had this "sound common sense," and the cunning to a degree. When the Métis in March 1885 hear that the police are coming north to arrest Riel and Gabriel, they gather for an emotional meeting and declare that no police will ever do to them what happened at Red River in 1870: force their leaders to run; they shout they will resist the police. Gabriel asks them carefully:

"I see you have quite made up your minds, but I think you will soon get tired and disconcerted. For my part, I will not give in. But how many will stand with me? Two or three?"

"We will all stay till the very end," all shout from every direction.

Then Gabriel uses his "good common sense": he organizes them into companies of ten headed by a captain: just as if he were organizing a buffalo hunt. But an army, like hunters, needs rifles and ammunition, so he sends one troop to every merchant in the neighbourhood to get what ammunition the stores have. He himself rides to the largest establishment owned in Duck Lake by the Englishman Hillyard Mitchell (a former army officer) who has been trying to persuade the Métis not to arm. Gabriel tells Mitchell: "If you won't give the supplies and ammunition to me, I'll take it anyway. So write it down on account and when the war's over either I or the government will pay you for it." When after several skirmishes with scouts Superintendent Crozier marches out of Fort Carlton with one hundred men to arrest the criminals, Gabriel does exactly what von Clausewitz would advise him: he conceals most of his troops behind a low rise and sends out two envoys to try and negotiate with the police to surrender; of course, in their entire eleven-year history the police have never surrendered so much as a single sack of flour, especially not the sometimes impatient but always extremely experienced Leif Crozier who expects within a year to become commissioner of the entire force and who knows that the retiring Commissioner Irvine with 150 more policemen is already in Prince Albert — almost at Duck Lake to help them; Crozier wants no help. So the police fire first: no police report mentions this, but all eyewitnesses seem to agree: Gentleman Joe MacKay, the police interpreter and scout,

rides forward with Crozier and he fires the first shot
(whether on Crozier's orders or not has never been clari-
fied), killing the old Cree envoy who he says later was
reaching for his rifle. And then quickly Isidore Dumont,
Gabriel's brother, is gunned down too before he can get
his rifle out of his stirrup.

Gabriel has watched all this from his hill; enraged but
still calm (von Clausewitz: "We must never lack the calm-
ness and firmness which are so hard to preserve in time of
war. Without them the most brilliant qualities of mind are
wasted.") Gabriel fires at the police head-on while sending
his concealed troops, which outnumber the police, around
on both sides through the brush and snow in two flanking
movements. Within fifteen minutes the police are about to
be surrounded and all, if not killed, captured. When
Crozier realizes this, he instantly retreats; it is his only possible move, and he gallops back to Fort Carlton leaving all
his volunteer dead behind.

Now the Métis are mounted; the police are in sleighs
and cumbered with wounded: so why don't the Métis prevent the police from reaching Carlton where Irvine and
his one hundred and fifty troops have already arrived?
Two factors: Gabriel had been severely wounded; a bullet
creased his skull (he always joked if his skull wasn't so
thick the bullet would have penetrated it!) and he could
no longer think clearly. His older brother Isidore had
been killed immediately, so the second in command was
now his younger brother Edouard, perhaps even brighter
and more energetic than Gabriel, though not as good a

shot and certainly not as experienced. When Edouard
screamed at Riel that the police were escaping, that they
must pursue and could easily capture them, Riel refused
to listen. He declared they had done enough for today,
enough people had been killed. Let them run. Clausewitz
would not have approved.

A day later about two o'clock in the morning the over
two hundred police and volunteers retreat from Fort
Carlton, trying to get to Prince Albert where civilians from
all over the country have been fleeing in terror. Gabriel,
still sick and dazed, his head bandaged, tells Riel they must
attack the police now; there are innumerable ambushes
possible on the Fort Carlton/Prince Albert Trail. They
will gain prisoners, guns, ammunition — everything they
need desperately — but again Riel does not allow Edouard
to take his Métis riflemen out on the trails they know so
well. It is "too savage" to attack the police by night.
Gabriel, never having heard of Clausewitz, nevertheless
echoes the general's thinking exactly when he tells Riel
gloomily, "If you give them all the advantages like that, we
will not succeed."

The question is: What did Riel want to succeed at in
this "war"? Two months later, in May, 1885, when
Batoche has been overrun by Canadian government soldiers and the Métis are trying to find some refuge for their
women and children, Riel finally asks Gabriel, "What are
we going to do?" Gabriel yells at him, "We must die! You
must have known that in taking up arms we should be
defeated. Very well, they must destroy us!"

In this shouted, furious conversation at the muddy edge of the South Saskatchewan River, domestic animals fleeing, children screaming, frantic women clutching them, running towards the barge to try and get across the icy river, men shooting, yelling at each other, scrambling about in terror, here I see the heart of the matter; the final breakdown between Gabriel's world and Riel's. One woman, Mrs. William J. Delorme, has hidden her baby in a tin washtub, hoping vainly to protect it from a stray bullet, and she heaves that precious tub down the ice-pan crusted bank. "I looked at the water," she remembers. "It was just like it was raining heavy. It was the bullets from the police." The Métis always call the soldiers "police", but whatever the volunteer soldiers are called: the Midlanders or the Royal Grenadiers or the 90th Regiment, the Winnipeg Field Battery — whatever their particular name, they were the vanguard of European Christian white immigrant civilization — or, push it back another step — they were the literate world of individualistic farmers and industrialists destroying forever the oral communal world of hunters.

Here is, if you want a Genesis parallel, the continuing Fall: Cain the agrarian kills his brother Abel the herdsman/hunter. It is in the very bones of human existence that the literate agrarian always destroys the oral hunter: how could it be otherwise? It is happening to this day wherever we can still find a hunter world (notice how easily the "sensitized" Canadians and Europeans are destroying the hunting, trapping world of Canada's northern

Indians and Inuit: we are "too sensitive" towards animal life ever to wear a fur again, thereby we are sentencing all native trappers to the sweet mercy of the Canadian welfare system). *"You must have known this,"* Gabriel screams at Riel. *"You must have known* [that] *we must die!"*

For though Gabriel did a certain amount of business, to the end of his life he was really a hunter and as a hunter he has a richness of perception that the educated, cerebral and intellectual Riel who writes everything down, over and over, can never have. Gabriel's true richness of perception is ignorance; ignorance is at once the glory of innocence and a straightforward acceptance of the sensory, perceptible world. Gabriel can at once claim to have fired every bullet that killed almost all the thousands of soldiers at Fish Creek — though there were actually only 440 men facing him and Charles Trottier and his 40-odd men surrounded all day in one turn of the creekbed must have kept some of them busy. (In fact Trottier reports he didn't even see Gabriel all day, leave alone hear him fire endless shots.) Gabriel can on the one hand claim to have demolished the Canadians mostly by himself and in the same breath state: "I attribute our success to Riel's prayers; all during the engagement, he prayed with his arms crossed and he made the women and children pray, telling them that we could come to no great harm."

Riel may know how to pray, and certainly he knows how to write and to speak the several languages governments can understand and he knows how politicians and priests and the prima donnas of white society think: Riel knows everything; what he doesn't know for certain he can always deduce with his powerful intellect or create with his overwhelming imagination. Indeed his knowledge incapacitates him with possibilities, with certainties. So Riel does not want to ambush the Canadians; that is behaving "too much like Indians." Harassing the long columns marching up from Qu'Appelle, cutting off their supply lines so that they will be at each others' throats — all of this Riel forbids because they might be in danger of firing on their Canadian friends, and when Gabriel protests, what kind of friends are these? They are joining with the English to kill and plunder us! Riel retorts: "If you knew them, you wouldn't try to treat them that way."

In fact, the educated Riel knows too much; he sees too many possibilities; certainty buries him.

The hunter Gabriel is far richer than Riel, richer in ignorance; he does *not* know, and is *not able* to imagine enough to be confused by the new life marching at him with rifles and cannon and Gatling guns. That one's friends can join one's enemies in a mutual attempt to kill you is impossible for Gabriel to imagine; just as he feels it would be more "humane," i.e., the better human behaviour to ambush and harass the Canadian army far from Batoche. His brother Edouard and their Indian allies have exactly the same one-stranded straightforward approach to life: during the battle of Fish Creek Edouard remains behind to guard Batoche, but at a certain point in the day he and his men ride for Fish Creek because, as the Indian Yellow Blanket explains, "when one wants to go and rescue his friends, he does not wait until tomorrow."

The fact is that Riel sees too much. And when the time comes to run (as he ran once before, in August 1870, at Red River, and thereby avoided capture), he spends days pondering what to do; he avoids everyone, especially his best friend Gabriel because he knows Gabriel will advise him not to surrender. But he also knows that, as always, he may very well win Gabriel over to his way of thinking; Gabriel says that himself, long after he has taken refuge in the States. For this time Riel will not run.

Gabriel of course runs. Moïse Ouellette, his brother-in-law, and numerous other Métis men surrender to Middleton "out of love for their children." Gabriel explodes: "Go to the devil! The government has skinned you like a sheep, it has taken your arms from you and now you are doing just as you are told!" For his trust of government, his love for his children, Ouellette gets three years in Stony Mountain Penitentiary; when Gabriel runs and leaves his wife Madeleine and daughter Annie at Batoche, he is sentenced to a couple of years shooting balls out of the air for the Buffalo Bill Wild West Show. His hunter mentality sees absolutely no problem with that; if you have spent your entire life imagining a possible buffalo herd over the next hill, if all life is the sheer chance of what actually is or is not there when you ride to the crest of the hill — well, the sheer chance of anyone walking through a door and paying to see you fire a rifle is really not much different. You live by chance, a certain always, either way, and Buffalo Bill is a lot more reliable than the accident of the hunt ever was.

But the learned Riel knows too much; in fact, he is so hemmed in by his knowledge that he can only try to know still more. He cannot, like Gabriel, ever stop, content in his present knowing. To read his writings is to wander into world history from the beginnings of creation to the eschatological resolutions of time beyond eternity and the archetypal relations of the godhead considering only itself. He can never be content, always more and more, he must be so impatient always for more that he can only keep on writing as it seems in desperation to the very last instant of his life. He cannot run away with people whose simple and only purpose is to escape. As Mrs. Delorme explains, after Batoche: "We decided to run away back to the Rocky Mountains. We were only three families. After three days [of hiding] then Louis Riel went back and he said, 'I don't think they'll do anything to me anyway.' We waited for him there for a week but we never seen him no more. A year later we heard he was hung."

We know Riel knew "they" would do something to him. Clearly Riel makes this unlikely comment to free the Delormes and their party from the weight of his necessary discontent at his own knowingness — to release them so that they can go on their way towards their simple, obtainable objective: to get away across a physical border. When he was younger he had crossed that border himself, but he will not cross it again; now he will stay to be chained, stared at, examined by endless lawyers and priests and doctors and political sycophants, and finally be displayed in the zoo of a court, tried, sentenced...but he will also stay in order to convulse all of Canada in a massive political debate still going on a century later. The hunters he has tried to help gain official title to land so that they can be somehow transformed into farmers, with whom he has tried to create a new society to the very point of renaming the days of the week and reconceiving their entire simplistic religion into a complexity comprehensible only by a theologian (certainly not by the Métis themselves and even less by modern political scientists and historians no matter how liberally intentioned), this destruction of a way of life from the chance arbitrarianism of the hunt to the sedentary rituals of farming, this *fall* from one world to another in which Riel himself has been the most active agent, all that is behind him now. He will now explain to all the civilized white world what he sees: what he knows. What no one he knows has ever seen before: how Western Canada can become a home for the dispossessed of the world; and particularly a homeland for his own dispossessed people — the hunters he came north to help.

Riel's trial words clearly tell us what he saw, why he did not run with Gabriel to Montana, what he wanted to succeed at in this "war". In his first address to the court, we find these words:

The day of my birth I was helpless, and my mother took care of me. Although she was not able to do it alone, there was someone to help her to take care of me, and I lived. Today, although a man, I am as helpless before this court, in the Dominion of Canada and in this world, as I was helpless on the knees of my mother the day of my birth.

The North West is also my mother. It is my mother country, and although my mother country is sick and confined in a certain way, there are some from Lower Canada who have come to help her take care of me during her sickness, and I am sure that my mother country will not kill me, any more than my mother did forty years ago when I came into the world. Because a mother is always a mother, and even if I have my faults, if she can see I am true, she will be full of love for me.

No hunter can speak this way; though it struggles with an English not quite idiomatic, the language is that of a literate, imaginative intellectual. And in Riel's second address to the court we find this "written language" of what he sees most clearly, though stumbling a bit more over the English idioms:

But someone will say, on what grounds do you ask for one-seventh of the lands? Do you own the lands? In England, in France, the French and the English have lands: the first was in England, they were first the owners of the soil and they trans- mitted it on to other generations. Now, by the soil they have had their start as a nation. Who starts the nations? The very one who creates them, God. God is the master of the universe, our planet is his land, and the nations and the tribes are members of his family, and as a good father he gives a portion of his lands to that nation, to that tribe, to everyone. That is his heritage, that is his share of the inheritance, of the people, or nation or tribe. Now, here is a nation. Strong as it may be, it has its inheritance from God. When they have crowded their country, because they had no room to stay any more at home, it does not give them the right to come and take the share of all tribes around them. When they come, they ought to say, "Well, my little sister, you Cree tribe, you have a great territory, but that territory has been given to you as our own land, it has been given to our fathers in England or in France. And of course, you cannot exist without having your spot of land also."

For this is the principle: God cannot create a tribe without locating it. We are not birds. We have to walk on the ground, and that ground is encircled of many things.

Saturday, August 1, 1885. It is an extremely hot day in a place once called Where the Bones Lie, though now its name is Regina, a town barely begun and already a capital. The small makeshift courtroom (which is really the new land titles office) is crowded with two judges, six jurors, four or five lawyers each for the Crown and for the defence, some twenty reporters from newspapers all over the world, and as many spectators as can procure tickets to be pressed together behind and around the judge and the prisoner's box and the jurors.

Two small windows facing the prisoner are open; they let in a little fresh air, the rhythmic sound of horses snorting at summer flies and the clink of bridles, but the windows are too high to see anything except perhaps sky. Riel has just spoken these words and the tiny sound of his uncomfortable, French-accented English has drifted over all these eager listeners, waiting for days now for something strange, something exciting, titillating, from this gaunt, bearded man continually, as it seems, contemplating his ball and chain and continually praying. The ladies are dressed in the finest of high fashion, the men in formal suits; many of them have travelled for days on the newly completed CPR from Winnipeg and even Toronto and Ottawa and Montreal to sit in this stuffy room on the measureless flat land because this charismatic, wild, possibly mad man who everyone already heard about sixteen years ago is on trial for his life. At least 53 white men are dead and 118 injured, to say nothing of assorted, uncountable Métis and Indians, so if it can be proven that he was "moved and seduced by the instigation of the devil" to levy war against the Queen, her crown and dignity, the only possible defence is his proven insanity.

And now his few words have been spoken in the small room, and perhaps they have found their way through the little windows into the immense sunlight shimmering over the prairie, which is empty now of the once numberless buffalo and all the animals and insects that lived there with them, and the people. His words at first seem simple, absolutely categorical, such homely natural images. Louis Riel says: "The North West is my mother; she is the mother country of my nation. We are not birds." But are they so simple?

Birds, for example. *Birds*:

> Any feathered vertebrate animal, most nearly allied to the reptiles, but distinguished by their warm blood, their feathers, and the adaption of the forelimbs as wings with which most species fly in the air. In common speech, fowl is used for larger, bird for small kinds.

"We are not birds."
Birds: The general name for the young of the feathered tribes

> — as — a hen and her birds,
> or — the name of the young of other animals,
> or — the name for a maiden, a girl, the endearing name for one — a bird / a chick?

"We are *not* birds." — We are not chicks / that is not an endearing name to us.

We are not birds of a feather flocking.

We are not birds of passage, shifty, temporary; we are of this land, of this our mother country.

Fine feathers may make fine birds, but they do not make us.

One Riel in hand may be worth three Gab-riels in the bush or out on the plains, *but we are not birds!*

Nor are we birdbrains!

What are we? Who are we? Sir John A. Macdonald, the Great Mother's Chief, once called us, derisively, "pemmican-eaters." He no doubt had never eaten any, his delicate, sensitive stomach far better accustomed to other much more easily absorbed foods and drinks. But Ecclesiastes warns us all:

> Curse not the king (or the queen), no, not in the
> thought, and curse not the rich in thy bedchamber
> (esp. if they have many bedchambers and you have
> none): for a bird of the air shall carry the voice and
> that which hath wings shall tell the matter.

O, that a bird had carried our petitions, and yes, finally our curses to kings and queens, to governors general and prime ministers, our petitions and finally our curses to the bedchambers of the rich in the East, in capitols where we could never ourselves speak, leave alone curse; where, though we were elected, we never dared appear for fear of being murdered; where our voices, if they were to be heard, would have required wings to climb the air over the magnificent stone towers and walls built against us there. No, such winged voices were never allowed us, birds never through air carried our words. For us the doors were shut in the streets, all the daughters of music might be brought low, the strong men bow themselves because man was going to his long home and mourners going about the streets but no one, no one, would rise up at the voice of this bird.

We are not birds. A little bird may tell us what we already know, we may have a bird's-eye view of the wide plains which are our home, but old birds cannot be caught with chaff. We need the full heavy grain of words to walk on the ground we know, of which we are; the wide ground of the plains that shaped us, out of whose mud we were first formed and where we first breathed the breath of life, both hunter and learned thinker.

And now we are faced with the simple stupidity of war. A hunter solution: if there are buffalo on the other side hill, we'll shoot them. Simple.

But not simple for Riel. He has never, and never will, shoot anyone. His well-intentioned, friendly lawyers tell him his only defence is a plea of "not guilty due to insanity." But that means that in order to defend himself against the accusation of high treason (i.e., levying war) he must consent to the inexpressible life of an asylum. He has been there before. "I do not," he tells Judge Richardson, "care much about [my] animal life if I am not allowed to carry with it the moral existence of an intellectual being."

He is too old a bird to be caught with chaff; but perhaps with the full grain of Crowfoot's words. Head chief of all the Blackfoot Confederacy, the hunter Crowfoot is credited with speaking words for all of them at Blackfoot Crossing on Friday, September 21, 1877:

> The plains are large and wide. We are the children of the plains, it is our home, and the buffalo has been our food always.... If the Police had not come to the country, where would we all be now. Bad men and whisky were killing us so fast that very few, indeed, of us would be left today. The Police have protected us as the feathers of a bird protect it from the frosts of winter.

Winter birds. Perhaps it is possible. Perhaps if we had a great orator's, a great poet's words, it would be possible. The poet Robert Kroetsch a century after the orator; the accumulated perception of five generations opening anew upon that solitary prisoner in a poem:

WINTER BIRDS

The winter birds   outside my window
feed in the sumac   hide in the green
juniper   eat and sleep

and in their season   lust
have their winter   and lust
again in season   while I...
unseasoned   open the door

(even the birds avoid me   fly
into the neighbour's maple)   feeling
a new desire   to know, to know

I go down the back steps   (avoiding
the ice, of course)   I climb up into
the sumac   clinging

I perch…
the birds return   I am pleased
they trust my   nest-like

head   my long bare arms
they speak   syllables only
and I   I am very still

I open my mouth   slowly
I try a grunt   a squawk
no answer   I try a friendly trill

no answer   I don't even know
their names   not owls
not jays   not magpies

birds, I ask them   how, how
no answer   birds, I ask them
what degree of zero   what

absolute cold   will make me
harder than   no answer
what length of night will satisfy

what iron winter will it take
to free   what polar
year   what ice cap

no answer   the birds
crowd against me   oh mother
mother, mother   is death

no answer   they peck at my
shoes, at my knees   they find
moth eggs   in my thighs

I am pleased   they find
winter buds   on my fingers
life isn't so bad   I assure them

life isn't so bad   they peck the
seeds from my tongue   they sleep
in my warm crotch   spring

will get here   I assure them
life isn't so bad   don't worry
spring will get here   don't worry

Gabriel would have agreed: don't worry. Spring will get here. In the 1885 war all Gabriel really needed was a von Clausewitz thinker to back up his arguments: treat them like buffalo / cut across their long supply lines / harass them at night so they never get any sleep / brutalize the dead so they become terrified. Or he needed a Cossack with a few swords to show him how to charge a regiment on horseback, screaming, and how to chop off a man's head or slice him in half while doing so. Gabriel's biggest problem as a hunter was that in battle he wasn't bloodthirsty and savage enough. If he had been as coldly savage as any good white nineteenth century soldier he could perhaps have piled up enough white bodies, cost Macdonald so much money that the P.M. would have been forced to bargain with him. Personally, I doubt that: Macdonald was too stubborn a Scot. But as a hunter Gabriel would instantly have agreed with the poet: we are birds. Don't worry — spring will get here. If your head still aches, you can't be dead. Look, Buffalo Bill stands smiling just across the border.

But Louis Riel is not a hunter. The certainty of all his knowledge has fenced him into this small box where he is on trial for his life. He insists: "We are *not* birds. We have to walk on the ground and that ground is encircled of many things." These many things are perhaps the imagination, knowledge, spirit of place, but that is all connected to people who have walked on this ground. It may be possible to let a hunter run for a few years to fire his rifle inconsequentially somewhere else, then pardon him and let him come home to tell adventurous stories to whoever will listen and to die quietly, forgotten, on his hide-and-fur bed. After all the government of Canada has no oral tradition. But Riel is a very different matter: he has written everything down; his acts exist in words upon words.

On August 1, 1885, he stated at his trial:

> It is acknowledged by the Canadian Government that 15 years ago the treaty of which I am speaking was a treaty of the North West...and if, by trying to say that [the treaty] was of the delegates of the North West, they wanted to avoid the fact that I was a being at all, the whole world knows it is not so; they cannot avoid me....It is not because I have been libelled for 15 years that I do not believe myself something. I know that through the grace of God I am the founder of Manitoba.

And it seems to me that a hundred years later this avoidance, this pretending that Riel never existed, is more impossible than ever. Some people cannot be done away with, no matter how often they are hanged. Riel's vision for the North West, the prairie and the poor bestrides us still; his cry for the dispossessed third-world nation now dispersed throughout every part of our society can be heard still: "I may be declared insane because I seek an idea which drives me to something right."

The Fish Caught in the Battle River

On Wednesday, May 27, 1885, southwest of the barracks in Battleford I met these two men with a fish they had caught in the Battle River that day. They had a young poplar stuck through its gills and on their shoulders, and then the tail trailed on the ground. It must of been at least six feet. I don't know what kind of fish and I forget the names of these men, but maybe they're still alive and still remember.

—

That's what I remember, a long dripping fish or the dust on this girl's ankle where her moccasin was cut through to her brown skin — dust, or grease on the top of long hair — but hardly ever names that didn't get written up from that time. Or numbers. There were exactly twenty-one yoke of oxen in our freight train divided into two

companies with a leader for each and a driver for every
three yoke. That way we were supposed to form two circles together fast when we got attacked or for night, and
we practised that too with all us men and teams inside.
They never give us soldiers for protection on the first
trip, nothing, not even a guard till fifteen miles out of
Battleford and the trail goes right by these big Indian
reserves and we camped like that and our leaders sent in
two men to bring a guard so we could come past and get
in. Then this Colonel Otter sends out a squad of twenty
North West Mounted Police to bring us in, but on the
second trip from Swift Current we never got that close
to Battleford and we sure never had time to form circles
among the young poplar of the Eagle Hills when these
painted feathered-up Indians were sprouting all around us,
Bang! without so much as a horse-fart to warn us before
they were all over like the grass itch. That was Thursday,
May 14, 1885. Ten o'clock in the morning. Late enough if
you've been switching ox-ass since half past five on that
Battleford trail. In a half hour we'd of been stopping for a
feed but there were these maybe six, seven hundred
Indians and half-breeds all looking only too happy to
blaze away and then nothing was ever luckier than us not
having more than a few hunting rifles or they'd of rubbed
us right out. I guess at least three hundred of them had
rifles and the rest axes and war clubs and stone-headed
clubs they were swinging over their heads like loosening
up for some nice game after a short night on hard ground.
I was on the last wagon and in charge of food for that part

of the train. So I had one of the rifles. One of our leaders
he still had his head on straight and he got up with a
white handkerchief — white as it was two hundred ox
miles from Swift Current — on a stick while I covered
him. I guess I could of gotten one or maybe even two if
Frank — yeah, that's his name, Frank — and lots of good
it would of done him too, but he says,

   "Cover me, Dan,"
and I guess that's the way it's supposed to be done, but
eight hundred Indians, what the hell. As it turned out,
there were heads worn straight with them too. They said
we had to leave the oxen and everything and they'd take
us men as close to Battleford as they dared. It looked to me
they'd been eating a bit pinched for a while and our heavy
wagons looked real good to them. We weren't more than
eighteen miles out of Battleford as it was and twenty men
started us in, all on horseback and us holding on to one
stirrup-strap, running beside them.

On Tuesday, April 28, 1885, we were starting from
Battleford to get this second load of supplies, over four
hundred miles round trip, and it wasn't actually us that
was so stupid. We wanted escort through the Eagle Hills
and we asked for it. Both for then and when we'd get
there coming back. That Colonel Otter sent a policeman
with orders to either move in fifteen minutes or get
arrested and our teams given others to drive. That Otter

should of stayed at home, in Ontario, yelling orders on parade and knitting spare time, thinking his two hundred men lying around the Battle River flats was shaking any Indian feather in the Eagle Hills. So our guys weakened and obeyed orders, and his little skirmish at Cutknife Hill on May 2 of attacking a sleeping Indian camp of over half women and children just got him eight men killed including a teamster name of Charles Winder shot through the head. He was no Custer at Washita Creek, that's for sure. And on the 14th he damn near got our hair creased and lifted too. These were Cutknife Indians, low on powder and tight in the belly. Poundmaker Crees with Stoneys thrown in, and they're madder than the Crees, any day.

We hadn't run more than a mile or so when these other Indians galloped out of the bushes on the left and stopped us. One of the half-breeds was translating a word here and there and said they were Poundmaker Indians too, but it came out we had to either go back to camp or these new ones that hadn't been in on the original agreement would maybe shoot us right there. And there were too many of them for our Indians to shoot it out, though one or two were waving their guns around, like what the hell, let's do it! I couldn't figure this out till after a few days. Our Indians, the ones we were running beside and who had first captured us, had given their WORD they'd take us close to Battleford alive but these other Indians, the same tribe and I guess the same chief and everything, hadn't given their WORD on anything. They hadn't been there to argue and so if they felt like it they might shoot it out with their friends so they could shoot *us*. You ever hear of such a thing? It wasn't as if we were enemies or anything, hauling supplies to a army that had already tried as hard as it could to surprise them and rub them out; our Indians had given their WORD.

One of the big troubles Indians have is they've got no general who gives out orders. Even if they are stupid. Stupid orders are anyways orders, but with Indians even a really big chief like Poundmaker or One Arrow can only say,
    "This is how I think,"
but if a lot of others don't think like him then it doesn't happen. If a war chief like Poundmaker's war chief Fine Day wants to lead, he makes a long speech and then he rides off and if anybody agrees with him, they follow; if not, everybody sits around looking at the ground and after a while the war chief comes back and he may still be war chief or he may not. Any Christian could tell them that's no way to run a war.

We got run back to the main camp and they had a council. All of them this time, about thirty of the main ones sitting down in a circle and all the other men standing around listening to the talk. Indians have any amount of time for talk. Talk, they're never rushing anywhere. We stood there too, looking out of the corners of our eyes and over our shoulders; the smell was pretty strong too, considering the leaves were out all over the hills. I wasn't looking that much at leaves then, and no nice dusty ankles either. This was business and the women stayed where they belong, over the hill. You didn't need a word of Cree to understand mostly what was happening. If the speaker wanted to kill us he'd dance around the circle with his rifle crooked in his arm, talking loud and fast. If he felt otherwise he'd leave his rifle or club on the ground and walk around, talking like he wanted to quiet a ox or horse. It was a long time touch and go but finally they agreed to keep us alive if nobody tried to run away. If anyone did, then any Indian that wanted to could kill as many as he wanted of the rest of us. So how do you like that? I mean us freighters weren't any tribe of Indians; we'd just been working together two trips up and down the Swift Current-Battleford trail and most of us hadn't known each other before that and sometimes you don't care to continue the acquaintance longer than absolutely necessary, if you see what I mean. We accepted the terms, of course, but I could see some of them bloodthirsty ones were counting on maybe one or the other of us trying a white act. Poundmaker talked to us then, wearing his foxskin hat like always and said our lives were safe and said we should thank God. He also gave us a nice quiet man to interpret so we would know what was wanted. When an Indian visited us and expressed a wish to kill one of us, this man always let us know his wish. They took our bedding and also my coat and vest. I had thirty-four dollars and I did not like parting with that (Scotch) but the interpreter said maybe I should let it go when one Indian was swinging a loaded rifle near my head. I did then, and the whole camp started to move southeast. A minor chief had me drive his oxen, his wife and I sitting on the front seat and he sitting behind on the supplies with a four-foot cutter bar of a grass mower in his hand, all the knives broken out except the top five. An ox-cart isn't actually that big and it bumps a lot. My Indian was sitting right behind me, that thing bouncing pretty loose in his hand going over the bumps.

On Monday, November 16, 1885, I was driving four yoke of oxen with four loads of fifty-two bushels of wheat each on my way to Regina. When I was just west of the North West Mounted Police barracks I was stopped by a policeman who told me to turn to the right and keep outside the stakes with a red flag on them. Nobody would come inside the red stakes. Going around the stakes was all turtleback, no road at all, just ruts and buffalo trails and prairie bumps. If these oxen hadn't been really trained to go by the voice alone I would have had a big job. We got back to the main road, then two miles and we were in Regina. The first words I got were, "Riel is dead." He was being hanged while I was going turtleback around them stakes.

We were travelling in these five columns and about half a mile wide winding between the poplar bluffs and just out on flatter country going southeast when the guard up front rode back waving everybody back into a ravine we'd just crossed. The rest of the riders went forward, and when they came back they said they'd shot a redcoat. It was a NWMP, or a scout at least, and who knows what he was doing there alone and I did not see the shooting, but heard it. He was shot in the back of the head by a Stoney and they buried him a little by carrying ground from a badger mound close by. We camped for supper about 5:30 and my Indian's wife and her sisters, all pretty young, and mother made supper of peeled potatoes, bannock, hard-tack, tea, milk and sugar, all from our supply wagon. We sat on our heels in the teepee around the food. I at the wife's right and she saw that I had plenty to eat. They didn't know about cans so I put a two-pound can of Armour's beef in front of her on a board and took the axe and cut it in half with one cut. They all looked serious but didn't move when I picked up the axe and all burst out laughing when the can fell apart and they saw what it was. I did it twice more but signed that they should leave the rest for another day. My Indian never opened one of the cans, he always gave me the axe and stood a little away like he could never be sure what might be inside those tight little white man's boxes. Once one lay too close to the fire and exploded; that one I had to take away and bury. I always had to take a bit too before they would, but the women were always good to me, both young and old. On passing a creek I let my Indian know I was going to have a drink and I let the oxen go themselves. When I got a drink I ran to catch the team and there was a old squaw. She just had her few things tied in a bundle on the back of a skinny dog and nothing in her hand. She took me by the wrist as I went past and I stopped and she rubbed my open hand slowly all over her head, smiling all the time at me.

The third night, Saturday, May 16, 1885, was very cold with maybe an inch of ice on the slough where we camped. The water was good, not a bit alkali. We were sleeping on the ground between two wagons with a canvas thrown over them. The first night we were in a tent and they gave us some blankets too but when these were divided I got none and not being much good at pushing for a place I got left to the door of the tent. Every little while a Indian would come to look at us and one of them saw me shivering and come back with a beautiful braided rabbit-skin blanket under which I went sound asleep and warm and forgot my troubles. I had that only one night and between the wagons we only had two double blankets for six men so two thought they would be warmer in the wagons and climbed up. We had a guard all around and every hour or so a Indian who didn't trust us come and counted to see if we were all there. All of a sudden there was a terrible racket. A Indian was standing with one foot on either side of my head, a burning piece of wood dropping sparks in one hand and using a butcher knife in the other as a pointer while he counted. Only four men on the ground — good, good — then they could start killing. I didn't move my head off my boots (my pillow), just covered my face with my hands because of the sparks and the interpreter was yelling for everybody to lie still, he was telling them again and again that everybody was still there, and after a while the guys in the wagons dared show themselves and so we were all there and everybody went back to sleep. Of course no Indian camp is ever all asleep. There's always something moving, a dog snarls sniffing around, a child stands up to take a leak, horses snuffle. There are night birds too, little night hawks that seem to split over your head with a whirrr — enough to really scare you with ghosts if you don't know what they are. There's just a shadow over your face and at the same time whirrrr. On cold nights there aren't mosquitoes and the sky lights up clear blue like a lake with diamonds. Sometimes the northern lights come too, washing back and forth over the sky all quiet. Then the Indians are really quiet. They say they can get you, the spirit dancers up there. I'd rather have slept with the Indians and was glad I was with them in the day. Then I'd get away from the only thing anyone ever talked about in English:

"How long do you think we'll live."

All I ever said to that was, "Maybe five minutes, maybe till our teeth rot."

We moved every day a little, talking and talking and waiting to hear from Riel. They were fighting at Batoche.

On Sunday, April 26, 1885, we were coming into Battleford with our first load of supplies and Colonel Otter sent out the police to bring us in when we sent in our two riders. We camped about eight miles from town, putting the wagons in a ring for protection, the men and the teams inside. I was put on guard on the west side and the police gave me a heavy revolver. About eleven o'clock a scout of Poundmaker's come close and had a look at us but not doing any more and so we didn't either. Everything was quiet about one o'clock, horses quit stamping and the oxen lay down with their long breathing groan, men went to sleep, police walking around with almost no sound. I was lying under a wagon with head and shoulders outside the ring under the sky, the revolver under my hand. Then I heard,

"Are you asleep?"

"No, sir," I said, and that was the truth or I would not have said anything.

Poundmaker was head chief of the big camp of quite a few reserves together and he was at least six feet, with very long hair in two braids hanging in front, a long straight nose and always wearing his whole fox-skin hat with the brush hanging down his back. He's the finest looking Indian I ever saw, dressed in blanket chaps, moccasins, buffalo-hide coat tanned and covered with rows of round-headed brass tacks and sometimes carrying his heavy pukamakin. It had four knives sticking out in four directions. The runners were expected to bring good news from Riel but they come and said Middleton had overrun Batoche and Dumont was wounded and going to the States. Then the Indians and half-breeds in camp put down their arms and after a couple of long councils decided to take us prisoners to Battleford and ask for terms. The squaws came often to look at us. They did not say much, just sat on the ground nursing their papooses that were mostly naked. The children would come and look too. Sometimes the children laughed at us but one old squaw who was poor and alone with all she had tied on the back of a spotted dog let me know she was sorry for me. We were taken to Battleford in four or five wagons and just as we were ready to start a Indian struck each of us on the shoulder with a quirt. That was on the 22nd. Middleton sent a message that they were to come in or he would come down and also defeat them utterly. On Tuesday, May 26, 1885, Poundmaker and his warriors came to Battleford and surrendered without terms. The flat between the Battle River and the fort called Fort Otter was covered with the white tents of the soldiers when the Indians come out of the sand hills to the south, a long, wide column of them with the two wagons piled up with guns and rifles, every kind ever sold by the Hudson's Bay Company in two hundred years, flintlocks to sixteen-bore single-barrelled to fourteen-shot Winchesters.

—

On Tuesday, May 26, 1885, a soldier pulled the tent-flap back. General Sir Frederick Middleton sat on a chair north of the Battle River facing west. At about fifteen feet sat Peter Hourie, the interpreter, on a chair facing east. The Indians sat a little lower in a semicircle on the ground to the south. I stood about fifteen feet north of the general, inside the soldier lines. Poundmaker got up from the centre of the Indians and stepped closer and held out his right hand. Middleton sat still leaning back in his chair, so after a while Poundmaker pulled his blanket tight and turned around and sat down on the ground again. Middleton asked why he had taken up arms and murdered innocent settlers. Poundmaker said he had murdered nobody and had defended himself when attacked at dawn which he thought he was entitled to do. Middleton asked why he had promised to help Riel fight the Queen with two hundred men, and Poundmaker said if he had promised that he would have done it. Middleton said he hadn't helped because he was scared, like a squaw. Poundmaker sucked on his long pipe and after a while he said,

"I am sorry. I feel in my heart that I am such a person as I am."

Middleton sat there and said very loud, "Poundmaker, you are accused of high treason. What have you to say?"

Then Hourie and Poundmaker talked back and forth for some time and soon Hourie made a statement.

"There is no such word as 'high treason' in the Cree language."

The general stared at him and the interpreter leaned forward talking back and forth with Poundmaker again. Then he announced:

"You are accused of throwing sticks at the Queen and trying to knock her hat off."

All at once a fat old wrinkled woman standing with the hundreds of Indians behind the seated chiefs started to talk and scream and wave her hands. The interpreter did not interpret. You could've heard her in the hills over the Battle River. Poundmaker said one loud sound without moving and she was quiet.

—

Sir Fred just nodded to Peter Hourie, and asked more questions.

A Night in Fort Pitt or (If You Prefer) The Only Perfect Communists in the World

Late one November evening in the thirty-third year of the reign of Queen Victoria, a solitary horseman might have been seen riding along the hills that parallel the North Saskatchewan River. He had been riding west since before daybreak, but now long after sunset the giant sweep of the frozen river suddenly confronted him, forcing him south, or as nearly south as he could surmise from the stars that glittered occasionally, momentarily, between storm clouds. And the wind which had been threatening snow all day now roared, it seemed, with a malignant fury up the cliff down whose steep slope he could not risk his exhausted horse, though he knew that he must somewhere, somehow get across the valley if he was to find shelter at Fort Pitt, the only white settlement along three hundred miles of river between Fort Carlton and Victoria House.

The night before the rider and his small party had endured among bare poplars in the fold of a creek; when they emerged that morning onto the prairie before dawn to continue their journey, they discovered the entire sky brilliant with aurora, torn sheets of light gently glowing and leaping into blaze above them and smouldering away again. The man had stopped his horse, watched, stunned; felt himself shrink as it were into and then grow incandescent in that immense dome of brilliance until sunrise burned it into sheer light, and he became aware that his Indian guide and Métis companion had vanished into the apparently flat earth; leaving nothing but the line of their passing in the hoary grass. The quick winter afternoon was already darkening before he caught up with them in their relentless track. The radiance of aurora still informed him and he told them they had veered too far south; sunset perhaps verified his perception, for after the long day's ride they still had not encountered the river. He refused to accept another night in the open and swung onto his weary mount. His men had already unburdened theirs, preparing to weather the storm they insisted was driving up from the west in a brushy hollow. So they watched him ride west alone, the prairie so open he could inevitably be found if lost, as impatient and as superior with all necessary knowledge as every white man they had ever met, riding into darkness following stars.

And now in stinging snow the stars were lost, though it did not matter since he had found the North Saskatchewan River. Well, it did matter, because he knew that every Hudson Bay settlement was on the north bank; he must cross over the river or he would miss Pitt, he could ride as far as he had already ridden in a month, another five hundred miles across prairie into the glacial mountains themselves and not encounter a white man. As if at the thought, his horse stopped. No urging could move it so he slid off, straightening his long legs against the ground with a groan. The horse turned its long, squarish head to him, nudged him, breaking the icicles off its nostrils against his buffalo coat and then finding the warmth of his armpit. Perhaps this hammer-headed bay from Fort Carlton could become as good a companion to him as Blackie had been — the storm shifted an instant and he realized they were on a point of cliff. Perhaps a tributary cut its way into the river here as steeply as the main river. Where was he? Even if he got down into the valley, if Fort Pitt was built half a mile back from the river in a bend like Fort Carlton, he would never find it. He sheltered his crusted eyes against the whistling snow that enclosed him: the air seemed as solid as any frozen prairie. He would walk on it easily as dreaming out into the sky....

The cheek-strap of the bridle hit his frozen face when the horse moved. He felt that, his arm slid onto its neck.

He knew he could not lose this one certain warm
body also, his mittens clamped on to its stiff mane

and so suddenly he was led forward and down, sideways and down, the incline almost vertical and shifting like relentless sand, but that one body was solidly with him, there, whenever they slipped they slid closer together, their six feet all one and always somehow set certainly into the side of that incline of what might be rock or frozen clay, deadly as ice, but so reliable, so trustworthy he would never let go of this horse, never leap aside even if river ice parted into water as it had when he leaped from Blackie sinking, scrambled to safety while seeing his horse sink into blackness and there was its beautiful head bursting up, its front legs, neck arched, and knees clawing ice with its deadly shod feet, trying to climb up into the bright air by sheer terror, nostrils flaring bloody and the ice smashing now again and again in ringing iron, and he turned away, sprinted for his rifle — he was an English soldier, soldiers can always offer the ultimate mercy of running for their bloody rifles — and he knelt there expert sharpshooter on the white, deceptive ice until the shots hammered back at him tripled from the cliffs and the long water ran flat again and implacably empty; on his knees, crying.

But this hammerhead bay led him so easily down...down five hundred feet or a thousand — instinctively he was counting steps, an officer must always carry some facts, even if they are estimated — and they scrambled out between broken boulders (or were they frozen buffalo?) and there was river ice again, certainly, hard as the cliff here and he was still clutching the horse. But with his arms and legs now, completely, and it moved with his frozen face in its mane, he could smell prairie slough hay, hear scrub oaks at Fort Garry scarlet as cardinals in October light, the chant of *Te Deum* prayed by monks in a roofless Irish ruin, and he became aware that the sting of snow had quietened: there was an upthrust, darkness moving beside him, a dense blackness, and he loosened one hand, reached out: it was most certainly the usual twenty-foot spruce palisade. Never anything in stone like the permanent ruins of Ireland. And a gate in the wooden wall; hanging open. Perhaps the Indians here were all dead, the gates hanging so open.

The bay followed him through that hanging gate like any dog and the storm was so abruptly quiet he felt himself breathing. High-peaked roofs, gabled, around a square, he could not distinguish a light or a sound. Perhaps smallpox had discovered them all, Indian and Métis and white alike, as in Fort Carlton. Winter would keep the bodies perfectly, death already blossomed over them like spring flowers. He limped across the open square to avoid what lay at the edge of every shadow, what might move, dreadfully: a door, darkness in the centre building. He seemed to have reached the heart of something, corpses were keening all around him, at the very hoared edges of his fur cap and he wheeled around, listening. But there was only his own small breathing, nothing but the horse snoring, bent low like grass behind him. So he turned back to the door and began to pound on it. Nothing. The plank door would not budge to his fists, its cracks blacker than its wood, and he tilted forward, hands, face clutching the frame, they were all dead, O open up, *o miserere mei* ... he heard a sound. Inside. Against his face an opening, of light, the skin of a face, a young woman's face. Impossibly beautiful.

Such materializations are possible out of the driving blackness of a prairie blizzard, lantern-light and such sudden woman's beauty as perfect as it is unbelievable? He found himself bending forward slowly, past the worn planks of the door-frame, tilting slowly into her light, his frozen cheek, his still tactile tongue ... and felt ... nothing. Those eyes, the black brows and exquisite nose, was it white, that skin in the golden light? Was it believable though impossible?

It is possible that when Lieutenant General, the Right Honourable Sir William Francis Butler, Knight Grand Cross of the Order of the Bath and member of the Privy Council of Ireland died in his bed in Bansha Castle, County Tipperary, on June 7, 1910, died as his daughter then wrote, "of a recent affection of the heart ... that was brought to a crisis by a chill," it is possible that on his deathbed thirty-nine and a half years later Sir William could still not decide: was that face he instantly loved at Fort Pitt on the North Saskatchewan River in the North-Western Territories of Canada on November 18, 1870, loved as only the truest Victorian male who believed all his life that Jesus Christ and Napoleon Bonaparte were the greatest men in all of human history could love, a latter-day romantic when romanticism was still acceptable in a male if he was also practical and above all heroic, dear god, was a man who championed the innocent and detested the brutalities of war all his life while becoming one of Victoria's most honoured and decorated soldiers, a member of Field Marshal Wolseley's brilliant Officers' Ring that fought for the Empire on four continents, and who dreamed for forty years of "the Great Lone Land" as he called the Canadian prairie and never saw again and idealized every Indian person he lived near for those few months in 1870 and 1871 when they were either dying of smallpox or more or less starving despite their unselfish greedless tradition of sharing everything, which makes Indians, as he wrote then, "the only perfect communists in the world, who, if they would only be as the Africans or the Asiatics it would be all right for them; if they would be our slaves they might live, but as they won't be that, won't toil and delve and hew for us, and will persist in hunting, fishing, roaming over the beautiful prairie land which the Great Spirit gave them: in a word, since they will be free — we will kill them"; this Butler who on the same journey contemplated the parklands of the Saskatchewan, observed their remarkable similarity to the English downs and found it "mortifying to an Englishman" that they were, as he so concisely put it, "totally undeveloped": this Butler was forced over an unseeable landscape by a November blizzard to be confronted by a woman's face, her thick black braids hanging to her hips; wearing a loose nightgown.

The nightgown was probably not thin. More likely it was heavy flannel since any Hudson Bay fort at the time (they were really nothing of forts but rather clusters of log buildings surrounded by log palisades, all of which could and did, as easily by accident as by design, burn to the ground) was badly heated by cavernous open-hearth fire-places, doubtless she wore that heavy flannel of solid red or delicate floral design which the company traded with the Cree and which those people suspended as gift offerings to the Thunderbird on the Centre Tree of their thirst dance lodges in June. And here it would hang as gracefully, draping between braids, shoulders and arms and nipples and hips a slender revelation. And the very handsome, six-foot-two and always brave and presently very hoarfrosted Lieutenant Butler, late of her Majesty's 69th Regiment in India and the Fenian Raids in Quebec across the Canadian border from New York, and most recently renowned as intelligence officer of the Colonel Wolseley Red River Expedition against the Métis founder of Manitoba, Louis Riel: frozen or not, Butler must fall instantly in love.

As he stood there, erect and frozen, clamped to the hand-sawn plank of the door-frame, his faithful pony having discharged its final faithful duty of carrying him to safety and about to collapse in faithful exhaustion behind him, did Lieutenant Butler say, "Madam, I very nearly gave up hope of ever reaching succour"?

And did she reply as stiffly, "O sir, our rude abode is but little better than the storm, nevertheless..."?

And he, accepting her hesitation: "Madam, if I may be so importunate...."?

And she, accepting his: "O sir, of course, do come in, sir, come in out of the storm"?

And did she turn to send the dark servant woman standing behind her scurrying to the kitchen to revive the fire that was no more than embers in the hearth?

Perhaps that was how Fort Pitt, named after the great prime minister but doomed never to be as famous as Pittsburgh, named after his father the Great Commoner, perhaps that was how Fort Pitt offered itself to him. Or did she exclaim out of the lamplight, "O la sir, what a storm brings you here!" and he, bursting into laughter, reply, "What you see is mere weather, my fine wench. There will yet be greater storms than this!" Staring so closely down into the luminous whiteness of breasts her nightgown made but small attempt to contain.

Her father, Hudson Bay Factor John Sinclair, had only a brutal litany of disease and starvation and death to offer him at Fort Pitt. He always kept the palisade gate locked — some damn Indian had tore it loose — every building locked, they were under siege and if thirty-two of sixty people at Fort Carlton was dead, including the factor, and half the McDougall missionary family at Victoria dead too, then Pitt had been saved because he wouldn't let one goddamn Indian into the place, trade or no trade, locked them all out, and he had been damn quick in summer when he first heard the smallpox spreading and he got some blood out of a Saulteaux Indian vaccinated at the mission in Prince Albert and used that to vaccinate everybody — well, damn near everybody — in Pitt and he had kept every Cree locked out, every bloody one of them: Butler could barely restrain himself. Use them, use them any way you can, use their very blood...but he sat at the kitchen table devouring (with perfect army manners, of course) the mound of buffalo steak and potatoes Mary (now properly dressed, of course) served him before the pine fire blazing on the hearth — where was the mother, the inevitable Indian, at best Métis, mother? The free traders, muttered Sinclair into his rum, had destroyed the hide and fur trade anyway, what did they care about Indians, just soak the buggers in whisky, steal all they could from them today and to hell with tomorrow, so now even at Pitt, the very heart of buffalo country, the beasts were gone, not enough robes this summer to make three decent bundles and he'd have nothing at all to eat except potatoes if Big Bear, that ugly little bastard that never got sick, hadn't dragged in ten to trade and he'd risked taking them even though half of Big Bear's band was spitting blood, they caught it fighting the Peigans near the border who got it from the American Bloods, hell, they said it was the U.S. Army deliberately infecting the Indians down there to wipe them off the face of the earth because it was costing them damn near a million dollars each to shoot them! The smallpox was sure cheaper, about as cheap as wolfers throwing strychnine all over the prairie, and about as effective. There'd soon be nothing but corpses stinking up the whole goddamn stinking North West.

Butler looked at him carefully: Sinclair was typical enough, a poor Scot forced to spend his whole life remembering home from the other side of the world, living who knows how in what overwhelming monotony of daily life and endless, endless miserable seasons repeating themselves, too old now for even the occasional Indian woman to rouse him, and suddenly a government official appears out of the night at whom he could momentarily blurt whatever he wanted, an official not on the summer boats but riding an assignment in the dead of a deadly boring winter on orders from the Lieutenant Governor of the Territories — there was one at long last — someone who had been within breathing distance of all those invisible Hudson Bay lords in London barely seven months before, who had often smelled the "goddamn heather" and seen the Queen herself who had finally survived her grief for Albert and was now the emerging mother of a world empire: what poor lonely sot of a homesick Scot wouldn't seize such an opportunity to snore every pessimistic worry he had aloud into his grog?

To be starving in Pitt, Sinclair suddenly roared, is like freezing to death in Newcastle! This is buffalo country, one herd moved over these hills for seventeen days and nights in '62, over two million, there was no end of them summer or winter and he'd fed every fort from Rocky Mountain House to Vermilion and the Pas, every god-

damn fur dragged out of this country and every bloody
ounce of stuff dragged back into it in every bloody York
boat — every fuckin' trader had Pitt pemmican in his gut
and now Big Bear brings in ten jesus carcasses and he has
to burn the hides and boil the fuckin' jesus christ out of
the meat! But at least that old bugger knew what he was
doing, telling his people to leave the fort and scatter in the
bush and maybe the winter would be cold enough to kill
the white man's disease, though what they would live on,
even their dogs and miserable horses so far gone....

Butler saw Mary Sinclair turn like a flame in front of
the fire. After a month of half-fried bannock and pemmican — which had all the taste of boiled shoe-leather — her
baked potatoes were beyond any remembered cream and
butter, dear god their very aroma — and she facing solitary winter darkness, a lifetime of that incredible skin dry-
ing up in cold and mosquito-and-blackfly heat, such a
shape hammered slack by year-after-year pregnancies. At
her bend by the hearth for another rack of buffalo rib he
felt his body thaw and stretch completely, his powerful
legs, toes flaring so fluidly, a kind of tensile vividness she
awoke in his hands hard from cold and clenched reins all
day, a touch of, somehow, flesh and resistance needed;
despite heavy cotton the length of her leg, her curved
thigh, her quick smile past her shoulder, her extraordinary
face even when seen sideways or upside-down. Her father
snored, fat arms flat on the table: every night such a lullaby
and every night lying somewhere innocent, somewhere in
this clumsy building, every night she was here naked

against cotton and he rolled in his deerskin sack on the frozen prairie, sweetest jesus why is there no comfort in the world ever *together*?

The Métis servant came sluffing down the stairs. The bed for the gentleman was warming with hot stones between buffalo robes, would he go up? It was Mary who spoke, Mary who led him up the narrow stairs through her own shadow to the door, opening it without so much as a glance: she gave him the lantern and was gone, not a gesture of her lithe body even at his stumbled good night, and thank you again…the hall was empty before he grasped her going. Wind moaned in crevices. Well, doubtless to help the Métis woman hoist her father back into bed again. He stripped quickly, blew out the light. The stones were too hot, the robes total ice; he felt his body slowly shrinking into a huddle. Be I as chaste as ice, as pure as snow, I shall not…he sensed a footstep and sat up: she was there, he knew. But it was several seconds before the rustle she made told him she was lifting the heavy cotton nightgown over her head.

Could he say anything when she came in beside him, he the Irishman of endless easy words, when she laughed aloud so gently at all his sweaty underwear? And she peeled it off him, chuckling again at the memory of his good night, did he think Pitt was a hotel and she a chambermaid? Hot stones in bed were no better than campfires: you were always roasted on one side and freezing on the other. He may have had a small hesitation.

The bed...is too narrow.

Wide enough for one is wide enough for two.

And her skin fit completely around him, her head warm as opening lips in the hollow of his neck. If despite twelve years of Her Majesty's army his body still did not know what to do, she doubtless helped him to that too; and perhaps his own skin and various tongues in that black room taught him something of her invisible shape.

Perhaps this happened to William Francis Butler in Fort Pitt in the North-Western Territories of Canada on the night of November 18, 1870. Perhaps, if he was *really* lucky and Mary Sinclair was, thanks to her mother (certainly not her father), one of the world's perfect communists.

There is of course another story; the one Mary Sinclair told forty years later. Before the rebellion, she said, when I was only a young girl, an English officer came to Fort Pitt. He was tall and very good looking and he talked and talked and he could talk so well I thought perhaps I could love him. He told me about his home in Ireland, he came out of the snow and storm one night like someone from a different world and then when his men arrived after him he rode on to Fort Edmonton and I could only think about him. But he came back again, and he asked me to marry him. He asked me to go live with him in the Old Country. There I was, a child of the Saskatchewan, what would I do in another country? Perhaps I cried a little, but I sent him away. And after a while I did not remember him so often.

I sent him away. That is how Mary Sinclair later told it; but not Butler. He wrote his story in a book, and he mentions her only in the same sentence as "buffalo steaks and potatoes." For these in Fort Pitt, he writes, "I had the brightest-eyed little lassie, half Cree, half Scotch, in the whole North West to wait upon me," and he mentions this "lassie" not at all on his return journey from Fort Edmonton at the end of December 1870 when bitter cold and a lack of sled dogs forced him, so he writes, to wait at Fort Pitt for seven days. Did she then also with steak and potatoes wait upon him? Serve him? Such a handsome Victorian soldier wrapped in tall furs on government assignment would perhaps not have remembered that she sent him away, especially not after he discovered in Ottawa a mere four months later that all the "excellent colonial ministers," as he calls them, had large families and that "an army officer who married a minister's daughter might perchance be a fit and proper person to introduce the benefits of civilization to the Cree and Blackfoot Indians on the western prairies, but if he elected to remain in single cussedness in Canada he was pretty certain to find himself a black sheep among the ministerial flock of aspirants for place." Premier John A. Macdonald's only daughter Mary was handicapped beyond any possible marriage, and the most beautiful girl on the prairies could certainly not have helped Butler be an "aspirant for place" in lumber Ottawa so, despite letters as excellent as excellent colonial ministers could make them for his excellent service, the tall officer returned to the heart of empire still a lieutenant, still without a permanent government appointment, still without a steady war in which to achieve the fortune that could purchase his promotion; he could not know that soon the kingdoms of hot Africa would provide him with a quarter of a century of men he could, with his enormous organizational efficiency, help to kill. In Fort Pitt on the North Saskatchewan in November and December, 1870, during cold so severe no Englishman could imagine it, a beautiful young woman "waited upon me," as he said; sent him away, as she said.

Or is a fourth story possible? Did they dream together, narrow bed or not? Did they see those enormous herds of buffalo that once flowed along the rivers there, such a streaming of life never again seen anywhere on the surface of the earth or even in the depths of the sea? And in the darkness did they see the long, hesitant parade of the Cree chiefs approaching Treaty Number Six that ordered them thereby to cede, release, surrender and yield up all that land forever, and behind them the one chief who would not, the chief Big Bear as the whites called him, but perhaps better translated "Too Much" or "More Than Enough Bear," who would ask them all how could one person give away forever what they had all forever had, who had more than enough of everything except the power to persuade his people of his defiant vision until Fort Pitt was burning, was becoming a great pillar of smoke bent over the river and the empty hills and all that flour and rancid treaty pork they had never wanted, had abhorred as soon as ever they saw it, surrounded them, rained on them, dripped black and stinking out of the very air they were forced to breathe?

She knows that darkness alone can offer what he longs to accept. Smell and touch and the tongue in the ear, yes, taste itself, yes, yes — but not sight. Eyes for him are impossible.

The fire locked inside each palisade log, the factor's house, the spruce walls close about their narrow bed springs into light, fire lifts Fort Pitt, transforms it into air and its place, here, on this earth, is lost to any memory, the valley and the hills changed as they are already eternally changed beyond the going of the animals and some day the Hutterite farmers will break through the bristly poplars, domesticate them into wheat fields and a plough furrow along the bank of the still relentless river one day reveals a shard of blue willow china; its delicate pastoral a century's confirmation of her waiting upon him, of her serving him?

Behind the double darkness of his clenched eyes he sees again the length of his rifle barrel and the black hair whorled behind Blackie's straining ear: the blood explodes exactly there! They had to cross today, the daily plan is irrevocable, iron shoes or not on thin ice or no ice they must cross, and his groans, his endlessly contained and most irregular, totally unplanned, tears.

They may have dreamed something together. Possibly they dreamed the scarlet riders of the police he would recommend the Canadian government establish to force English law upon the western plains, the police whose thin implacable lines would weave the red shroud of the old Queen's authority over every child of the Saskatchewan until Inspector Francis Jeffrey Dickens, the great novelist's third son who aspired to his appointment by patronage, not by excellent merit of excellent colonial service, would at Fort Pitt become the most infamous officer in the history of the world-famous force. Force indeed.

Or they dreamed again the gaunt Cree dying, scraping their pustulated legs and arms and breasts and infants' faces along the gates, the door-frames, the windows of the locked fort to force the white man's disease back upon him, to somehow smear him with his own putrefaction. And perhaps they also dreamed Big Bear walking so emaciated among his people, his magnificent voice persuading them they must scatter to the woods and the animals, that only on the solitary land would they be given the strength to destroy this invisible, this incomprehensible evil that rotted them, his words and his scarred face proof of his lifelong power over the white diseases, his name certain and forever More Than Enough Bear for everything except the white words on the white paper, words that would one day endlessly whisper to him behind the thick, sweating walls of Stony Mountain Penitentiary.

Was it Big Bear who helped her say to him then:
go away.

Only she could dream that. It is impossible for
Lieutenant William Francis Butler to dream such a hope-
less dream; even in a narrow bed in Fort Pitt, even in
Mary Sinclair's warm and beautiful arms.

The Skull in the Swamp

To write means arranging words in a certain, implacable order. To try to recount, after twenty-five years, how one's first novel was published, forces you to try and explain the beginnings of your literate life as if it had plan and system and perhaps even personal purpose; even if, at the time, you were aware of none.

During the three years I wrote and rewrote *Peace Shall Destroy Many* I thought I learned something about story and about words: about their kind of immovable independence, about their inertia, about their irreducible force. And then, suddenly, incredibly, the book is in your hand. Anyone can pick it up, read any line here or there, the worst or the best sentence, anything; they can even buy it (a few always do), a thousand different people can take it home and sit down and read every word of it at their leisure, study it, return to certain bits again and again, ponder; they'll lend it to their friends and you can do nothing about what it creates in their mind. The book is there, you can change nothing — and yet you are still responsible.

I was living in Winnipeg and editing a weekly Mennonite Brethren Church paper when *Peace Shall Destroy Many* was published in September 1962. By March 1963, I was no longer editor and by August had left Canada. O, words have power, power beyond what I had imagined in three years of wrestling with them.

A first novel is always the purest because in order to make it you must use everything you know or can imagine. In 1959 what little I knew about life and humanity had to be pushed to the utmost limits of my conception, and then another notch farther, and then another, towards whatever I was discovering of what was good and new and moving and beautiful. No one knows you, there seems to be no chance that the marks your pen or typewriter are tracing across blank paper will ever get beyond that paper and so you grab everything conceivable and imaginable into your hands, spin it around into one compact ball and hurl it as hard and as far as you can and you never expect to hit anyone. And then, by some miracle it gets published and you do. Hit someone. Again and again.

A first novel is also the purest because it has the least chance of publication. For six hundred years the primary meaning of that English word "publication" has been "the action of making publicly known." To have a construct of whatever you know and can imagine about life "made publicly known" is a dangerous act, and once it has been done you will never be the same again; nor never so innocent.

To use a hunting, or guerrilla war, image: you have once and for all blown your cover.

In *Peace Shall Destroy Many*, Thom Wiens and his friend Pete are cutting hay in the huge slough east of Wapiti district; they are walking to find how close to the swamp water they can cut.

After a moment they pushed back, their teams waiting, the still-cool day seeming to hesitate over the ancient lake-bottom to see what they would do with it. Thom stumbled suddenly, feeling something abrupt against his boot. He bent to see. Pete, peering with interest, said, "Shouldn't be any rocks here in the swamp," as Thom felt the broad turn of the horn. He tugged hard and it came up with moss and roots dangling. The lower nose had rotted away; the roll of bone at the skull-top and the thick jutting horns were all that remained.

"Must have been a wood-buffalo. Man, look at that, eh!" he held what was left of the skull at arm's length, a finger on each horn-tip. They looked. The top was a perfect bow-line turning almost back on itself. One horn was clean, the other mud-grained, but both were scarred with rot. Below the gnarled horn only a broken suggestion of the great blade of the skull remained. Thom gripped the clean horn at the base with his hand and, huge as they were, his fingers did not go halfway round. He wished he had seen that horn when it gleamed in ponderous dignity below the massive shoulder.

"How long has it been lying here, you think, Pete?"

"Don't know. Not too long here — the water would have rotted it quick."

"These haven't been around for at least fifty years. Must have worked its way in with the spring run-off, year by year. Odd you haven't hit it with the mower." Staring at the broken skull, its heft heavy in his hands, a vista opened for Thom. Why was Canada called a "young" country? White men reckoned places young or old as they had had time to re-mould them to their own satisfaction. As often, to ruin. The memory of the half-Indian woman he had met last winter in a house where he would never have dreamt to find her forced itself upon him. As he thought unwillingly, the aura of impenetrable consciousness of her own being that she carried like a garment somehow enveloped him, now as then. His enforced habit of avoiding that scene asserted itself and, still holding the skull, he welcomed the thought of Two Poles at the picnic. Perhaps some lone ancestor of his had lain all day under the willows with the insects and bugs, spear or gun in hand, waiting for this buffalo to graze closer.

Pete moved forward and Thom followed. The horses were shaking their heads as the sun tipped higher over the meadow.

"You know, Pete, it's funny. There are stacks of European history books to read, yet the Indians — a people living in nearly half the world — lived here for thousands of years, and we don't know a single thing that happened to them except some old legend muddled in the memory of an old crone. A whole world lost. Not one remembered word of how generations upon generations lived and died."

"If you look at what's left on the reserve, we haven't missed much. A couple o' them came to buy eggs yesterday. Told Papa they were out digging seneca roots. This morning we were missing five chickens. Just a bunch of thieves now. Until the law came West, Papa says they were nothing but packs of cutthroats; whoever killed most was greatest. They would kill now too, only they're scared of the Mounties."

They were beside Pete's mower then. Abruptly, Thom hurled the skull as far as he could into their own quarter where the hay quivered untouched.

Pete said, "You'll run into it with your mower now. Why did you do that?"

"That's okay." He strode to his waiting team. "I better get cutting."

Thom's anger is clear: he appropriates the skull for himself, hurling it into the Wiens' hay lease.

The skull in the swamp is memorial fact/artifact. Only the heaviest horn and massive roll of forehead bone remain, and even these are eroded by rot, but this is indelible fact suggesting far more than merely itself. It is also "the broken suggestion of the great blade of the skull": the rest of that massive body moving through that landscape; it is there in his hands, visible to the one who has eyes to see. Oddly enough, the body and landscape of *Peace Shall Destroy Many* in 1959 grew out of just such broken suggestions of stories, sketches I had written earlier: rolls of bone that resisted the short teeth of time and retained their artifactual power three and four years after I had written them in F. M. Salter's English 65 writing class at the University of Alberta.

These artifacts are there in the very first words of the novel, where the two boys play hookey from school and go looking for frogs' eggs. Perhaps only those who have lived through the cold, the darkness of a northern prairie winter can comprehend the miracle of warm earth and water and spring green leaves and frogs singing; can comprehend the incredible feeling that the bright morning spring air fondling your nostrils releases you into.

The largest artifact, truly the bone skull of the fiction that determines the entire body of the novel, is the story of Elizabeth and her father. They first appear in a story I wrote in the last weeks of October 1955 for English 65. "Unto the Third and Fourth Generation" (my biblical title) was then thirty-eight pages long. In early November I revised the story down to twenty-three pages. But that skull still haunted me and in March 1956 I tried another version of twenty pages. Salter had encouraged all these revisions; he had been writing his usual cryptic comments ("I think you might omit this whole scene"; "too much is almost worse than too little"; or "a situation strong in itself is weakened by too much gab about it.") Now suddenly he commented: "this story was better before." It could not be chopped down to skull only. I did not work on it again for three years, and I certainly had no idea of the body of the beast that would emerge to carry that skull into the soggy mosquito-burdened hayslough of Canadian fiction where, it seemed to me, the dazzling gleam of bright water was then only very occasionally visible.

When I look at those manuscripts and re-create in my mind how I groped about trying to discover the shape of Elizabeth's story, I am not surprised at the fumbling, clumsy mass of it. It is, in fact, so long ago that I can consider it the effort of a disinterested third party: a young man of barely twenty-one who cannot bring that woman into the foreground, who must begin the story with a debate between a young man and her father, the preacher of the community. In many ways this young writer cannot see how all-too obvious and really *surface* Elizabeth's story is; he tries by careful parallels (which totally disappear in the later novel) to find some depth in these people, father/daughter/young man. In the story Elizabeth is nineteen, an only child, and her father before her had once been a wild Mennonite youth who on a dare one night rode into a Russian village and was quickly seduced by a Russian prostitute. This act is instantly known to everyone in the Mennonite community and, alone and humiliated, Peter Wiens flees to Canada and eventually establishes a small Mennonite settlement on the prairie which he dominates and where the sexes are, of course, kept separated to a ludicrous extent. Indeed, he himself "had not talked ten words to his wife before he asked her father for her in marriage." Now, his only daughter becomes pregnant by his own Halfbreed farm worker, and she dies in childbirth (much the same way the older Elizabeth dies in *Peace*). The preacher's youthful seduction, when he discovers himself "alone in a room with an animal woman," is described in strictly obvious terms: "he could feel the present in his limbs and in his own animal body," but in the story Elizabeth, dying beside her aborted four-month-old foetus, recalls her seduction differently:

> The living smells of blood and birth and death were mingled inextricably in that terrible, half-shaded room... "father," the sound seemed almost voiceless... slowly, dreamily in pain she talked, "He said such nice things to me — so gentle — so kind. He smiled when he saw me.... I knew you'd beat me if you knew, but it was so nice — you never told me that was wrong — you never told me anything.... When I was with him I didn't care about you or anything.... When he touched

me — he did what he wished — it was so beautiful under the black spruce in the spring night."

Whatever my understanding of the differences between male and female sexuality was then (and to get their full minimal range you'd have to read the entire clumsy manuscript), I was at least groping towards something more subtle. As can be seen when Wiens, again in a scene not retained in the novel, walks blindly out of the house of death:

> ... he did not see the patiently waiting horses or the half-filled hayrack — it was as if the farmyard were suddenly filled, crowded, with the whole settlement — the grazing red cattle, the small green-gold fields, the little log houses filled with people — the mental Utopia he had built where the strength of his will protected them all from evil and the world. And suddenly the people came out and looked at him, they saw him as he stood in the yard, and then they lifted long, terrible, accusing fingers and pointed. Slowly, the pointing fingers grew and grew together into one massive finger pointing at him and it came slowly towards him ... and he was terrified to his soul.... He had judged, forbidden, condemned! Was he a God?

I had struggled with three variations in six months, and I still had no more than a presentiment of what

Elizabeth's story could actually be. For over three years I left that, but there was a great deal of body attached to this skull.

Similarly, the last chapter of *Peace* was based on another short story, one I wrote in 1958. It is called "To Cry Peace" and concerns a young man sitting on his skis one winter night and staring at a one-room school, remembering a fight at a school Christmas program just past.

The story placed second in a Canada-wide writing contest for students, but Salter's spidery notations on it took a drastic turn. After a lapse of three years, he laid down the law: "For the health of your soul," he wrote, "you *must stop reading Faulkner*. For the next ten years you must take total abstinence…otherwise, your style will become more and more sloppy, slipshod, sleazy and formless."

Those were orders, all right. Three years before he had told me he "had often found me impossible to teach" and I certainly did not now abstain from Faulkner, may my soul rot as it will. But the fact also remains that it was Salter himself who placed the temptation before me soon after I completed that story. It wasn't until 1982 — twenty years after the novel was published, and twenty years after his death — that I finally dared to accuse him of this ultimate temptation (and you might note the style):

I was perfectly resigned that summer of 1959 to a job as an insurance investigator and then you got me listed as top alternate for a Queen Elizabeth Scholarship and sure enough one of the top ten

winners didn't accept theirs and I got it and needed
to do nothing all summer but start on a thesis and
I told you I wanted to do it on Shakespeare of
course — a perfectly acceptable subject, to investi-
gate, reveal, analyse, maybe destroy Shakespeare's
attitude on war, whatever it was I said — and you
just sat there, "yes, yes," while I got carried away
or carried myself there, who knows, you weren't
even in your office then, we were sitting in the
June sunlight of your porch, your house which the
University has now destroyed and levelled into a
parking lot, "yes, yes," with all those stacks of thick
books piled around you *in your porch* and letters
from scholars and thinkers and writers from all over
the world lying everywhere like gold, "yes, Mr.
Wiebe, yes, a great many people can write perfectly
acceptable, or dreadful, theses on Shakespeare, but
as you know, the University of Alberta has the op-
tion of a novel for an M.A. thesis. Perhaps only you
can write a fine novel about Mennonites." Leaking
that into me like... poison.

Ahh, what a poison; the poisonous temptation of the
possibility of fiction. No matter how carefully you sip, no
lifetime is long enough to build up a permanent immu-
nity to that. In 1958, in the underground vaults of the
Rutherford Library, among the dry backfiles of newspapers and magazines, sprouted some strange summer
mushrooms: Thom, Deacon Block, Elizabeth, Mrs. Wiens,

Herb Unger, Hal, Razia Tantamount — drawn out of such unlikely soil, I suppose, by the intermittent rain and lightning of imagined character and Wapiti landscape and Mennonite beliefs and sensuality and language and an enormous amount of blind, ignorant bullheadedness. Those catacomb notes and lists of names, characters, plot outlines, books read, chapter headings, 1944 news items, incidents, weather reports, scene ideas, various dead-end directions (a whole "animalistic" family named Wolfe was to provide Thom with some alternatives to his heavy religious thoughts; according to a Salter note, even in 1959 my favourite word remained "animalistic"!) — for me to try and remember that summer is to remember happiness. I had worked my way through university with labouring jobs; now I was being paid to imagine, to write. Salter had once suggested, with his wry cynical wit, that if I as a Canadian really wanted to write quality fiction I had best go to London and find a rich publishing heiress and marry her quick. Certainly his spidery comments in the margins of my manuscript remained as caustic as ever; one on an overwritten paragraph is indelibly carved on my memory: "Mr. Wiebe, you are exuding — poplar trees exude but writers write, carefully." That first draft was completed by September and I have no idea where it has vanished to. Perhaps in a Salter-provoked rage I shredded and fried it in liver, onions and gall and ate it.

The second draft was written in the bathroom of our small apartment because that room had the only door that could be closed against our mobile eight-month-old daughter. There I placed my typewriter on a board laid between the bathtub and the book-raised toilet seat; the plumbing helped nothing, but the blank windowless walls did. I lived inside my head from October 5, 1959, when the very last chapter of the book was finished first, to December 23. The whole second draft, 90,000 words, hammered out in not quite three months. Twenty-five years later that still seems an extraordinary pace for the formative draft of a novel.

By March the third draft was done. The 257-page manuscript was examined by a proper university committee and found "acceptable". It is typical of Salter that for my outside examiner he chose the historian L. G. Thomas, the man who earlier in his Canadian history course had given me the lowest mark I ever received at any university.

After I had left Edmonton, Salter sent me this letter:

Dear Mr. Wiebe,
Thank you very much for your letter. You do "kiss the rod." I trust that what you really mean to say is that I am forgiven.

I have just written to Mr. Jack McClelland and hope he will give your novel the careful consideration it deserves.

Sincerely yours, F. M. Salter.

I don't remember what my letter had said. What did I have to forgive him for? Probably plenty, if my own supervision of graduate theses is any indication. But whatever

that tongue-in-cheek comment meant, his recommen-
dation to Jack McClelland was crucial. On the same day,
May 30, 1960, McClelland and Stewart acknowledged
receipt of my manuscript; on August 18 McClelland himself sent me a two-page letter explaining they wanted to
work with me to make it into a novel they would be happy
to publish. A stunning letter.

A few years before this, it was Salter who convinced
McClelland to publish Sheila Watson's *The Double Hook*.
That publication in 1959 gave McClelland and Stewart
the distinction of having published the first modernist
novel in Canada, though at the time McClelland was so
apprehensive he had Salter write a "Preface" by way of
introduction. Salter had also introduced W. O. Mitchell to
Edward Weeks, editor of *The Atlantic Monthly*, and the
first two Mitchell stories published there in 1942 grew
into *Who Has Seen the Wind* by 1947. So when Jack
McClelland in 1960-61 paid two editors, Claire Pratt and
Joyce Marshall, to work with me on a total rewrite of
Peace, he was gambling on Salter's perceptions honed by
twenty years of reading new student writing.

In September 1962 the book was published and I
immediately sent one copy from Winnipeg to Salter in
Edmonton; his daughter Elizabeth wrote back to tell me
he had died on August 25. I still believe what I wrote to
her then:

> [he] influenced me the most in my first six years at
> university. He had the enviable quality of driving

the best in a student to the surface; if praise would not do it, certainly his knife-edged criticism would....

The first jacket of the new book announced in dramatic red and black:

In his first novel, Rudy Wiebe, a young theologian, writes of prejudice and bigotry erupting to destroy the people of a small Canadian community.

I had argued as much as any first novelist can about that cover; I thought "theologian" pretentious, and still do since I've never been one. For about a year and a half, in keeping with my position as editor of the largest Mennonite English paper in Canada, I had preached in most of the twenty Mennonite Brethren churches in Winnipeg and a few beyond; I was widely known for my sometimes critical (some said "unspiritual") editorials. I could probably have weathered the various storms my editorship raised among conservative church members (many had never read English before), but now *Peace Shall Destroy Many*, the first realistic novel written in English about the Mennonite experience, brought an inevitable explosion. I had been naive about that too.

Let me draw a quick, thin path through the wide range of letters from Mennonite people that I received, from January to June in 1963.

— a woman from Saskatoon:
Thanks be to God! Finally something has been written about which we can't say, "Now wasn't that a nice book!" We are talking and wondering and feeling vaguely uncomfortable.

— a man in Minnesota:
As far as I know, it is the first novel in a totally Mennonite setting, and written by someone combining sympathy and honesty. Much of what is in the book has needed to be said a long time, and you have said it well … to make our people consistent with the obligations of their heritage.

There were many other letters like that from people I had never met, but the ministers who finally wrote (some after months of pressure from constituents about "Wiebe's dirty book") had quite a different tone.

— a minister from Snowflake, Manitoba:
…what prompted you to write as you did [everything] portrayed in the negative sense, backward, isolationist, language barrier, and outwardly a pacifist, but underneath beware! … And the level to which you reduce the women is scandalous, portrayed as pure animalism [!], I'm sure that the same subject gets better treatment in "shunt literature" [junk literature].

— *a minister in B.C.* (who had officiated at my wedding):

The spirit of the book from its first page to the last one is a purely negative one. You have pointed out some of the dark spots in the history of our people, leaving the reader under the impression that this is the general situation. Nothing is being said in defence of our people. It is like washing one's dirty wash in the front yard of a neighbour.... I may tell you this, that in Mennonite circles the idea prevails that you have described the Coaldale [Alberta] Church. It is possible, because you grew up in that community and no doubt have suffered a lot under a certain legalistic spirit, which was predominant there in the past. It is not the same any more. Now it seems you are pouring out all the bitterness which has accumulated in your heart in your book.

The final, necessary quote is from the leading minister in the Coaldale church, where as a teenager I was baptized:

For some time I had been urged by members of our church to read the book. Younger and older members had read the book and classified it as "filth".... I have read the book from cover to cover... our Mennonite people, the M.B. church and authoritative men have been degraded, and sorry to say, our young people plastered with shame.

So, for some time, I wrote lengthy responses to these lengthy letters. As a friend has since pointed out, perhaps it had seemed that I would become an "authoritative man" in our church; with this book, however, that possibility was betrayed. On March 21, 1963, I sent the following note to the Conference Publications Committee which was my employer:

> Since I understand that I no longer have the confidence of the Publications Committee, I would herewith tender my resignation as editor....I should like to thank the Committee for the original trust that was shown me when I was appointed to this position.

About that time an acquaintance in Elkhart, Indiana, a true theologian, wrote me:

> If you feel that you have acted responsibly in the publication of this book (my own evaluation of it is quite irrelevant here) you will be tempted on the one hand, to justify yourself, and, on the other, to become bitter and resentful against your critics.
>
> It is at this point that I wish to register my concern that you have the grace to retain your own personal integrity, realizing that what is true need

not be defended, and that sometimes it is better to let "error" live than love die.

Besides the leading minister, only two people from Coaldale, my old home community some thought was portrayed in the novel, wrote me; both of them were women. In fact, all the many women who wrote me were, with one exception, totally commendatory. An unmarried woman (she identified herself as such) from Kitchener, Ontario, wrote, "I especially liked the insight which the Elizabeth-Louis affair revealed," and a high-school girl from Dalmeny, Saskatchewan, added to her church report, "how thoroughly I enjoyed [your novel]." The Coaldale letters, however, were the most revealing. One unmarried woman wrote at some length:

> I want you to know that I have had some interest-ing times defending it [the novel] before relatives and friends. The sentiments expressed by one friend seem to be prevalent: "Why does he portray the negative so vividly? What kind of a mind does he have to dwell on such immorality?" [But I say] please don't bury any of your talents because of this.

The most interesting letter was from a woman whose daughter I had known at the Alberta Mennonite High School in Coaldale ten years before. This letter needs to be quoted completely because there is an intensity and high seriousness in it which cannot be evaded.

Coaldale, Feb. 9th, 1963

Dear Rudy,

When [my former classmate] came home at Christmas she asked where she could buy your book *Peace Shall Destroy Many*. I told her as soon as we had one and read it we would buy all our children one. Now Grandpa R...gave me his to read. I had such big hopes for that story since the person who wrote it we knew. When I started the book there were so many people mixed up in it that it was not interesting. Finally I made up my mind to read it anyway but many times I felt like throwing it in the fire (and would have had not you been the writer). You must have heard stories in your home which puts your parents on a low level. If you had not been a church member when you wrote this book things would be different. I also know that the young people in Coaldale did not have a chance like they should have. We both me and you promised before *God* and people not to *talk* about church happenings to the world but take them in prayer before God. With this book you scattered it like opening a pillow with feathers and worse, hanging it on a pole. My parents taught me *man plaudert nicht aus der Schule, wie viel mehr aus der Gemeinde* [one does not gossip out of school, how much more out of church]. Some day when your children will read that book they will surely be ashamed of it as I am. To think such things are horrible but to put them in book form is more than I can understand. As you know and will see by this letter I have had not much school-ing but I always was proud of our young people that went to University and came back and give testimonies for our Lord and Saviour. There are so many nice things to write about and the Bible tells us what to talk about *wass wohl lautet* [things of good repute]. So many people talk about your book that I thought it would be best if I let you know how I feel about it.

Sincerely
[signed]

There are so many double meanings in this letter; every line echoes with far more than is overtly said, and at the time it made me very angry. Especially infuriating was the reference to my parents and the kind of smutty gossip they must have promoted in our home. I do know that my parents (who never read *Peace* because they never learned to read English) suffered a great deal from impli-cations like that and for years this made me bitter towards that community where they continued to live until their deaths. I do not believe my parents ever doubted me, in fact, my father told me once he was proud that I, the son of someone as unimportant as he, had created such a flap among all those "*groute Manna*" (big men). The idea that my children years hence would be so ignorant as to be ashamed of what happens in the novel — in contrast, say, to how it is written, which is quite a different matter — struck me even then as ludicrous. But the letter is transparently, intensely honest; the woman writes to me, while "so many" only talk, and the most revealing element is that she does not argue about the believability of the events in *Peace*. Clearly such things happen, *but* they should not be spoken of in public.

And I then remember clearly an old lady phoning me one miserable winter day in Winnipeg and telling me in Low German that I shouldn't let all this silly talk bother me: things like I'd written about, and worse, happened among Mennonites all the time, both in Canada and Russia. She herself could tell me a lot worse, and she laughed her lovely grandmother laughter. I'd written a good book, I shouldn't worry about it.

I did not, of course, carry any of this controversy in the paper I was editing. Frank Epp of *The Canadian Mennonite* did, and a reply to certain critics I wrote for him at that time has since been reprinted in *A Voice in the Land*. I received a great deal of support from numerous people (many of whom are friends to this day), though in the end the best revenge is to write better. Or outlive them — which is, as Marion Engel used to say, perhaps the best thing. But to continue working for a church organization was clearly impossible, and I never argued with anyone on the Publications Committee about retaining my job.

In May that year I accepted an offer from Goshen College in Indiana to teach literature and writing at that Mennonite liberal arts college; what some found offensive, others found creative. We were given a surprise dinner: over seventy friends came to the Oak Room, the St. Regis Hotel, to eat, sing, talk and wish us happier days in the United States. *The Winnipeg Free Press Weekly* was condensing *Peace* for its magazine section, but at the end of September, when I'd been teaching at Goshen for a month, the editor called me. Problems had developed with certain large Steinbach and Winnipeg Mennonite advertisers when they announced publication of the novel, and actually a three-man delegation had come in to have a serious talk. The upshot was the serialization did not run; then. But the *Free Press* had paid a few hundred dollars (they doubtless paid the condenser more than me) and five years later they ran it in seven instalments: November 30, 1968, to January 11, 1969. As far as I heard, not a word was said about it then, one way or the other. Perhaps no one read it; they merely glanced at the illustrations by Peter Kuch.

Before I began editing the *Herald*, in November 1961, I had received a letter from a gentle old man in Coaldale I distantly knew. He congratulated me on my announced appointment and said (I translate): "In your work you will get to know many people, and will also learn to know their weaknesses thoroughly. . . . I would wish for you a Jonathan, to whom you can empty your heart when it all becomes too heavy."

There is perhaps no more thorough way to learn to know the weaknesses of others — and oneself — than by editing a church paper and by publishing a passionately felt novel at the same time. I do not believe I have ever had a single Jonathan, though at times different individuals played some of that role. On the other hand, perhaps David did not need a Jonathan to be a poet; perhaps he only needed one to be a king. Certainly solitariness is necessary for some people; perhaps that too is part of the effect of a lifelong indulgence in the subtle, lovely poisons of fiction.

To return to *Peace Shall Destroy Many*: Thom Wiens is still standing in that hayslough, the swamp water seeping about his feet, and contemplating the buffalo skull. He cannot say, "Alas, poor Bison, I knew him well" — he has never known him in the flesh, and he never will. Nevertheless, that half-rotted skull does suggest greater possibilities: the rest of the head, the shoulders, the great humped body of the beast, suggest its startling and absolute discreteness. This very discreteness, this particularity, empowers Thom to see beyond the mere bone he holds in his hand, to see into that surrounding landscape, that air, those particular people who once lived here with their desires, their endless human necessities. Thom in the swamp does what a novelist can do: lends us eyes, ears, tongue to go beyond fact into artifact. Because clearly the skull is not the artifact; the word "artifact" comes from the Latin "arte" meaning art and "factus" meaning to make, that is, artifact is *that which is made by art*. The novel, not the skull, is the artifact. It is the thing made through the art of and with words, and when you order words that way and publish them, that is, make such artifacts public, you better beware. A lot of people like Pete won't be able to see past their five missing chickens. But you, for the health of your soul, you better be able to do so.

SAILING TO DANZIG

MY NAME IS Adam Peter Wiebe. As far as I know, there hasn't been an Adam in the family since the name Wiebe was first recorded in 1616 in Danzig, which is now of course Gdansk, Poland. The first Adam Wiebe was Frisian, and in Danzig he had two sons, Abraham and Jacob. Oddly enough, my own father, who was born in Chortitza Mennonite Colony, the Ukraine, was called Abraham Jacob, which in the Russian Mennonite tradition of naming meant that his father's name before him was Jacob. My oldest brother, who was born in a Mennonite village in the foothills of the Ural Mountains, was named Abram Abraham, my second brother Daniel Abraham, the Daniel coming from my mother's father. How is it then, I asked my parents years ago, that I, the last son, was named Adam Peter?

"Actually you weren't," my mother tells me without hesitation. "In the government papers in Saskatchewan, wherever they have them, your name was Heinrich."

"Heinrich?"

"In the papers, yes, and Abraham your second, like always. You were Heinrich Abraham."

"I'm not Adam?" At age seventeen I am about to discover my name?

"Of course you're Adam," she says calmly. "That was just those government papers. But we were living so far in the Saskatchewan bush when you were born it was seven weeks before your father got to town and he registered your name 'Heinrich Abraham.'"

My father, across the kitchen table from me, has continued to study his *Mennonitische Rundschau*; his reading glasses, bought at a counter in Eaton's, tilt at the end of his long, almost patrician nose. He sits this way every Sunday afternoon, the only day of the week he does not have to feed cattle on the farm where he will work as a hired man until he is sixty-nine, another seven years, never able to find the one Canadian dream he still has: a job where he can work inside and be warm all winter. He says nothing now, not even at my mother's teasing irony which, we all three know, will prick him eventually into some response.

"He had the day wrong, too," my mother continues suddenly. "He remembered it was a Saturday but he got the date wrong a whole week and when we got the registration when he was going to become a citizen Mrs. Graham says to me, 'My Lloyd was born the same day as your Adam, the midwife came from you to me, how come your day is wrong?' and then I noticed that too."

"It was eight weeks after, not seven," my father mutters finally; as if correcting her fact will balance his.

"But my name, Pah, you didn't remember my *name*!"

He seems particularly intent on the *Nachrichten*; he will never understand more than the barest English and it is in the weekly *Rundschau* that he learns what he knows of the news of the world.

"Mr. Graham wrote the names in them," my mother says, "'Adam Peter,' and so we corrected both the date and your names."

"When was this?" I ask.

"Well, Father, when was it, you became a Canadian citizen?"

"Nineteen forty-one. You want my registration number too?"

My mother is knitting and ignores that, easily. She knows he memorized the number immediately in case he was ever forced to cross the border again; when they got to Canada at last on March 5, 1930, he vowed he would never leave of his own free will and he never has.

"But you always called me...."

"Yes, we always have."

"So how come you called me that, Adam?"

"Oh," my mother looks up from her knitting, dreamy like the look I now see again on my daughter's young face, "there was a little boy, a Penner, he was a little Adam and he died just before you were born, he was so beautiful, always singing and only four and so good, laughing in the children's room in church and playing with all the babies to make them laugh too, it was so sad when he drowned in the slough behind their barn. That was a nice name, he was an Adam, so good."

"Well," I say bitterly, "you tried your best, with the name."

"Adam," my mother says softly, and touches me. For an instant her voice and fingers seem about to find tears behind my eyes, but my father says gruffly,

"Where did you find out about this Adam Wiebe, in Poland?"

"In a book."

"Books, books, all your books they'll ruin you."

If I only had the chance. What's ruined him? Being born in 1889 in Russia he always says, a Mennonite hauled into the Czar's forests in lieu of compulsory military service and he had finally finished his four years and come back to his village to marry my mother when World War I erupted and he was dragged back again, another four, or three rather, because the glorious October Revolution ended all that, they got so busy killing themselves, all those Communists, and playing games with him forever, what could anyone do but do what he was told? But finally, at forty, he did one thing: he left what little he had, they were poorer than Russian meadow mice, and took his wife and six kids to Moscow to try and get out of there; forever. Astonishing, he did that one thing, after a Mennonite father and four older brothers and over seven years of the Czar's army and then ten years of Communists, the Communists, oh he had learned to do what he was told.

"What was this Adam?" my mother asks.

Adam/Peter — ground/rock, surely a name significant enough for anyone. Adam/Peter/Abraham —
ground/rock/exalted father of a multitude, dear God
more than enough, all earth and exaltation too, with
Wiebe a solid Frisian name to anchor it; a people stubborn and implacable as water. In a class I taught years
later at the University of Leeuwarden there was a long
blonde girl named Wiebke den Hoet, her father the dike
master on a new polder slowly forming itself out of the
North Sea. But I could not know this when I was seventeen, did not yet know Wiebe was a Frisian given name
transformed by deliberate centuries into a patronymic,
my mother knitting mittens for poor children on a hot
August Sunday in Alberta. That first Adam Wiebe sailed
from his fishing village of Harlingen on the North Sea for
Danzig in 1616 because that Hanseatic free city needed
a water engineer and he was the best in the world.
Harlingen is still a village in the Netherlands; its laby-
rinth of dikes and canals, many of them probably built by
Adam, still thrust it out in alternating loops of earth and
water against the grey sea. The aerial (KLM) photo I have
shows it almost as neat as the 1624 copper engraving of
Danzig which in the top-left corner features the city's
coat of arms and the top right a portrait of Adam Wiebe
himself.

"Look," I say to my mother, and read for my father's
benefit, since he won't look up, "Wybe Adam von
Harlingen."

"That's your father's nose," my mother says, and so it is. But a higher forehead, heavier eyebrows in a narrower face; an unstoppable genius who served Danzig thirty-two years and before he died had streets and gates and even squares named after him.

"Where's my long nose?" I ask.

My father laughs then. "It got lost for a turned-up Loewen. Her mother's family."

"Does your book have pictures of a Loewen?" my mother asks.

If I could answer her now, I would tell her the Loewens were Flemish believers from the other great Hanseatic city, Antwerp, probably jewellers who escaped religious persecution and arrived in Danzig even earlier than Adam Wiebe. But perhaps now, rather than parade all my dubious facts of history, I would ask her to sing, that beautiful soprano now lost forever except in the folds of my memory. Any of the songs she sang when the leaves came out green as frogs in the Saskatchewan poplar May and she began to cook on the stove outside to keep the house cool for sleeping. It would be a song from the *Dreiband*, their pocket-size Mennonite hymnal without notes but of course a person who sang in a church choir then knew at least five hundred songs from memory, and my father across the yard somewhere within earshot would answer her in tenor harmony, their voices floating like lovers hand in hand high in the bright air. By some genetic shift more drastic than my nose the two musical rocks of Flemish Loewen and Frisian Wiebe have faulted into my tunelessness: though I can recognize any melody, I cannot reproduce or mirror one either close or at a distance. Not even the overwhelming choir of thirty-six Peter Wiebe descendants in Gladbach, West Germany, last year helped me to one tuneful sound — the over two dozen children from two families finding hours of melodies in that tiny apartment, their heads filled endlessly with identical words and notes.

"Peter Wiebe," my father would have slowly raised himself erect. "That was my brother, the rich one with us in Moscow in 1929, he always — "

"Leave that old story," my mother would have said quickly. "We have to forget such things."

"Forget!" my father's thick worker hands are crumpling the paper. "You forget when your own brother who's as rich as the dead Czar keeps saying to you, 'How do you think you'll get out to Germany, you and your Marie and six kids, when you don't have three kopecks to rub together?' How do you forget that?"

"Abraham," my mother murmurs, "God needs money for nothing."

"And the Communists don't either, thank God," my father laughs sardonically at his own wit. "Having money in '29 was the end of any going, no beginning."

"So forget that old story, it — "

But I would have to interrupt her. "This isn't your brother Peter, Pah, it's his son, he was in Moscow with you too, young, he — "

"Peter Wiebe is in Germany now? Did he finally buy his way out, now?"

"It's your nephew, not your — "

"That young Peter was nineteen in '29," my mother says dreamily. "Short, very thin and very bright eyes. Such an open Wiebe face."

And he still has it the first time I see Peter Wiebe. In 1982. He was coming towards me through several thousand Mennonites at their annual reunion in Germany to celebrate their '70s escape at last from the Soviet Union, exclaiming, "That's a Wiebe face, a Wiebe face!" And for that moment he appeared to be my father reincarnated in a slight, short body, his thin blond hair which would never turn grey and that patrician nose and square jaw, limping towards me through the crowd that turns to stare and then laugh aloud at our happiness, at our embrace and enfolding double kiss. I had to bend down to him, over him, my arms surrounding his narrow bones, and suddenly between my fingers there spread an enormous, overwhelming silence. I might have been holding my father, alive again after seven years; though he had never in a lifetime held me like that.

"I never wanted a Peter in my family," my father says. "An Adam I didn't care, but a Peter, another Peter...."

My mother is singing. She will be singing not to avoid my father: they did not live sixty-one years with each other that way; rather, that wordless sound suspended by her voice, a broadening colour which does not hesitate at

sadness or laughter, or break because of anger, unforgive-
ness, even hatred; it is a sound which slowly, slowly
threads brightness over the glowering, stifling Sunday
afternoon. It is like the story young Peter Wiebe, now sev-
enty-two, will tell me of his second arrest and his second
transport to the Gulag in the last fierce days of the dying
Stalin. He will say:

"We had religious freedom, of course, it was official,
guaranteed by the Soviet Constitution. But no more than
three people could talk politics together and the police
must suspect everything so when our village met every
Wednesday evening for Bible reading, faith became politics. I had the only Bible and the room was full, always
tight full and I read in German, no one ever said a single
word not used by Luther — where would you get a
Russian Bible? This German Bible from my father was
the only one in the village, and even if we had spoken
Russian, who knew what person had been pressured by
what police, and why? Your own sister or cousin or even
husband would never dare tell you if they *had* to inform
to prevent something worse. That was the way they controlled us, fear, and if *you* had to inform, at least you knew
how to protect yourself because you knew at least something they knew because you'd told them — well, why
would Soviet police or party members believe us when we
told them again and again we never spoke anything at all
but the words of Jesus? And sometimes his words, well,
the way you say them can sound like something a little
slanted and people will smile as if they know something,

just for a second they know and can think, something. So
that time they came in as I was reading John 15: 'I am the
vine, you are the branches. They that abide in me...' they
were pounding loud on the house door, and of course it
takes a while to get the door open and there's always so
many big men and women around the door that they
can't actually get in for a while and when the knock came
I had to leave the room, like I'd done two times before but
this time they are smarter: two of them greet me by the
kitchen door as I come out. 'We just want to ask you a few
questions, nothing more, don't worry, Katerina Petrovna,
he'll be back for night.' Of course, but which night? Four
years later, when Stalin is dead three years and Khruschev
reviews all the ten or eleven, maybe it's thirteen, million
political prisoners' records, I am released just as quick, I
can go not even into free exile as they call living anywhere
in the Soviet Union except within five hundred kilometres of your home village, I can go, go home. I am alive
only because I am small, and because I can keep books.
Even sitting on a stool in a heated room all day you get
barely enough food to keep a body as small as mine
breathing year after year, but if you have to labour in the
mines or the forests in the terrible cold, especially if your
body is big like yours, you don't last a month; the smaller
people last longer, sometimes almost half a year, but me
they would have stuffed with black bread gladly forever,
sometimes even a fish-head in the soup because every
camp administrator has to have a bookkeeper who will
keep him ahead of his boss — you cannot imagine the

unbelievable records that have to be kept, every turnip peel weighed and written down to whom it went and to have a prisoner in camp who can add and is honest, well, honesty is so unbelievable that every camp boss I ever had kissed me and cried when he had to let me go. By God's grace there I am, four years of a twenty-five year sentence, the food ration is the same whether you have to meet an impossible quota set in the Kremlin of trees cut in waist-deep snow or add numbers all day, columns like forests down page after page growing themselves green in your head until you are an adding machine, your eye sliding down their wrinkled bark and clicking so exactly even the unexpected Kremlin inspector with machines can't do anything faster, leave alone find a mistake in books stacked to the ceiling, thank the dearest God who gives you this year after year mind of numbers and denial, nothing more, 'No, I did not.... No, I never said.... No, I know of no one...' the unending questions that come to you at any time of any night, always only at night, and only the numbers are constant, solid as rock and the frozen spruce piling up like corpses around the camp you have no idea where it is buried in the taiga but you know exactly how many bodies there are, trees or people. You become numbers; soon an axe blow no matter how feeble in the farthest swamp is already written on the paper of your mind, eleven to seventeen chops per tree up to thirty centimetres in width for a fresh prisoner, seventy-six to ninety-three for the same tree for someone who will be dead in her bunk rags tomorrow, the skin stretched stiff across her torn teeth and you have another statistic: longevity calculated in relation to declining rations, in relation to quotas not filled, how long can rations be cut for the prisoner coming in weighing thirty to forty kilos, forty to fifty kilos, do women last longer than men even though their initial production is never as high and they have the same quotas, same food ration? The largest men always die first. But I am small, I work inside where it's warm, I last four years; until Stalin is dead. It is Wednesday evening again when I get off the train and walk to my village along the empty farm roads and I open the door of our house, the same door where they took my father in 1936, and the woman inside who is reading stops and she gives me back my father's German Bible and I open it and read as if I had never left, read aloud in that room crowded with the same white, silent faces the words of Jesus, 'They that abide in me and I in them, the same bring forth much fruit, for without me you can do nothing.' That was my second return, the first time was in the war when I was falsely accused and our collective farm worked two years to get me out. But my father never came back the first time. They came for him in 1937, and Stalin still lived then for almost twenty years."

This story, and all the other stories I will hear from Peter Wiebe are already there in my mother's song as she sings until my father joins her, their voices singing this story which has already taken place but which they will never hear nor speak about sitting at the worn kitchen table in Alberta, Canada, my memory of them like their memories of Moscow, like Peter's memories of his father, my uncle Peter Jacob, the rock and the deceiver, my father's older brother having to live on in the Mennonite village in the Ural foothills to which he and his family are returned from Moscow in 1929 while my father and his family travel to Germany and finally Canada. My uncle has to wait seven more years until that knocking on the door he has always known will come finally comes, and he disappears into the winter darkness leaving only memory and his German Bible, a tall, strong man like my father who has no mind for numbers either but can chop down a thirty-centimetre tree in nine strokes of an axe, easily, and so fill his quota. At least for the first three or four days. With the square Wiebe face we all have, but a nose unlike mine; a patrician nose like Adam Wiebe in 1616, the year Shakespeare died and Adam sails to Danzig to lay the city's first wooden watermains and set artesian wells in its squares and drain the marshlands along the Radaune River by building dikes and canals and wind and horse-driven mills that lift the turgid water up into the slate-grey sea.

"What is this," my mother says, pointing with her knitting needles, "these strings here?"

She is studying the grey picture of the copper engraving of Danzig, the coat of arms in its top-left corner, the narrow, energetic face of Adam in its top right. Below the coat of arms is a line drawing of a high hill labelled Bischoffs Berg, the centre is low sagging land along the river and marshes with the church spires and gates of the city beyond; but below Adam's picture on the right there is an elevation almost as high as the hill: it is labelled Wieben Bastion.

Adam built that fortification to protect the city from the army of King Gustavus Adolphus of Sweden, and he constructed the city walls and the bastion above the swamps of the river by using earth from the Bischoffs Berg. The strings between the two my mother is puzzling over is the double cable Adam Wiebe strung on poles so that, by means of an endless stream of moving buckets attached to this cable, the earth could be carried over the river and the swamps from hill to bastion. So exactly were these buckets designed, so precisely were distance and weight calculated that no power was needed to make them move: the weight of the filled buckets at the top of the hill carried them down across the valley to the bastion while returning the empty buckets back up to the top. And though the gigantic Gustavus Adolphus and his mercenaries destroyed much of Europe for hire and the unending glory of the Protestant Church, they never got inside the walls of Danzig, leave alone near its central bastion, because in 1622 my ancestor invented the cable car to defend a defenceless city.

"When did this Wybe Adam von Harlingen die?" my father asks abruptly.

"Sixteen fifty-two. Pah, he built all that for them, and Danzig never even made him a citizen."

It is then my father looks up. "Yeah, yeah," he says, heavily, "that's the way. It always is. When those Communists hammered on our door in Moscow and told me to get on that train to Germany, they gave me a yellow card. 'Stateless refugee,' that's all it said. A hundred and fifty years in Russia and they send us out, a piece of yellow paper and fill in your own name. 'Stateless refugee.'"

I had not known that either. I suppose it doesn't really matter. After all, over how many lakes and rivers and parts of oceans, across how many fairgrounds, up how many mountains on how many continents have I sailed through air suspended somehow from a cable and not known about my ancestor Adam Wiebe? My ignorance has, of course, never made any of those cables less real, any sailing less beautiful. Or potentially dangerous.

And in my memory my parents sit at our kitchen table in Alberta suspending the thin thread of their songs across the marshes and bitter rivers of their memories building what bastions? Against what fearfully anticipated or remembered war, against what knock at what door, "We just want to ask you a few questions, come, you'll be home for night"? Slight, bent Peter, the rich Wiebe's son having to live a sort of a life in the Soviet Union, I the poor Wiebe's son living a different sort in Canada: which would one actually prefer? Peter Jacob who vanished in 1937, Peter Peter bringing that Bible to Germany when he is too old even to keep other books and still so immovably honest and absolutely immovably stubborn and he is told to go at last, go, who wants you, you old bastard, you troublemaker — these are facts, were already becoming facts one August Sunday afternoon long ago when I was a teenager and discovering that my mother and father could tell me so little about the names I had, could tell me only small facts that explained nothing; facts like intermittent needles in compassionate wool, or poles sticking up out of sinking ground, holding up cables no one could explain what genius, what vision had once made them possible so that all that solid earth could be moved so beautifully over swamp from the Bischoffs Berg to build the Wieben Bastion.

Wybe Adam von Harlingen, where are you now? Your cables are gone. Only the memories of songs remain.

RIVER OF STONE

To follow a river, whether it has a name or not, means you travel linearly. Your movement is a line across the area which the globe offers you in that particular place.

Line and area. Now it is a characteristic of Inuktitut, the language of the Canadian Inuit, that every spacial concept and every thing or motion in that space can only be expressed in terms of either line or area. An actual grammatical change (like changing the verb "move" to "moved" when you indicate a difference of tense in English) is required when you speak of either one or the other. In Inuktitut, a person or caribou standing still is, linguistically considered, an area; however, a person or caribou moving is linguistically considered a line.

English, of course, makes no such distinction and for me to try and explain it becomes a study in prepositions. But let me try. A canoe (which is linear in that it is much longer than it is wide), a canoe *in* a river (which is also

linear) moves *with* the river *across* a limited space —
which is an area. However, the canoe also moves *on* the
river — which makes it and the people in it (since they
are moving *with* the canoe *on* the moving river), doubly
linear.

So much for a river in a space with discernible limits
as, for example, one which runs between trees or mountains. However, a river in a space whose limits are not
readily discernible to the human eye behaves differently
again. In Inuktitut, space without discernible limits is considered linear also — that is, for the Inuit such space is
always longer than it is wide. Perhaps that is an under-
standable characteristic of the language of a nomadic,
hunting people who for eight thousand years have lived in
the apparently unlimited (at least to the unaided human
eye) the unlimited space of sea and ice and Arctic land
beyond the treeline. Theirs is a heritage of movement in
order to stay alive: a movement necessary both to gather
food and to keep warm.

Therefore, when I step *into* a canoe and paddle *on* a
river passing *through* an Arctic landscape whose limits are
beyond my discernment — as in the Arctic beyond the
treeline they invariably are: I am surrounded by nothing
but horizon — in the language of the people who live
there, I am linear three times over:

    — myself in motion;

    — the river in motion under me;

    — the landscape boundaryless around me at whatever
      spot I may choose to consider it.

That is journey indeed. A journey worthy of the quintessential human story, which I take to be that of humanity always and forever wandering, of the peoples on the earth eternally without rest, and searching.

I did not understand this very well when several colleagues and I planned a summer's water journey in the Northwest Territories. We intended to travel the watercourses between the Obstruction Rapids on the Coppermine River, via Starvation Lake and Little Martin Lake to Winter Lake and the 1820 site of Fort Enterprise. We knew we would be almost two hours in flying time north of the nearest large settlement — Yellowknife — and days by canoe away from the nearest Dene village. So we needed six people in three canoes to ensure some measure of safety. And in fact, during the fourteen days of travel we did not encounter a single person other than ourselves. But at home in Edmonton, I glibly say I made an Arctic journey by canoe.

What was the journey we took? On my office floor I spread out the maps: those scaled at 1 to 1,000,000; then those at 1 to 500,000, and finally those at 1 to 250,000 — that is all I could get. The Department of Mines and Technical Surveys of Canada informed me nothing in that particular area has yet been drawn to a larger scale. But even on the small-scale maps the space pulses larger and larger: more blue for lakes, more delicate tracing for rivers and occasional streams and rapids and contour elevations, more centipede lines for meandering eskers.

But the greatest office-floor revelations are the aerial (here meaning both "air" and "area") photographs. Each picture 9 x 9 inches photographed on Kodak Safety Film through a 6-inch lens pointed straight down from 30,000 feet: recording that world sometime in the summer of 1955. These photographs provide details clearer than an inch to the mile. Match them to the maps, pattern for pattern, and the very grain of that world leaps into texture: every particle of it as distinctive as a snowflake or a fingerprint.

Nevertheless, these pictures are black and white, and my own eyes have told me that that is certainly not accurate. These Army Service Establishment photographs declare a world existing only between the extremes of white sand and black, motionless water. Perhaps that is enough for the army; it isn't for me. On the floor I spread our Fujicolour aerials taken from a Twin Otter at 6,000 feet, July 10, 1988. Instantly, beyond the breathtaking variations of colour in water, land and sky, I recognize that these pictures were taken at an angle, not straight down. Beyond the multi-shaded bodies of lakes outlined by tan sand and the blue, green and white lines of rivers, the pictures invariably catch a horizon. And it is that seemingly simple line of the horizon, not the incredible colour, which makes that journey for me expand suddenly, endlessly into a memory without discernible limits.

It is clear I cannot speak of "our journey." The only meaningful question is, which journey did I take? The one traceable on variously scaled maps of the Geological Survey of Canada? Or the more problematic one (because it has more alternatives) which can be deciphered on the army photographs? Or the possible route we plotted for ourselves across lakes and the height of land connecting waterways, using both these sometimes unreliable sources of information? Or was my journey the plane flight we took to get to what we then thought would be its beginning, or to get away from its end?

Even more particularly, was my journey the track of the canoe I helped paddle across lakes and down rivers, lined or pushed through and over rock gardens, carried on my shoulders across miles of portages, or as bowman in the rapids we ran, tried to slow down in white water or aimed directly into standing waves or angled at the correct split second through water folded in vees between rocks and never quite tipped, though once, at the end of the most amazing run of a mile-long rapid, the last quarter of it paddled *backwards* after the four-foot standing waves whipped us around, we emerged in the lake below kneeling up to our chests in water, the canoe and all its cargo totally submerged under us but held by our braced knees and us balancing there, delicate and shifty as a sunken feather, facing the long wash of white water above us which we had just traversed, somehow, in one unforgettable, ecstatic rush?

Which was the journey? The several hundred pictures, instants caught and held as if furiously paddling canoeists or foaming white water could be frozen motionless forever? In written Inuktitut, is the language describing a moving person or a river in a picture grammatically area? A picture always has a frame, no matter how artificial. Is one's memory of such a person or river linguistically line? I do not have to make that distinction thinking or writing in English, and that is unfortunate, since that might have forced me to consider such a "journey" even more seriously before I attempted it.

So now, beside the maps and pictures and routes, I must place my notebook on the floor as well. It is filled with the precise discreteness of English words and sentences, with hand-drawn maps, portage lengths and numbers, named and unnamed lakes and watercourses, details of times and impressions and moods and stupidities and rages and walks taken and heat and cold and mosquitoes and wind endured, and rain, the experience of sleeping for several weeks beside my son on ground where the permafrost will retain the thawed, hollow print of our bodies long after we have passed on; of our trying to become, together, the complete cooperative personality two people in a canoe must become in order to survive a lake, a river, any rapid.

Which was the journey I took? Or *what* was it? If I could decide, I would perhaps tell you. Tell you whatever we have time for, since we western Whites are always circumscribed by moments. I am as time-bound as anyone, but two years after the fact I long for the kind of journey a Dene storyteller would have time to make with you, here. I have sat with a few of them, and listened. Their infallible courtesy, even in a language as inflexible to them as English, cannot be rushed, and they will usually tell you something. Or they may not, and you must accept that too. However, if they do offer a story, unexpectedly, you had better take whatever time it requires to listen because that experience may not come again.

One of our original purposes for the journey I am talking about was to see the landscape where, between September 27 and November 2, 1821, eleven of the nineteen members of the First Franklin Expedition to the Polar Sea died horribly of overwork, starvation and murder. Franklin was, of course, capable of much more: on his Third Arctic Expedition twenty-five years later every one of his one hundred and twenty-nine men on two ships died in misery, including himself. But for me, our journey between Obstruction Rapids and the site of Fort Enterprise where the stumps of the trees Franklin's men cut are still perfectly preserved by dryness and cold even after a hundred and sixty-seven years, our travel came to have almost nothing to do with Europeans and what they in massive arrogance call "discovery." As Stephen Kakfwi, a Hareskin leader from Fort Good Hope, has said of Alexander Mackenzie: "[In 1789] my people probably wondered at this strange pale man in his ridiculous clothes, asking about some great waters he was searching for. We've never understood why our great river [Dehcho] is named for such an insignificant fellow." The longer I travelled, and the longer memory creates that journey, going far beyond any details of map or photograph or notebook, the more I understand that, if there were any significant human beings in this awesome land-scape, they are those who have lived there for fifteen thousand years: the Dene, in particular the Dogrib People and the Yellowknife People.

We did not physically meet any of them. The Yellow-knives as a distinct group no longer exist, and the Dogribs live in small settlements several days away by canoe. There were no Dogrib hunters in the area because the caribou migration does not return from the Arctic coast until the middle of August. However, the marks of human pres-ence were everywhere: campsites at the heads of portages, faint carrying trails we sometimes stumbled upon over esker and muskeg, the numberless paths made by caribou worn deep as cattle trails across the tundra and leading always to a river crossing above a rapid. And there were graves. Solitary on high points of land, or an unexpected cluster of them the size of a woman, a man, a child, on a small island in Winter Lake. And each is always sur-rounded by the peeled pickets of tiny treeline trees, a tall picket cross at its western end draped with red prayer-beads or a medallion of the Virgin.

In a landscape that is still strange, still without identi-fiable proportion, kneeling in a canoe and seeing these human-size structures over long, close water against sky makes them mysteriously large, like distant cathedrals you know cannot exist there. And then you stand beside them, looking down at them for some time. That evening you write: "I love the landscape where they put them, of far rocky ridges of hills and whitecapped lake. When you walk into the wind there are no mosquitoes or flies and for a moment it seems you are in a friendly landscape. But that's not really true — it is merely a landscape that does not care one way or another."

No Dene would ever write that. Rather, as George Blondin of Great Bear Lake has said, "The land, and all it provides for our people has been the very spirit of the Dene. From the land came our religion…from the land came our life…from the land came our powerful medicine…"

In the Genesis story of creation, Adam in Paradise discovers the enormous difference between himself and all other creatures while inventing language: as Adam names the animals, he finds there is no "help meet for him" among them. Thereupon, Yahweh makes him "a help meet" from his rib, that is, Eve, who within three verses has been so extraordinarily helpful, so the story goes, as to assist him in destroying Paradise and laying an immeasurable burden of sin and guilt on their offspring for all eternity.

The Yellowknife People, who guided Franklin on his first expedition and without whom the entire expedition would have died, the Yellowknives had a very different creation account. In 1835 a Yellowknife man named Old Soul told that story to Richard King on the Back River. Old Soul did not pretend to know where man came from, but he must have appeared in summer, he said, when there were plenty of berries and plants to eat. However, the deep winter snows made that impossible, and chasing animals extremely difficult. The man realized he needed larger feet to run over the snow as swiftly as the hare, and so his fresh imagination conceived of snowshoes. He bent the frames into shape, but then he was stuck: he could not make the webbing because, as Old Soul pointed out, that was woman's work and as yet no woman existed. The man struggles to hunt on foot in the snow, and is on the verge of starvation when one day, as he returns exhausted to his hut, a ptarmigan flies out of it. Going in, he sees the snowshoe frames have a bit of webbing woven through them. This happens again, with more webbing filling in the frames. "The bird has done this," the man decides, and next day comes back early from his hunt, surprises the ptarmigan at its work and catches it before it can escape. The bird turns into a woman in his hands, and of course she completes webbing the snowshoes so that the man can easily hunt in the snow and she can cook and sew for the comfort of them both.

I find this Yellowknife creation story of "The Snowshoe" inexpressibly more inspiring than the Judeo-Christian one of "The Rib and the Apple." Help meet indeed. Living in a land as harsh as any on earth, the Yellowknives emphasized not individual temptation and disobedience and sin, but true complementarity.

The Dene also emphasize the close relationship between human and animal. In this story, woman comes from bird. The Dogrib People are named that because, they say proudly, they are descendants of a Yellowknife woman and a handsome stranger who at night became a huge black dog. The woman's brothers killed the dog in a rage, but the woman gave birth to six puppies. She loved them, but was afraid for them and so she hid them in a sack. One evening she noticed children's footprints around her tent. The next day she hid to watch, and soon the sack opened and out jumped the six puppies, turning into three boys and three girls as they did so. Ecstatically happy, the woman sprang out and tried to catch the children, but three leaped back into the sack before she could hold them. The three she caught, however, two boys and a girl, became the ancestors of the Dogrib People.

Human beings descended from dogs? What kind of people would tell such a story about their origins? Only those who understand their inextricable closeness to the land and the animals that live on it. The dog is, of course, a slightly domesticated wolf, and the wolf, like people, lives by hunting caribou which, in turn, live on the mosses which grow on the land. In fact, all Dene races consider the wolf taught them how to hunt the swift caribou. As anthropologists have noted, the hunting patterns of wolves and people are to this day remarkably the same. Until whites came with their demand for furs, the Dene did not hunt wolves, and do so now only reluctantly. The murderous villain wolf of European folktales does not exist in their stories.

On our canoe journey we did not see a wolf. But that was, as usual, a problem of our ignorant eyes. The wolves were certainly there because we heard them. One evening,

just as we were setting up camp on an island in Little
Martin Lake, the wind suddenly rose and the lake began
to run high, breaking whitecaps. While we tried to anchor
our tents, a wolf howled from the mainland, long, long,
the sound carrying to us in a brief quiet of wind across the
wild water smashing below on the rocks. My brother the
wolf, trying to tell me something. Immediately two of our
party, with the invariable instincts of "civilized" male stupidity, threw back their heads and bawled a cacophonous,
barbaric bellow in response. I could have, with great joy,
kicked them both into the lake; after that the wolf did not
deign to make another sound. And the wind marooned us
on the tiny island for over twenty-four hours.

Actually, the journey I wanted to make was none of
the ones I have mentioned. I realize now that, exciting as
it was, I did not want to paddle a canoe in a river crossing
the tundra. I really wanted to walk on a river: all its motion
my own.

This too is possible in the Arctic, and not only in winter when water turns to ice — which is, of course, water
pretending to be land. For in the Arctic there are great
rivers of stone: we call them eskers. They are the narrow,
sinuous ridges created by the sediments of glacial melt-
water streams flowing in tunnels through or under the
glacial ice. Since the northern half of North America was,
until as recently as ten thousand years ago, covered by the
immense Wisconsin-Laurentide ice sheet, eskers snake
parallels across the tundra everywhere — often twenty,
fifty or two hundred kilometres long. I looked down at

their white lines flying, I looked up at them often, with longing, kneeling in the river of water. At their sides precise as pyramids at the angle of repose, at their white-sand tops level and smooth as highways, at the erratics (glacial boulders) sitting on them so massively elegant the ancient Egyptians themselves, those grave lovers of great rocks, would have blanched to see them.

To cross the Arctic on those high, prehistoric skyline rivers of stone — now that would be a journey. A journey indeed.

On Refusing the Story

AKLAVIK IS A CLUSTER of seven hundred and fifty people almost invisible in the enormous Mackenzie Delta. The Anglican Church Cemetery there contains the grave of a man who tried to hide in the Arctic. Albert Johnson, as he is called, should have known better. He never saw Aklavik alive; he was brought there only to be buried on March 9, 1932, and since he had killed one policeman and almost killed two others, he was interred as far away from the tiny log church as possible, on the very edge of church property.

However, since 1932 the town has grown; the old brown church has become a museum and a new prefab structure stands there bluer than the sky; the town is now so large that the main street with its two stores, hamlet offices and fire stations runs along the back of the cemetery. As a result, Albert Johnson's grave is now on the very edge of the main street: the long entrance to the cemetery is right there beside the two broken tree stumps that stick

like symbolic rotten columns out of the white picket fence
outlining his gravesite. One stump has a large white *A*
painted on it, the other an even larger *J*. Beside the grave
stands a square sign with roughly painted scenes from
Johnson's life; it bears the following legend:

> THE MAD TRAPPER
> ALBERT JOHNSON
> ARRIVED IN ROSS
> RIVER AUG. 21, 1927
> COMPLAINTS OF
> LOCAL TRAPPERS
> BROUGHT THE RCMP
> ON HIM HE SHOT TWO
> OFFICERS AND BE-
> CAME A FUGITIVE OF
> THE LAW WITH HOWL
> ING HUSKIES, DANGER
> OUS TRAILS, FROZEN
> NIGHTS. THE POSSE
> FINALLY CAUGHT UP
> WITH HIM. HE WAS
> KILLED UP THE
> EAGLE RIVER
> FEB 17, 1932

The slender white crosses, the white picket fences of
the graves of the good burghers of Aklavik crowd about,
spreading to the far corners of the cemetery; only this

once-ostracized "fugitive of the law" whose true name is not known to this day receives so much attention. Tourists are always there, taking pictures. Why are murderers so much remembered?

I submit that Albert Johnson is simply the most obvious example of a human being in the North with a secret, and in contemplating his, some of the wider secrets of the Arctic landscape will become clearer.

In one of the most beautiful short stories ever written, "The Lady with the Pet Dog," Anton Chekhov has his protagonist recognize:

> The personal life of every individual is based on secrecy, and perhaps it is for that reason that civilized people insist so strongly that personal privacy be respected.

Chekhov's protagonist, Gurov, is thinking of the double life he personally leads. Gurov recognizes that "he had two lives, an open one" (which is the conventional life that everyone knows) "and another life that went on in secret...that no living soul knew of.... Everything of importance...everything about which [he]...did not deceive himself" is in that second, secret life.

Now despite a massive manhunt and fifty-five years of sporadic search by police and private persons, we know nothing whatever of Albert Johnson's personal, secret life; in fact, his public life is known only from July 7, 1931, when he arrives in Fort McPherson, N.W.T., until he is killed "up the Eagle River" on February 17, 1932, and he becomes a motionless dot on the Yukon ice. His most elementary secret, that of his name, defies discovery. The legend (I use the word advisedly, in two of its possible meanings) on the grave board on Aklavik's main street which states that Albert Johnson "arrived in Ross River Aug. 21, 1927" is fact only if we identify him with a certain man who in Ross River called himself Arthur Nelson. Ross River, Yukon Territory, is as the raven flies at least five hundred kilometres from Fort McPherson, Northwest Territories; it is almost twice that far by mountainous river, which is how Albert Johnson arrived there.

Historian Dick North of Whitehorse has identified Johnson with Nelson; but Nelson's past, his story, seemed untraceable before Ross River. Now, however, after twenty years of "obsession" (North himself uses that word) with Johnson/Nelson, North is at last positive he has found the man's real name, and with it all that vast revelation of human activity and personality, of family and past and birth and place which a public name must expose, that immense factual story which every human being in the retrospect of memory has lived.

Strange to say, North believes that the fugitive's name really was Johnson. Only his given name was different: instead of the relatively distinctive "Albert," North says it was, of all most ordinary names, "John." This John Johnson was born in Norway and from the age of one grew up in North Dakota; he was a convicted bank robber and horse thief by age seventeen (1915), and spent several years in various U.S. prisons before apparently disappearing into Canada in 1923. After years of following every shred of evidence to build his case, all North lacked to make the last, indisputable identification between the two Johnsons was Albert's fingerprints. However, the prints taken from Albert Johnson after his death have disappeared from the Royal Canadian Mounted Police file.

How it is possible that one of the most famous police forces in the world has not kept the ultimate record of an unidentified criminal I will not try to explain. North writes, "This left only one recourse for me, and that was to dig up Albert's body.... He was buried in permafrost and consequently his skin probably would be in good enough shape to 'lift' the prints." On April 27, 1987, the news went round the Yukon by radio and newspaper that the hamlet of Aklavik had given Dick North permission to exhume Johnson's body.

Oddly enough, on that Monday, April 27, I was in Old Crow, Yukon. That evening I met some twenty Kutchin people of the Old Crow community who came to talk with me about my writing, and particularly what I knew about Albert Johnson. We were talking quietly, slowly comparing bits of information, when one man who had not sat down when we began suddenly asked on my left, very loudly: "Do you know who shot him first, that Albert Johnson?"

His tone was incredibly loud in the, until then, friendly room. Everyone was peering at me intently.

"I'm not sure," I said. "Do you?"

"Sure I know," he declared. "Everybody here knows that, it was Johnny Moses right from here, Old Crow, he was a special constable for the police and he had permission to shoot, he was the best shot and he fired and hit him first in the foot so he couldn't run to the bank and get away, he'd have got away, they'd of never got him, that's why he was stuck there in the middle of the Eagle River. It was Johnny Moses."

And then the man was shouting. "What they say is all bullshit in all them books! Bullshit! When they got him there on the Eagle River the police shot him so full of lead they couldn't lift him into the plane, ten men couldn't lift him, he was so full of lead."

Some of the people were smiling a little. What this Old Crow man said was obviously impossible, but it was not ridiculous. Something beyond mere facts was being told, a truth only words, not facts, could create. But before I had to say anything, the man continued even louder:

"It was Christmas, Jesus Christ! Christmas when the goddam police bang on his door, so why didn't they bring him a turkey and say 'Merry Christmas' and leave him alone? Eh?"

My mind was stumbling, but I tried to turn his rage a little. "Well, even if the police come banging on your house at Christmas and disturb you, you're still not supposed to shoot them through your door."

Some of the people chuckled with me, but for a few more moments he ranted almost wildly. I was stunned;

could not quite believe this: but it was certainly in keeping with the whole, extraordinarily beautiful day.

It began by flying north from Dawson City, the brilliant spring sun on the granite slabs and snow of the
Ogilvie Mountains, the sinuous bends of the Porcupine
River and the tiny village set against the airstrip at the foot
of Old Crow Mountain, its green spruce and streets packed
in solid snow of all-skidoo traffic. That afternoon I had
given a long reading and told stories at the school and then
I was taken back to the airport where the band had
arranged that a plane fly me to the Richardson Mountains
and the Eagle River. "We're gonna show you where Albert
Johnson got shot," the pilot told me. I had never been
there. With us came two Old Crow high-school students
who had read my novel *The Mad Trapper* and two band
elders. One of them, the venerable old woman sitting
beside me in the Cessna, introduced herself as the sister of
Johnny Moses, the RCMP special constable who had been at
that shootout fifty-five years before, though she did not tell
me her brother had shot Albert Johnson first.

So we flew east, over the widely scattered, still deserted
summer fish-camps and hunting camps in the snow at the
caribou crossings, along the frozen river, further east until
the Richardson Mountains appeared, abruptly, like enormous unglaciated pyramids folded into each other irreg-
ularly like a white random scattering of conical shapes,
and all so deadly white with their creeks outlined by black
spruce. Clouds covered the Barrier River Pass which

Johnson crossed in an impossible blizzard after killing
Constable Edgar Millen, so we could not fly there, but
the twisting loops of the Bell River, the deserted roofless
walls of the three buildings of La Pierre House, the beautiful circle sweep of the Bell River west around a mountain to join the Porcupine and there, just like a map, the
Eagle River entering the Bell from the south.

We droned a little lower. We saw a moose feeding
among willows and then the pilot laughed, "Oh, what the
hell," and he bent down to one hundred and fifty feet,
tilted, and I saw tracks, mink and marten trails, looping
out from the riverbanks, even the tiny spoor of weasel,
everything so icy sharp in the incredible air, I need not
breathe, only look. And then the plane made a wide turn,
and I saw what I had imagined, tried to imagine years
before again and again: I saw the tight reversed S turn of
the narrow river outlined by the straggling black spruce,
the tight reversed S where Johnson, deceived at last by the
twists of the river, ran backwards in his tracks because he
thought the posse was already ahead of him and, rounding the tight bend of that betrayal, suddenly met the dogs,
the men, the rifles racing after him head on.

It was so exactly as I had imagined it, in the plane I
knew I was dreaming. It seemed I saw through that window, past the strut and the motionless wheel, under the
shadow of that bulk and wing the actualization of what I
had dreamt sixteen years before and then dreamt again
and again trying to snare that in the words of a short story,

of a movie script, of a novel. There, on exactly such ice, between those precise, tiny, bristled trees; fifty-five years ago. Though of course the river under that ice could not be the same. But perhaps it was. Precisely every particle how many diurnal cycles later?

The man in the community centre at Old Crow, standing in the steady 10:30 p.m. daylight of April 27, had stopped shouting. He was talking quietly now, but with very great intensity.

"Men go crazy, you know," he said. "I've seen men, anybody here has seen men go really crazy. You can't help that and you should just get out of the way, leave them alone, they'll be okay, just leave them alone. Why do you have to bother a man when he goes really crazy, huh?"

Such words did not seem to expect words in reply. After a while I asked them all, "What do you think, should they dig him up now to get his fingerprints?"

Nobody said anything. "They'd find out for sure who he was then," I said.

A woman at the back said, "They should leave him alone."

Next morning a skidoo stopped beside me as I walked down the street; it was driven by a lean, handsome man about my age in a wolverine-trim parka. We'd met at the hall the night before and now in the sunlight he wore dark glasses so I couldn't see his eyes.

"I was gonna say something," he said, "but then that guy got going...." He shrugged.

"Oh, yeah," I said. "We talked after. He told me his father was a Danish whaler who came to Herschel Island on a whaling ship, so I asked him where were his blue eyes and blond hair."

But the skidoo driver would not laugh. He said, "Johnny Moses was my uncle. My mom lives over there, she was with you on the plane."

"Did your uncle ever talk about that manhunt?"

"Not to me."

"How come?"

He said thoughtfully, "I guess he didn't want to. He talked to my mom a lot, I know, but that's all."

"Would she talk to me about that?"

"I don't know." He was silent for a time, but made no move to go. The morning sun was almost stunning on the snow. "Once a few years before he died he was working with a construction crew near the Eagle River, they got close to that place on the river and one of the workers made a joke about it, said something like, 'Hey, Johnny, isn't this the famous place you shot Albert Johnson?' and he just put down his tools and walked away from there. Just disappeared. The foreman got worried and radioed my mom and I went out to look for him. It took me two weeks. He was camped in the bush way up the Porcupine, just his rifle and knife. Not even a tent. He knew how to live in the bush like that."

"He came back with you?"

"Yeah. I stayed with him a few days and then we came back."

I didn't know how I could ask what I wanted so badly to ask, and finally I said something unnecessary; totally obvious. "He wasn't working for the police any more?"

"No. He never did after that," and it was clear from his tone what "that" was. "There was something about that Johnson...something strange."

That was the same word a Hareskin man from Fort Good Hope used to describe the Dehcho, their prehistoric name for what we call the Mackenzie River. He said it twice, very thoughtfully, remembering perhaps his own lifetime beside its heavy brown darkness and all the people that had vanished into it: "The river is strange... strange. It will roll a body along the bottom for six days before it lifts it up so you can see it, forty miles away." That had happened to his best friend that very spring who with his girlfriend was late one night following him in a riverboat back to Fort Good Hope and in the morning they found the boat, its kicker still idling slowly turning circles on the river and the girl sleeping huddled in the prow, still unaware that she was alone. "His body was way past Good Hope six days later, it come up. We only recognized him from the bits of clothes left on him. Sometimes they won't come up at all, if the water's too cold. Maybe in the spring, somewhere. By then you don't know them anyway."

One looks into a moving, dark, strange river like the Dehcho and you will see nothing; only yourself. You follow a moving, dark strange man in linear (like a river) pursuit for six weeks along Arctic mountains and rivers and what else can you expect to see? Some who took part in that pursuit cannot bear ever to talk about it; some will talk a little; but none of them will do it again; they refuse that story.

There were only three Kutchin men in that police posse on the Eagle River on February 17, 1932: Johnny Moses, Peter Alexis and Lazarus Sittichinli. Only Sittichinli is still alive; in fact, he is the last man left of the entire hunt.

Lazarus Sittichinli now, in his small red house two blocks from Albert Johnson's grave, opens the door to me whom he has never seen or heard of: a tiny dark shrunken man, a few hairs bristle on his face, oddly powerful hands still with heavy horn-like nails. He walks to the kitchen table supporting himself on a four-point walker; he gestures for me to sit down. He is ninety-seven years old and he says he lifted Johnson up out of his hollow in the snow on the Eagle River, and turned him over so they could look at him. Peter Alexis and Karl Gardlund, who had been shooting from the same side of the river as Sittichinli, had advanced with him. Behind them came trader Frank Jackson and the police inspector.

"You know this man?" the inspector asked.

Alexis said, "I never know him."

In the warm house Mrs. Sittichinli sits dozing in a soft chair while the old man tells me that whole story again. Without prompting, as easily as if it had happened yesterday and acting out all the parts, changing voices, brown hands gesturing the shape of scenes, and I know it so well I can only hear details that no one else can ever give me: "Johnson had a bullet cut all across his belly; he had no grub, he'd been eating spruce gum and whisky-jack; he had a string with a rag tied to it in the barrel of his .30-30 to keep out the snow so it wouldn't clog and explode; he could jerk the string out, clean the barrel and shoot almost in the same motion."

I listen, and watch Lazarus' high-boned face move in his slightly off-beat English, or his ancient wife, a soft mound breathing, her moose moccasins laced up under her long cotton dress. They have been married seventy-six years and twelve of their fourteen children have already died. But there are plenty of grandchildren and great- and great-great-grandchildren around. He's fed them hunting caribou at the river crossings and sheep, lots of Dahl sheep, in the mountains. "I'm always lucky hunting," he says. "All the men from town here always follow me hunting in the Richardson mountains, sheep. All my life we live on hunting and trapping, we always live in the bush."

"Could you do that, working as special constable for the police?"

"I never did after that," he says. "I quit, then."

So then I could ask him why. He is tired now, and clearing his throat of phlegm, his toothless jaws moving sometimes as if he were eating Kutchin words which my white ear could not understand anyway. The story is long, but he wants to tell it long, how he brought his dog team back then from the Eagle River over the mountains after four days and the inspector, who had flown in with the badly wounded Hersey and Johnson's body, told him he should take a holiday after so much hard work on the two-month patrol. He was only earning seventy-five dollars a month. But next morning the inspector (Lazarus never calls him Eames or Alex; he names him only by function) was at his door as usual, told him to haul in four big trees for flagpoles. Several other things happened then, but now Lazarus shifts erect at the table, his black eyes suddenly fierce, bright. "I get the trees but I was mad," he says. "I tell him I'm not working no more. I quit now, you break your word, I break my word. I go home. A little later the inspector he come to my house. 'Why you quit?' 'You're asking too much.' 'No, no, you stay with us.' 'No.' 'Well, be the town police.' 'No,' I say. 'I won't police my own people. That's no good.' So I go home and I stay quit."

Like every storyteller in the north, he has acted all the parts as he speaks them, his voice changing to suit authority or obedience or anger. But at times there was something else in his tone; something like the man in Old Crow remembering his uncle Johnny Moses who had followed the twisting, spiralling river of Johnson's self-mocking flight almost as far as Lazarus Sittichinli, and who had been there when Lazarus lifted that frost-blackened, starved body out of the snow. "I said I have a good place on the Husky River," this ancient man tells me in that strange, abstracted tone. "Good for trapping. And I work sometimes in the hospital. But not the police."

William Nerysoo spoke the same way. He is ninety-four years old, living alone in a one-room house in the middle of Fort McPherson on the Peel River. He took no part in the six-week hunt; he was the man who originally reported to the RCMP that he believed Johnson was disturbing his traps; which report started it all. When I visited him in 1983, almost the first thing he said to me was, "I won't tell you anything about that. Everybody comes here and asks me, I go to the store and the little boys yell after me, 'Hey, Mad Trapper! Mad Trapper!' I don't tell you anything."

"Okay," I said. "Okay." What else could I say? A neighbour man came into the little house then, we talked of the spring caribou moving north to their calving grounds, and suddenly Nerysoo said, "Maybe I'll tell you one thing." So he did that, and then we talked about the caribou some more and suddenly he said again, "Maybe I'll tell you one thing." After a while, he had told me his whole story, and though I will not repeat it, his tone and his gentle, gradually insistent return to that trapline telling me more than his words about that trap and the fatal report he had once made.

What is it about these men? They are, in Chekhov terms, "insisting so strongly on preserving someone's personal secret." It seems they are, for that insistence, the most civilized of people. I asked Lazarus Sittichinli about digging up that famous grave down the street.

"I don't like that," he said. "There are people who do all kinds of things to themselves — if you want some fingerprints, take theirs. But no digging. Johnson, he had enough suffering. Leave him alone."

Alone with his locked, his unlockable secret. His untold, untraceable story. It is all so un.... The long river of his flight is as opaque as the Peel on which he first appeared, the gigantic Dehcho whose opaqueness it somewhere, indecipherably, enters.

But those Dene men who remembered their roles in the hunt for that man who defended his aloneness with such single-minded and truly horrifying intensity, they remember their roles with no joy, no recalled heroism; those men were the farthest thing from being "loners." White people like Albert Johnson appearing somewhere from southern Canada may be that — leave them alone — but a Kutchin or Inuvaluit "loner" seems incredible. It is a contradiction by very concept. Both Dene and Inuit have extended families that stretch beyond children in all possible directions of cousins and nieces and parents and adoptions and in-laws. It seems in the Arctic that everyone lives in a community; in any one community everyone, except for the few whites, is related to everyone else; when any community has a celebration, all the other relatives within a day's flying from all the other communities will arrive by chartered plane to help in the celebration. When they do that, they tell each other their continuing stories even as they live any number of new ones: stories here are a living construct of spoken words by means of which we remember.

And this oral storytelling, so refined and perfected by millennia of skilled practice, is the very affirmation of their non-aloneness: the storyteller and the poet/singer presuppose a community of listeners; otherwise nothing could be told. One may read a book alone (in fact, most of us prefer that) but one cannot tell a story alone. That is why any language changes so drastically when it moves from oral to written form. Now the most minimal word, spoken or written, about any human being is name, and everyone who hides even that goes beyond secret into enigma. That is, into intentional obscurity. There is then no story to tell and the original people of the Canadian Arctic living in tiny communities on the immense land-scape find such a refusal of story especially strange, disturbing, puzzling as only an oral, communal people can; but they respect it. Leave him alone. There is no story to tell; or, as William Nerysoo tells me, I won't tell you the story I know is there. Yet he is too much a person of his people and his landscape to ultimately refuse it; all you have to do is wait.

Nevertheless, Nerysoo's refusal to tell me his stories until he had some confidence in me underlines their enormous power. Songs, stories are the memory of a people, the particular individual rivers of the sea of life which constitutes us all. And when you hide that, when you insist the river of your life is as opaque as the Dehcho or Peel, you are defying the ancient assertion of that sea: you still do have a story (you cannot not have a story: you had a mother, you had a place and time when you were born, you have moved because you were alive) but if you persist so absolutely with silence, motionless silence, even unto death, then we will respect your refusal of your own story.

We will leave you alone, though we will continue to tell what little we do know because that is the only way human life continues.

Death continues to hide Albert Johnson. Experts disagreed about the permafrost at Aklavik being strong enough to preserve his body so well that fingerprints could still be taken. "Hell," one Aklavik resident told me, "I've lived here for twelve years and I've seen the Mackenzie flood the graveyard so bad there were bones floating around. There's nothing left of him." The river, hiding a secret again. Besides, the territorial governor explained to me that between 1932 and 1933 three suicides had been buried beside Johnson and now, even if the bodies were well preserved, no one would know exactly which body was whose. Ironically then, the iconoclastic Johnson, who in life refused to live near anyone, in death is now protected by what he would have considered a crowd.

In any case, soon after the April 27 announcement, a petition against the disinterment was signed by more people than actually live in Aklavik. It seems that historian Dick North with his implacable white obsession to know is not going to get his clinching evidence. Johnson remains an enigmatic secret. Perhaps fifty-five years is enough to leave him at that; to leave him alone.

THE BLINDMAN RIVER
CONTRADICTIONS

an interview with Rudy Wiebe

INTERVIEWER: *Maybe you could begin by telling me where you were born and where you grew up.*

WIEBE: There's a story around that I was born in Saskatchewan to a Mennonite refugee family but that's not true. I was really born in Alberta quite near Edmonton, a tiny hamlet which has now disappeared. My father was the son of the inspector general of the British army and he came here to homestead when my grandfather got tired of him sitting around home: he was nineteen years old and still had no idea what he wanted to do, so grandfather said, "Go out to the colonies and see if you can make something of yourself." My father ended up in Nova Scotia while his father was going to Bermuda to inspect the

British military installation there. From Nova Scotia he gradually worked his way west, like everyone else.

How did a Mennonite family end up in the military?

There was no Mennonite. I'm not a Mennonite.

You aren't?

No, I'm British, I'm English. I never had anything to do with the Mennonites; that's a fiction I made up because of course in Western Canada there's much more point to being ethnic than to being English. Actually, a Canadian writer has an enormous disadvantage in being English, as you perfectly well know, rather than Ukrainian or Greek or Icelandic, or Mennonite. I had the races of the world to choose from and I made a really bad choice; I should have chosen Jewish, which would have given me tremendous literary contacts in ways I can never have as a Mennonite (Mennonites generally don't read and never buy books — at best they borrow them) but really, I'm English, and I was telling you about my father who detested militarism but his father was the inspector general of the British army, a professional soldier who kicked him off the family estate in England and so he ended up on a homestead near Falconer, Alberta. Of course, Falconer didn't exist at that time but he rode up the Blindman River trail from Lacombe to Buck Lake I guess, and he found a homestead easily enough.

Really? What was Falconer like as a place to grow up?

Well you see, my father and his cousin created that hamlet because they were such terrible farmers. They were archetypal Englishmen, they chose homesteads for the scenery they wanted on their estates and the Blindman River valley is really beautiful, but the place they chose had the worst soil in the entire district. If they had gone just a bit west of Lacombe where the black soil is two or three feet deep, they could have done very well, but they had to have a rippling stream, scenery an Englishman could appreciate, wooded riverbanks, hills, ravines, and they didn't bother to find out that three inches of good soil is all that covers the clay. So they couldn't make a living as farmers, especially gentlemen farmers; they had to do something else. They were perfectly literate, they could keep accounts well, so they ended up building a general store on the banks of the Blindman River. There were several families living nearby already so they named the place Falconer after one of the families.

Your name wasn't Falconer?

No.

What was it?

Are you the police?

Of course not.

Exactly.

Am I to assume you went to a one-room schoolhouse?

Of course I did, but the reason I became a writer was because I sat on the knee of the Governor General of Canada. You see my grandfather, this general above all British generals, finally got perturbed about what his son was doing in the wild Canadian west and after thirty years he decided to visit him. I was born in the middle thirties, that is a fact, and was still too young to know what was really going on, but when my aged grandfather visited us he brought the Governor General along — it was John Buchan, Lord Tweedsmuir. By that time Buchan had written several novels, *The Thirty-nine Steps*, *Greenmantle*, which I read a few years later — I was reading by the time I was three or four though I wasn't old enough to do that at the time he showed up — but I knew he was a very famous man and he came to have tea in Falconer one afternoon when my grandfather finally visited my father, the one and only time either came to Alberta. Lady Tweedsmuir came along with a huge vice-regal party and Lord Tweedsmuir picked me up, I remember this with absolute clarity, he put me on his vice-regal knee and patted my head and said, "You know, there's certainly good stuff in this boy; just keep him growing," and then he drove back to Edmonton because tea was over. History was made in Falconer that day. The house still stands where it happened, you know. It was very exciting; everyone had such English accents.

Was it a house filled with books?

No. My father rebelled against all things English. He detested the English military tradition of the nineteenth century and basically he hated English books because they propagated that militarism. I did go to a one-room school, that's a fact, but my father became secretary-treasurer of the school and he went through the library and took out all the books like *Tom Brown's School Days*, and *Great Expectations* and *Rob Roy*, all those classic books that describe English life — *Winnie the Pooh* and *Wind in the Willows* — and I wasn't to read one of them so of course I read them clandestinely. I almost burned the house down once because I was using a match to read, if you can believe this, a match to read *Tom Brown's School Days* under the blankets! He punished me for it of course, but beating simply made me a more compulsive reader than ever.

Did you have any favourites that you especially enjoyed reading?

I really liked reading the nineteenth-century English novel where everybody knows exactly what they're doing. You have an ordered sense of the world in the great novels of the nineteenth century: you must get married, and get married well. You start with Jane Austen — I also read Scott but he's too romantic, so far away in chivalry and honour and impractical principles like that — the thing I loved about the English novel was its simplicity: money and marriage. Of course George Eliot messes it up by having Miss Brooke marry well and then the problems start, but basically Dickens, Thackeray, Trollope create a world that makes total sense: once you have married rich you're set, the story is finished. I liked that.

Were you a prose reader all along or did you read some poetry too?

I liked poetry a lot, famous poems like "The Highwayman" and "Sheep" and "Dover Beach," that enormous English melancholy of tides rolling endlessly up and down the naked shingle of the world. I loved that perhaps because I never saw an ocean; my father wouldn't take me any-where near one. He himself returned to England to fight in various wars that England always has and Canadians feel obligated to help them with but he would never take us there, me or my sister. He always said, "See an ocean and before you know it you'll be standing at attention, saluting something," and he didn't want us to be cor-rupted by the English genteel world either so we didn't eat with napkins on the table. Now I know that English peo-ple really do eat with napkins on the table, and fine bone china, they always have that and any amount of silver cutlery. It made me angry because the one time I met my grandfather and his friend the Governor General I experienced this clear sense of class, of *correctness*. You know? The contradictions of my father were very strange; he hated the army but he served in two world wars, he wasn't any good at farming and he wasn't any good at business either.

But my father did know how to write speeches and he ended up being a member of the Alberta legislature here in Edmonton. The thing that got him elected was building the railroad between Lacombe and Breton; he worked on that for twenty years, around wars, and the MLA salary certainly helped keep the store going and then when he got the railroad built he lost his seat. Typical of Canadian politics of course, but it enraged my father even further. He got kicked in the teeth again and again for the kind of person he was; he sort of lived his life seething.

On the other hand I really did like the liberal melancholy I found in Tennyson and Arnold. Tennyson's great question standing in Westminster Abbey, that magnificent structure built to faith and the state Church, "But God, what if it is not true? What if there is nothing up there?" Is Darwin really right, or the Bible? That kind of liberal melancholy — focussing the human need for doubt — it's heady stuff.

Your father was a politician and a great speaker, he must have been a pretty good storyteller too.

Well, he controlled himself when he was at home. My mother often said to him, "Don't bother, so much control!" but you know my mother was Ukrainian and he did this again in defiance of all things English. I mean what Englishman would marry a Ukrainian peasant girl, eh? And that she certainly was. My mother was the warmest, most loving person who had a far better knowledge of everything human than did my father, and her blood was the rawest, barefootest, most up-to-your-ankles-in-the-cowshit kind of peasant that could be. This ancestry really gave me my dichotomy; I mean I go in two different directions: I don't mind calves and chickens wandering around the room and at the same time I long profoundly for white linen on the table. I can't imagine a better start for a novelist. But I felt I had to disguise this basically unbelievable dichotomy when I began writing so I invented this Mennonite persona that I'm known by, now.

Did your mother sing Ukrainian peasant songs, and tell you anecdotes, proverbs, enrich you from the treasury of Ukrainian folk culture?

She certainly did. But she had to do it clandestinely or my father would swear at her. Every time she started singing one of these beautiful lyric songs, getting all weepy the way Ukrainian people do when they get into the old songs, he would come in swearing and cursing, and if he hadn't truly been an Englishman, he would have hit her. Of course he didn't; as an Englishman he could just yell at her or slice her fine with cold sarcasm, but he never touched her in anger in his life. I would sometimes hear them through the bedroom walls, "You know, Charles, if you would hit me sometimes, you might get over it." I understand this now. I didn't then, that if couples really love each other, sometimes if they can fight physically they can settle some things. My father could never do that; an Englishman's sense of fair play will not allow him to beat women or children. It's impossible, so they lived this kind of profound, almost terrifying contradiction unresolved.

Did you have any teachers that made a lasting impression on you, that helped you develop the promise the Governor General saw so intuitively?

What can I say? I was the archetypal Canadian prairie kid who always has to walk three miles to a one-room school; always through deep snow at forty below, always poor and during the Depression. Well, we *were* poor. My father and his cousin owned a store but it was a terrible business. People think that storekeepers have lots to eat, but they don't unless they eat their own wares and then they're just making themselves poorer. And the multiracial "ethnic" Canadians all around us never believe you can possibly be poor if you spoke English like my father. You should have heard his accent when he was mad.

When did you get bitten by the writing bug?

I had a good childhood to be a writer because I had all these contradictions at home and I longed for a world out there that I believed must be really attractive. It was, and so I read more and more. Reading is a way of ordering the world better than the world that surrounds you. If you can say that a critic is a reader of a text, that a critic takes a text apart and orders it more clearly, then the writer takes the world apart in effect and orders it according to his thinking. And that was always appealing to me. The world I lived in was such a miserable world; why not make a better one? You couldn't make it any worse.

So you picked up the pen to do social work?

No, no writer is a social worker but one of the effects of writing, of thinking and putting stories on paper is that you do create a particular worldview, if people are patient enough to read it all, carefully. Most of them aren't of course. Many readers just want a diverting story but if you write serious fiction, as I hope I do, then eventually you do create a particular worldview; it is there in your work, hidden, and reading uncovers it. A good reader has to be willing to follow wherever the writer leads. Many people aren't; if the trail is too tough, they'll just go off and ride easy on some railroad track laid to somewhere else. But if they have to walk and cut their way...you know, following a good writer is like following a good scout through Alberta bush. Maybe the trail is half disguised and you even have a hard time finding it. Most people would rather sit in airplanes and circle around the world that way, looking down serenely on everything from ten thousand metres and actually feeling nothing much at all except comfortable.

Were you a child prodigy in the literary world of Falconer?

No.

Do you remember some of your earlier stories? Were you shoved up in front of the class to read, or be the star performer at the Christmas concerts?

No, no, I had a lot of miscellaneous ability... I was fairly well coordinated so I could play sports quite well and I could sing pretty well, I could tell stories pretty well. It would have been much more convenient if I had one particular ability, you know some people really have a voice and that's good because then all your choices are limited: either you sing or you're dead. Some people have good logical minds and they know they're going to be lawyers or doctors and of course every immigrant offspring wants to be that because they make money. But if you have a miscellaneous mind that goes in all kinds of directions, you've got no help. I could have done about fifteen different things and been sort of average at any one of them. I had problems.

When did you decide you were going to be a writer?

I am still not sure if I am one. Every book you write, you're still trying to find out if you can write it or not. I've been involved with publishing fifteen or twenty books, but that still doesn't mean they're very good or that I'll be able to write another one. You're always trying to find out, well, can you or can't you? And every time I start again I — I mean I don't even think in some ways that I *write* a story; it seems to me rather that I'm finding it. I don't know if I'll ever find another one. How can you tell?

When did you write your first story? How old were you?

Oh, probably about the time my sister died. That was right at the end of the war. It wasn't a story, actually it was a poem. Or a song. I made it up riding to school. Falconer was so small the school was in the country and I... this...thing had nothing to do with my sister who was lying in a coffin in our storeroom because there weren't any undertakers around to take away the body of a person you loved and bring it back packaged like they do now. My father was in England of course, training soldiers, but it was spring luckily so the body stiffened up nicely and didn't smell too much among the leather harness and barbed wire. I made it up...it was a kind of a song I guess, I was riding my horse to school. I was about eight years old, and crying.

How about your first publication? Was it in the Falconer Gazette *or where did you publish first?*

Well you could hardly call it publication, a local newspaper article. The write-up of a school party which I disliked so much...I didn't like parties even then so I was the perfect reporter. I stood there and watched kids my age, fourteen or fifteen, going through the charade of a party and it gave me the perfect kind of writer's stance. I was standing back and watching everyone, including a goofy, long-boned kid like me ladling out the punch, watching the older boys trying to pick up girls and the girls simpering and giggling and some of the sensible ones I admired not knowing what to do because being silly is really the only expected behaviour there. That experience gave me a sense of distance, of being an observer at the same time as a sort of participant...this sense is a necessity to any writer. In one way you are totally involved and in another you are quite apart, watching. That's a fine thing about being a writer. You're split. It helps if you're a Gemini.

Are you a Gemini?

No. I wish I was.

From what you're saying, it must have been quite traumatic for you to go from Falconer into the big city. Was it a difficult transition to make, have you ever really left Falconer?

I don't know. I'm a Libra and I balance two things at least, all the time. All my life I'm holding two things or more in my hands. Now the fact is I've never literally lived on a farm; on the other hand Canadian newspapers have sometimes had agricultural journalists review my novels. All my adult life I've lived in cities, yet I like the land, I like farms. But I can't stand the thought of myself being a farmer. It's ridiculous.

Do you enjoy going back home?

Where's home?

Falconer.

No, I never go there. It doesn't exist. I know this is a cliché but really, you can't go home again.

What else would you still like to do? Do you have any second careers in mind outside of writing?

No. Writing is one of the great arts and anybody can spend a lifetime at it and still not be satisfied with what he's done. I suppose it's that way in making the other arts too, say music, painting, but those arts aren't quite so close to daily life. Nobody naturally uses musical sounds all the time, nor makes pictures or designs, but everybody uses language. Language, both poetry and fiction — it's so close to the way we conduct our lives in one sense and in another so far away that there seems to be no connection at all with what a marvellous writer like James Joyce or William Faulkner does with language and what we do, writing letters or talking, and yet in a mysterious way there is a connection. Far more so than what Picasso does with images, or Stravinsky with sound, story is always a living closeness; there's an endless fascination in making them. Anyway I don't even think I write stories; I find them. I'm more archeologist than inventor. You never know when, or where, but you're always looking and suddenly you unearth a marvellous archeological site and then, if you're smart, you dig very carefully indeed.

Do you think your awareness of language or your apprecia-tion of it is heightened by the fact that you grew up in a com-munity with so many central European kids, people talking so many languages?

Oh, that is certainly true. I can't imagine myself being a writer without my mother who spoke to me only in Ukrainian or her mother in German. My father had been sent to one of the best schools in England, not exactly Eton but close, because his father had military plans for him. But the polyglot world of languages in which I grew up gave me a magnificent start and my mother always said that the first word I uttered was "Baba," it wasn't anything else; it was Ukrainian.

Then why have the Mennonites laid claim to you? What's in it for them?

Oh well, heck, they're just glad to grab any publicity they can get. I mean, they have so little artistic reputation, until my generation they've never had a writer writing in English in this country worth reading twice.

Then how did they end up with you? Couldn't they have chosen someone else?

They've certainly thought so many times since, I assure you, but after my first book came out the die was cast. They couldn't do anything about it and they just have to put up with it, now. As Osip Mandelstam says, no more than you choose your own parents, do a people choose their own poets.

Thank you very much.

ACKNOWLEDGEMENTS

These pieces first appeared, sometimes in a slightly different form, in the following publications:

Forward: Love Letters from Land and Sea: *En Route Magazine*, July, 1992.

Passage by Land: *Canadian Literature*, #48, 1971.

The Darkness Inside the Mountain: *Alberta, a Celebration*, Edmonton, Hurtig Publishers, 1979.

Tombstone Community: *Mennonite Life*, #19, 1964.

Where is the Voice Coming From?: *Fourteen Stories High*, Ottawa, Oberon Press, 1971.

All on Their Knees: *The Mennonite*, #46, December 17, 1968.

The Beautiful Sewers of Paris, Alberta: *The Road Home*, Edmonton, Reidmore Publishers, 1992.

The Naming of Albert Johnson: *Queen's Quarterly*, v.80, #3, 1973.

The Angel of the Tar Sands: *Alberta, a Celebration*, Edmonton, Hurtig Publishers, 1979.

Did Jesus Ever Laugh?: *The Fiddlehead*, #84, 1970.

After Thirty Years of Marriage: *Canadian Forum*, 58:685, Nov., 1978.